Anonymous Mom Posts

Anonymous Mom Posts

Jenifer Goldin

Book Cover by Stuart Bache
Formatting by Alt 19 Creative

Paperback ISBN 979-8-9874456-0-0

1st edition 2023

Published by Anchor Head Books

This book is dedicated to my children Anna and Micah.
You don't know where you'll land until you fly.
(Because I'm obsessed with Harry Styles),
and to Jonathan.

Contents

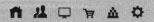

Hamilton Beach Moms
PRIVATE GROUP — 5,327 Members

Kara Thompson
Today at 7:03 a.m.

Hi Moms. I need recommendations for a party company that dresses ponies like unicorns. My daughter loves unicorns, and this would make her second birthday perfect. Thanks in advance!

10 👍 68 😮

Comments

Isabell Whitmore: Light money on fire much?

Faye Carter: My friend used Dream Parties for her one-year-old's Coachella-themed birthday. They provided body paint, tents, desert-themed decor, and even a small yurt. It was insane!

Simone Jackson: Save the money for the therapy your daughter will need when she realizes the world doesn't cater to her every whim!

Maggie O'Donnell: What happened to having a kid's birthday party at McDonald's?

Hilary Solomon: Everyone is being a bit harsh. Let this mom celebrate her daughter any way she wants.

Aya Wang: CANCEL

CHAPTER 1

Laura Perry

M Y NOSE BRISTLES with irritation at the recent rash of snarky comments on the Hamilton Beach Moms' Facebook page. Is it bringing this community together or tearing it apart? Earlier, a mom posted looking for a company that could provide "unicorns" for her daughter's birthday. The comments were ruthless.

Naturally, I'm a fixer, so I'm hoping the new anonymous posting feature will decrease the cattiness and remind these moms we're here to support each other.

Pulling my SUV in front of the Edge of the Water Hotel, I'm glad my new client, Julie Wu, took my suggestion to stay at the waterfront property. House hunting goes much smoother when my clients are dazzled by the blue of the ocean.

As I inch my car around the hotel's white brick, circular driveway, I notice the building gleams with an iridescent hue. It reminds me of the day I married Troy at this hotel eighteen years ago. My heart thumps in my chest as I consider the ups and downs our family has experienced over the years.

An image of my sixteen-year-old daughter Nora's face flits through my mind. Her best friend moved to Florida last spring, and her other close friend is busy with a serious boyfriend. Nora's having a hard time finding a new place to land.

Julie raps on my passenger door, and my mind shifts away from thoughts of Nora. I roll down the window and give Julie my big, wide, real-estate agent smile. "Hey. So nice to meet you, Julie. Hop in."

She smiles, opens the door to my Volvo, and folds her slender body into the beige leather bucket seat next to mine.

"I'm sorry to meet you in my car," I say as we pull away. "Normally, I'd come inside for coffee, but this first showing is at eight-thirty."

Julie runs her hand through her dark, tight, curly hair. "Not a problem. I'm on East Coast time since we live in DC. I've been up for a few hours."

As Julie talks, I'm struck by her beauty. She's gorgeous, but not in the blond California way. Her skin is creamy white, and her eyes sparkle green, like the gardens I frequented when times were harder. The color grounds me in nature. Instantly a warm, tranquil wave courses through my body.

As we drive along the windy coastal road leading to the upscale neighborhood of Hamilton Beach Estates, I review several points I've made over email. "The schools here are top-rated, so there's no need for private school."

"That's appealing," Julie replies. "Right now, Talia and Van attend private school. They're getting a great education, but everything is so controlled. There's also very little diversity."

I nod my head as I listen. Julie's voice is calm. Her energy is laid back considering she was just hired as the head of legal for the most prominent dot com in the area. Her simple white t-shirt and brightly colored tote bag make me believe she's not flashy or concerned with high-end labels, like many of my clients. I like her already.

"If you're looking for a diverse community, Hamilton Beach is the right place. My daughter, Nora, went through various stages, where she demanded to celebrate Hanukkah, Kwanzaa, and the Chinese New Year." I laugh out loud, but then worry maybe I've offended Julie.

When she chuckles, I'm relieved. "Well, we celebrate just about everything in our house. I'm Jewish, and my husband, Eric, is Asian. It's a real cultural hodgepodge."

"I love that," I say, envious of the varied outlooks that shape Julie's family.

"Eric and I always say the biggest benefit is all the different foods. Traditional Jewish brisket, scallion pancakes, and Asian dumplings. Oh my god. The dumplings. But we digress. Tell me more about Hamilton Beach."

My mouth waters at the thought of homemade dumplings. I swallow hard and continue. "We have gorgeous beachside neighborhoods, swim and tennis communities, single-family homes, townhouses, apartments, and even a retirement community. Everything in Hamilton Beach is clean and California coastal. Lots of white buildings against a bright blue ocean and sky."

"It looks lovely," Julie says as she glances out the window.

"Oh," I continue, "be sure to join the Hamilton Beach Moms' Facebook page."

"The Hamilton Beach Moms' Facebook page?" Julie cocks her head to the side. "You'll have to excuse me. I'm not a social media person. What's that?"

"Oh!" I reply. "Well, are you on Facebook?"

"Van created an account for me a few years ago. But I hardly use it. I notice, every year on my birthday, I get assaulted with messages from people I haven't seen or spoken to in over ten years."

"Don't you just love that!" I gush with enthusiasm.

"To be honest, I think it's disingenuous. It feels like spam." Julie shrugs.

"I get what you mean," I reply as I pull into the entrance of Hamilton Beach Estates. "But I love connecting with friends, even if our current relationship lacks face-to-face interaction. Plus, the Hamilton Beach Moms' page is a great resource for anything you need—doctors, restaurant recommendations, tutors. The moms in this community are all-knowing. Their collective wisdom rivals Alexa and Google."

Julie looks at me and smiles. "Well, that's interesting. We'll need new doctors. Van will want to continue private coaching for soccer. I want to find a book club."

"Yes! The page can help with all of that." My tone of voice jumps an octave, but it's hard to contain my excitement. "This is exactly why I started the page a few years ago. Why don't you open Facebook on your phone, and I'll direct you to the page? You can leave the group if you find it spammy and annoying."

"I haven't opened Facebook in months, but okay. You sold me."

"Ha! Great. Now let's see if I can sell you this amazing home."

Julie opens her bag and hands me her phone. I pull up the page as I wait behind a car in line at the gatehouse for Hamilton Beach Estates.

"All set. Now you'll be in the know for all things Hamilton Beach." I give Julie her phone and pull up to the guard on duty.

"Hi, yes, I'm Laura Perry from Perry Properties. I'm here to show my client the property for sale on CoCoplum Way. The homeowner should have left my name."

The guard glances at a paper inside the small gatehouse, searching. "Yes, here we go. I'll buzz you in." He looks at Julie and smiles. "Welcome to Hamilton Beach Estates."

CHAPTER 2
Julie Wu

> Can anyone recommend a great dermatologist for teenage acne?

> My husband and I need a new mattress. Who has one they love?

> Where can I find tops for my 10-year-old daughter that cover her stomach? This mama is struggling to find appropriate clothes.

GLANCING THROUGH POSTS on the Hamilton Beach Moms' Facebook page, I get the sense it's harmless enough. Maybe it's time to embrace social media. It could be a way to make friends. I've always envied women with good friends and a strong sense of belonging. I'm still hesitant to be my true self in personal relationships, and this leaves my friendships feeling hollow.

As Laura parks her car on a stately driveway, I marvel at the perfect green grass and curb appeal of the home before me. It's gorgeous—two stories and three times the size of the house we have in DC. It's one hundred percent California vibes, with its red clay roof and white stucco exterior.

"So, this is it. As you can see, the home's style is Mission Revival. A popular style in Southern California. It's five bedrooms, fully renovated, with an open floor plan. The backyard has a pool that faces the ocean. Let's go inside and look."

Glancing at Laura, with her tan complexion, thick blond hair, and athletic build, I want to run away. Moving to California, buying a house on the beach, starting over with friends. It's so much at once. But my new job at Click Com is the opportunity of a lifetime. And when Eric and I looked through the real estate links Laura sent through email, we fell in love with the idea of living the true California dream.

"Look at that ocean!" Eric said when we clicked through Zillow images for this home. "Perfect balcony views every single day."

"Do you enjoy cooking?" The image of Eric's excited face disappears, and I land back in the gorgeous kitchen where Laura has asked me a question.

"When I have time," I say, picturing myself preparing Rosh Hashanah dinner in this unbelievable space.

"Well, this kitchen has everything you could ever want—a double oven, two dishwashers, a warming drawer, a chef-grade stove and range, a beverage station."

"It's beautiful." I run my hand over the gleaming white countertops, shimmering in the sun.

"The natural light in here is fantastic," Laura says, looking toward the immense glass doors that slide all the way open to create a seamless flow between the inside of the house and the ocean.

Laura leads me outside to get a good look at the pool. It's large and square-shaped, surrounded by a deep indigo tile. I can't help but ooh and ahh at the stunning ocean that sits behind it.

"Oh, and I almost forgot to tell you. The owners planted a vegetable garden on the side of the house. It has tomatoes, bell peppers, garlic, broccoli, and several herbs."

"Talia will love that," I say as I follow Laura to the garden. "She's an environmentalist and wants our family to live an eco-friendly lifestyle."

"Perfect!" Laura says. "Talia will love it here."

I nod in agreement but can't help thinking about what Talia said a few days ago. She admitted she's nervous about making new friends.

"What do you mean?" My heart fluttered. Fitting in has always been a struggle for me. I never want Talia to feel like she doesn't belong.

"Look at me, Mom. I'm not blond, I'm not girly, I don't wear makeup. I'm Jewish and Chinese. I'm afraid I'll be surrounded by blond robots with big fake boobs and perfect teeth."

"Oh, honey," I said. "I get that. I totally do. For God's sake, I grew up in Georgia in the 1980s."

"Yes, Mom, you've told me a million times. You were the only kid in Daisy Springs who was Jewish."

"I've saved the best for last," Laura interjects as I push away my concerns about Talia. "Follow me, so you can see the ocean and get a complete view of the back of the house." Laura slips off her metallic sandals. Following suit, I pull off my flats.

As we step onto the beach, I see a woman about my age jogging along the shore. She's quintessential California. Tall and blond, with a Barbie-doll figure, barely covered by a tiny sports bra and itty-bitty running shorts.

"Isabell!" Laura yells in the woman's direction, waving her hand furiously. "Isabell!"

The woman stops and rolls her eyes, appearing annoyed by the interruption.

"Isabell and I grew up together in Hamilton Beach. We've been friends forever." Laura walks toward her and motions for me to follow. "Hey, Isabell. I was wondering if I would see you running today. I know you never miss a day."

Isabell smiles, but her lips spread out tight. It's obvious the smile is forced.

"Julie Wu, this is Isabell Whitmore. She lives in the house next door." Laura points to the enormous mansion nestled in a private area down the beach. Her house may be *next door*, but it's secluded and set apart on its own.

"Julie and her family are moving here from DC," Laura continues.

"Nice to meet you," Isabell says as she jogs in place. She's clearly more interested in exercising than making conversation with a potential new neighbor. I can tell she's growing impatient by the way her eyes wander down the shoreline.

"I'll let you get back to your run," Laura says as she moves back toward the house.

"Thanks. I need to get this run over with." As Isabell picks up her pace and passes me, her large breasts hardly move. Maybe Talia was right to be concerned about blond robots with fake boobs.

Turning away from the ocean, I cup my hands around the top of my eyes, bringing my dream house into focus.

"It's a gorgeous property." Laura's eyes shine with enthusiasm as she heads back to the house.

Following behind her, I wonder if this piece of coastal perfection will really be my family's new reality. I picture Talia and Van tossing a football on the sand after swimming in the ocean.

Suddenly, my lungs deflate, and my body sags. I am reminded that one child is missing. There should be *three* children frolicking on the beach in this daydream, but there are only two.

Immediately, I'm struck by the thought that Eric and I don't deserve this life. We absolutely don't deserve any of it. I wonder if he's ever tormented by our past? We never talk about it.

A line of sweat forms around my hairline. I must look unwell, because suddenly Laura is fanning me with the glossy brochure that describes the beautiful home before us.

"You look hot. Are you okay?"

Composing myself, I ignore the sharp stabs in my gut. "It must be the heat," I say. "It's warmer here than in DC."

"Do you want me to run inside and get you water?" Laura asks with genuine concern.

"No, that's okay. Just give me a minute to catch my breath. I'll be fine." But the words are a lie.

CHAPTER 3

Isabell Whitmore

MY FEET POUND the dense sand as I sprint away from Laura and her client. Irritation fuels my fast pace. I hate when my run is interrupted. I love to be in constant motion. Once I start to exercise, my body takes over, and I'm in a zone. It's both an escape and a distraction. But my beast mode's been disrupted, and I'm agitated.

While it's true Laura and I have been friends since childhood, our only connection is history. Our relationship should have ended in our twenties after I broke the lease on our New York apartment and moved out.

A wave of heat grips me as I remember how Laura's voice shook with emotion on the day I packed my bags and left.

"I don't understand why you're moving," she said.

"I'm just over having a roommate," I said as I zipped up my suitcase and walked out the front door. The truth was, I had to get away from Laura's watchful eyes. She always wants to fix everything, and some things can't be fixed.

I'll never understand that time in my life. I was weak, and it sickens me. I quickly hurl the distressing memory into a black abyss where I keep all my unpleasant experiences. My past will never take me down.

Laura should just let our friendship go. But she clutches onto our past like a baby to a warm bottle of milk. I have no desire to prioritize her over my schedule. It's a myth right out of a Disney fairy tale that female friendships should last a lifetime.

Suddenly, my watch vibrates against my skin. I glance down and see a text from my husband, Harris. The first time I met him, his solid good looks, quiet nature, and immaculate appearance reminded me of a stale catalog model. Our relationship quickly progressed into something dull and predictable—sleepovers on Wednesdays, Blockbuster, and takeout on Fridays. But I needed an out when we met, and he was the perfect exit strategy.

> **Harris:** We need to talk about Lola and Grace. They're out of control.

Our twin girls are constantly smoking pot and barely passing their classes, but that's how it is. Their behavior won't lead to anything life-shattering. Plus, I'm not the kind of mom to catch my kids in a parachute each time they plunge off a cliff. Sometimes, taking a hard fall is the only way to learn how this world works.

> **Harris:** Also, I need to work late again. Won't be home until midnight.

Some wives would be upset that their husbands work nonstop, but I love it. I barely see Harris. Being on my own is a special kind of freedom, and it's glorious!

Who cares that he's lying about work and meeting up with his flavor of the month? We have an unspoken agreement about our affairs. As long as we stay away from people in each other's circles, we're free to do what we like.

Right now, I'm violating that rule by dating the new tech whiz kid Harris hired for his multimillion-dollar software company. What can I say? It makes each illicit rendezvous more exciting.

Nevertheless, I'll never tire of maintaining the pretense of my happy marriage. There's too much to lose, including, but not limited to, my obsession with Gucci handbags. And let's not forget, Harris never bothers me for sex. Thank the stars! I've got little interest in faking orgasms at this point in my life.

Sweat drips from my brow as I adjust my sports bra. It's been rubbing against the skin on my shoulder for the last five miles. As I climb the stairs that lead from the beach to my veranda, I wonder if my new housekeeper, Mary, will make it past week one.

When I step through my French doors, I see her hunched by one of the majestic side tables flanking the couch in our sitting room. As I walk closer, I notice the ornate frame that holds our most recent family photo has fallen. Glass shards are strewn across my reclaimed pine wood floor. Harris and I had the wood flown in from a historic building torn down in Pennsylvania. It cost a fortune. But it's only money, and we have plenty.

"Oh, Miss Isabell. I'm sorry. I knocked over your picture as I was dusting."

Glancing at the photo, I notice Lola and Grace's snide smiles. They were angry I made them wear Diane von Furstenberg wrap dresses for the family snapshot. My son, Warren, smiles widely, even though I'm sure the stiff Saint Laurent suit I had him squeeze into was uncomfortable. If he'd only cut back on soda, he could lose those eight pounds that make him look puffy.

"That frame was expensive. Harris and I bought it on our recent family trip to Bora Bora." My eyes narrow as I speak.

Mary's cheeks flush. She pushes a long red curl out of her eyes as she scurries over the frame. "I'm so sorry," she says again. "You can take the cost out of my pay."

"That won't be necessary," I say gruffly, knowing that frame cost more than her monthly rent.

"I'm going to shower. Then I'm leaving to meet my tennis team for lunch. Can you put away the new top and dress I bought yesterday at Neiman's? There's also three new handbags that need to be shelved by designer. The shopping bags are in my car."

Mary looks at me, her red brassy eyebrows arched high. "Which car? There are three in the garage."

"In my Cadillac Escalade."

"I'll do that as soon as I'm done cleaning this up," Mary says as she puts shards of glass into a trash bag.

I curtly nod and take the back staircase to my bedroom. Will things work out with Mary? I go through housekeepers like my husband goes through mistresses. Apparently, it's hard to find good help, and good blow jobs, these days.

HAMILTON BEACH MOMS
PRIVATE GROUP — 5,328 Members

Laura Perry
Today at 10:03 a.m.

Good morning, moms of Hamilton Beach! We all know, it takes a village to raise a child, support a partner, and find time for self-care. The Hamilton Beach Moms' Facebook page has allowed our village to go virtual! Solutions for every dilemma imaginable can be crowd-sourced and are just a click away.

Need to know where to find pants that will fit a boy who is equally tall and skinny? Or how to get a toddler out of your bed and back in the crib? The Hamilton Beach Moms' Facebook page has the answers. Wondering which cosmetic surgeon is best for natural-looking Botox? Or what restaurant offers the most delicious gluten-free options? The moms of Hamilton Beach can provide you with the information you need.

Many of you have asked me to post your personal questions anonymously. While I'm humbled you trust me with your most private matters, I'm thrilled to announce that you can now post anonymously. 🍪🍪. Instead of messaging me, click the new anonymous post link. I hope this feature will be helpful and am glad the moms of Hamilton Beach can continue to receive advice and emotional support without fear of being exposed. One last thing, I'm still looking for someone to co-moderate this page. We have over 5,000 members. I could use some help. PM me if interested.

Hope everyone enjoys the perfect weather out there!

267 👍 68 🖤

Comments

Jodi Loar: @Laura Perry This page is the best resource. In fact, I was struggling to figure out which joggers would be most flattering for my figure. I posted on this page and received 67 comments 😄.

Allison Skatoff: Joggers always border the "is she wearing pajamas" line with me. I'll stick to leggings!

Amy Beyer: I'm on the hunt for joggers that are flattering, fitted, and professional-looking enough to wear to a meeting. And oh, they must have pockets.

Jodi Loar: @Amy Beyer You are looking for a 🦄.

Jasmine Lewis: Yessss! There's nothing more entertaining than an anonymous mom post! It's seriously better than any Netflix show, scandalous movie, or New York Times best seller. Keep the anonymous mom posts coming! 🍿 🍿 🍿 🎥 🎬

CHAPTER 4

Maggie O'Donnell

M
Y BED MAKES its usual squeak as Doug leans over to grab his phone from the side table. Scrolling through sports news is always the first item on his agenda.

Unsettled by the morning's blackness, I roll over and curl into his back.

"Morning," I say. An artificial blue light outlines the back of his head like a halo as he scans his phone.

"Good morning—I guess I should get in the shower." Stepping out of bed, he doesn't even turn around to look at me.

My jaw tenses as he walks away. *Something's off.* And it's been two months since we've had sex.

As soon as he shuffles into our bathroom, I grab his phone, hoping to scroll through it before it locks. I do this occasionally, although I'm not sure what I'm looking for. Perhaps a glimpse of the last web page he was reading, a text, or his last email.

I've only timed the morning snooping right a handful of times. And each time has confirmed he is who he appears to be. One time, the lingering page was an article on college football recruiting, the next time an ad for a new set of golf clubs, and finally, an email from one of his producers pitching a story idea.

Yet, I can't kick this feeling that he's hiding something. But then I have to remind myself that there's a difference between a marriage having *secrets* and a marriage having *privacy*.

It wasn't always like this. He used to wake up, turn to me, and smile. "Hi, gorgeous," he'd say as he pulled me close and stroked my hair. Then, before mindlessly scrolling on his phone, he would play me a morning song. The ritual started with CDs while we were both students at UCLA. In college, he was never without his yellow Sony Discman.

When we were falling in love, it was a cheesy song like "Lost in Love" by Air Supply, or "I Will Always Love You" by Whitney Houston. And, of course, Rod Stewart's "Maggie May" became a standard.

Eventually, the song revealed the state of our union. The morning after our first big fight, he played "Hard to Say I'm Sorry" by Chicago. When we had a spat over blowing the budget we had set for ourselves as newlyweds, I woke up to the song "All Apologies" by Nirvana. When I was pregnant, he chose songs like "Ice Ice Baby" by Vanilla Ice and "Sweet Child of Mine" by Guns N' Roses.

As life got busier and busier, the daily morning song ritual whittled away to Sunday mornings only. By the time we had our second child, it disappeared altogether, along with my perky breasts.

As soon as I hear Doug step into the shower, I tap my finger on his phone's home button. My body stiffens when it prompts me for a passcode. Defeated, I carefully place it back where he left it.

Ten minutes later, I walk into our bathroom. Doug stands in front of his sink. Picking up my toothbrush, our eyes meet in the mirror's reflection. "Hey," I gurgle as I spit toothpaste from my mouth.

"Morning," Doug says as he slaps citrus-smelling aftershave on his freshly groomed skin. His face glows from the sun pouring in through the windows. "Oh, I almost forgot," he says as he smooths gel into his hair. "The media department wants you to post another photo on the Hamilton Beach Moms' Facebook page with a link to my piece on local soccer star, Joy Brashton. Can you do that today?"

A few months ago, when the public relations department at WRB TV was struggling to increase Doug's female viewership, I offered to post links to his sports stories on the Hamilton Beach Moms' Facebook page.

"Sure, will they send me an updated headshot?"

"Actually, they want to try something more organic. Can you post the link to my story with a family photo? They want these posts to show I'm a hometown family guy."

"I don't love that idea," I say. "I hate the thought of people I don't know looking at our photos and knowing our business. It's not the same as when I post to my own page."

"Totally get that, but you're married to a local celebrity." He winks. "And the PR team at the station thinks you're a genius. My female viewers have increased ten times over since you started posting on that Facebook page." Doug raises his hands in the air, cheering silently.

"The sway of that page over this community is ridiculous," I say, exasperated. "But I suppose it's my go-to place for advice and recommendations."

"See. The page is great and helps my ratings."

"Okay, I'll find a picture to post today." I comb through my thick, straight brown hair and then peer at myself in the mirror. The fine lines around my eyes are starting to bother me. Pushing my body against the counter, I pull my skin taught.

"You're as gorgeous as you were twenty years ago." Doug smiles and exits our bathroom.

A few minutes later, I help Sophia and Evan collect their backpacks. I watch out the window as they board the bus to Hamilton High School.

"See you tonight," Doug says as he fills a huge Yeti with coffee. He kisses the top of my head and walks out the door.

As soon as he leaves, I go upstairs to shower and dress for my lunch meeting at Trendy Greens with Valerie. I opt for jeans over my usual yoga pants, paired with a white top and a colorful scarf. I always like to look stylish when I see my old roommate from college.

Once dressed, I upload the family photo and link to the soccer story onto the Hamilton Beach Moms' Facebook page. As I wait for the post to load, my phone pings with a text.

> **Doug:** Can you bring in the dry cleaning? Need my gray suit for an interview.

> **Me:** Sure.

> **Doug:** Thanks, and thanks for being understanding about the family picture. You're the best!

Walking into my closet, I pick up the dry-cleaning bag, digging through it to make sure all the clothes inside need professional cleaning. A few weeks ago, my favorite lace dress slipped off a hanger and landed in the bin without me knowing. The dry cleaner ruined it.

As I toss around the clothing, I see a piece of bright red fabric sticking out of Doug's gray suit pants. *What's that?*

I pull out the pants and give them a shake. The pant legs tumble down and straighten out. A pair of red, racy underwear falls to the floor.

I stare at the lacy undergarment for a minute solid before formulating a clear thought. *Is Doug having an affair?*

My feet burn as if the floor is on fire. I bend down to pick up the underwear. Holding them up, I realize they're mine. But the fabric is pulled out into an odd shape, the elastic stretched beyond repair. It looks as if *Doug* has worn my underwear.

I crumble the lacy garment into my hand and step over to our bed. *Is Doug wearing my underwear?* It doesn't make sense. Doug's a real guy's guy. When we first met, I couldn't stand him, or the way he paraded around UCLA wearing cotton muscle tanks that had slits down the sides, exposing tufts of his coarse dark chest hair for the world to see. Could this former macho guy's guy really be wearing my underwear?

My head swells with memories, pieces falling into place. The time we were on vacation and several pairs of my underwear went missing. The time I couldn't find the new underwear I had just purchased at Nordstrom's Anniversary Sale. And of course, that time in college. The evidence was right in front of me, but I'd missed it.

Oh my god, is Doug wearing my underwear?

What should I do? I know I can't tell anyone, but I'm desperate for advice. I sink into my bed, grasping the underwear to my chest. In a moment of pure panic, I grab my phone. I pull up the Hamilton Beach Moms' Facebook page and make an anonymous post.

> **Anonymous Mom Post**
> Today at 10:23 a.m.
>
> Today, as I was gathering clothes for the dry cleaner, I discovered a pair of red lacy underwear inside my husband's suit pants. At first, I thought I'd caught him having an affair. But then I realized the underwear was mine. If I think back, there are many cases of missing underwear spanning the entirety of our relationship. I've always written it off as the dryer monster, but now I'm second-guessing myself. I think my husband is wearing my underwear. I don't know what to do. Should I confront him? What would you do? Is my marriage over?

PAPERS FALL AND scatter around my feet, almost as if in slow motion. My eyes fix tightly on the rude woman who just pushed past me at Trendy Greens. It's her fault I dropped my file folder. Moments ago, I saw her yelling at the valet when she got out of her Cadillac Escalade.

The woman glares at me. "You should be more careful. You were in my way."

"Excuse me?" I say, confused.

"Yes, you bumped into me. And now your papers are on the ground." Her face barely shows any expression. It must be the Botox.

"Isabell, over here."

She turns her focus on a group of women standing a few feet away. "Coming." She walks toward her friends, without even offering to help me gather my things. Her behavior is astounding.

My heart pumps wildly in my chest like a fizzy soda that's exploding out of the can. But it has nothing to do with the rude woman.

My head is still racing after finding my underwear in Doug's pants this morning.

The hostess rushes over and bends down. "Let me help you with that."

"Thanks." A flush of heat rises to my cheeks. I desperately need to sit. "My friend hasn't arrived yet," I say once I've gathered my papers. "But I'd like to be seated, if that's okay."

"Sure, follow me this way."

Taking a seat, my head spins with thoughts of earlier.

Why did I make that anonymous post? My mind shuffles through this morning's events. Looking up from my table, I peer at the entrance looking for Valerie. She must be running late as usual.

Why did I make that anonymous post? I think again. Suddenly, everything around me blurs into a mishmash of colors. Dread mixes with terror as I pull out my phone to see what other moms have to say.

> **Lexi Tate:** Shock and awe. I'm sorry, anonymous mom. Call a divorce attorney. PM me if you need a recommendation.

My stomach rolls around itself as soon as I see the word "divorce." *I have to get out of here.*

Gathering my folder and phone, I hustle to the restaurant's exit and text Valerie.

> **Me:** Sorry, not feeling well. I just left Trendy Greens. We'll have to reschedule.

I dash to the valet, feeling dizzy, and hand the young kid at the carport my ticket.

"Ma'am, are you okay?"

Before responding, I leap toward a small plot of grass as vomit spews from my mouth.

HAMILTON BEACH MOMS
PRIVATE GROUP — 5,328 Members

Laura Perry
Today at 7:12 a.m.

Attention Hamilton Beach Moms! I am excited to announce our Facebook group's first-ever in-person fundraiser to help our community food bank. This amazing event will take place at Edge of the Water Hotel. Let's help feed families in need. Follow this link to register. https://www.facebook.com/HBCMomsgiveback

Tickets are $50 and include lunch, one drink, and a raffle to win a weekend getaway at Edge of the Water Hotel. Enjoy a silent auction, with jewelry, art, Harmony Spa gift certificates, and much more! Come meet your fellow Hamilton Beach moms and donate to this fantastic cause. Also, I am still looking for a co-moderator for this page. It's a fun way to get involved and be on top of community happenings. PM me if you are interested!

202 👍 139 😃 108 🖤

Comments

Meredith Lee: I love this idea! Buying my ticket now.

Tawana Williams: Yes, happy to give back to those in need!

Colleen Hapsher: $50??? That's a bit steep for lunch. I think the page moderator has lost touch with reality.

Shana Sheffield: @Colleen Hapsher If you think it's too expensive, don't go. I think $50 is reasonable for a nice lunch and a glass of wine. Plus, we are going to be helping the food bank.

Isabell Whitmore: I can't believe you are providing Harmony Spa an opportunity to market its services. I had a gel manicure there last week, and it chipped on day two. Unacceptable!

Laurie Rubin: An excuse for day drinking. I say yes!

CHAPTER 5

Laura Perry

N ORA SITS ACROSS from me as I read the comments on my post. She refuses to look at me. She's been wound up since meeting deaf teenagers at the mall six weeks ago.

Distracting myself from her anger, I glance at my post. I'm excited this community will come together for a good cause. It may get Hamilton Beach positive press, which is always good for home sales.

> **Colleen Hapsher:** @Shana Sheffield $50 is a lot of money! Not all of us in Southern Cal have endless bank accounts and drive around in luxury SUVs. Many of us are the people working around you, making your almond milk lattes, repairing the broken straps on your Louis Vuitton handbags, and fitting you with your perfect pair of $500 Golden Duck sneakers. (I still don't understand why anyone wants sneakers intentionally made to look dirty?)

Is the event too expensive? I wonder. But lately, it's impossible for anyone to post on the Hamilton Beach Moms' Facebook page without a blowup. Last week, someone innocently asked where to get her hair colored, and a war broke out about which hairdresser is best at covering grays.

I shut my laptop as Nora takes another bite of her avocado toast. Standing abruptly, the ends of her long blond hair brush against the green mush on her plate. She rushes over to the sink to wipe away the mess. Her lips round into a slight pout. When she exhales, the surrounding air thickens with discontent.

Walking by me, she makes sure I see she's not wearing her cochlear implants, then takes her car keys off the hook hanging by the back door. She stomps out of the house without saying goodbye.

As soon as she leaves, fear bursts through me. I try to remember this doesn't mean there's actual danger, but I can't reason with myself. Nora is deaf and about to drive away without her cochlear implants. She won't be able to hear anything. What if a car honks its horn to alert her to danger? What if a crazy driver revs a loud engine and sneaks up on her before she realizes it?

Grabbing her implants off the kitchen table, I push open the door and run toward her. *I have to fix this.* She doesn't notice I've caught up to her until we're both standing next to her car.

"Please, Nora, at least wear these while you're driving for safety reasons." I can tell she's doing her best to read my lips by the way her forehead creases up as I talk.

"I'm not wearing those things! Deaf people drive safely all the time. If you bothered to understand deaf culture, you would know that." Her pupils widen in anger.

"Yes, I know that, but deaf people were taught to drive deaf; you were taught to drive hearing. It's dangerous." I shudder as I think of Nora pulling away without her implants.

"Don't you get it? I'm deaf. I was born deaf. But you and Dad decided my deafness meant I was broken. You forced me to be a hearing person." Her voice is shrill. She can't regulate her volume without hearing herself through her implants.

Watching her, I can't help but recall the first time we learned Nora might have a problem hearing. A middle-aged female hospital technician, dressed in faded blue scrubs, had tried three times to get a "pass" on a hearing screening for newborn babies.

"Many newborns fail the screening," she said as she placed Nora back in my arms. "Babies still have fluid in their ears after the birthing process. It's probably why I didn't get a pass."

The technician's words floated above me with little consideration. I was too focused on getting Nora to latch onto my breast.

"Maybe I'm not supposed to be a hearing person!" Nora continues frantically, pulling my mind back into the moment. "Maybe I'm not supposed to wear these cochlear implants and be a cyborg who is part machine and part human. Why did you think I needed to be fixed?"

Her words are a violent punch that will leave a large, misshapen purple bruise on my heart. Her rebellion against her status as a cochlear implant user is new. Teenage rebellion—I get it, I do. Most of her peers are equally furious with their parents for making them dedicate their childhoods to pursuits like soccer, piano, or chess, without considering what they might have chosen for themselves. Nora, however, is furious with me for reasons much more profound.

I clasp my hands together to calm the emotions swirling through my body. "We explored deaf culture. It's a beautiful and vibrant community. But your dad and I are hearing, so implants were the right choice. Every decision we made was from a place of love."

Nora's lips curl into a seething scowl.

Feeling like a hyena who's been fatally bitten by a lion, I let my words fall limply to the ground.

"I'm going to school deaf today, whether you like it or not!" Nora screams. She looks at her implants resting in my palm and shoves my hand away.

I can't help but wonder if her intense emotions are fallout from losing her friend group. But before I can ask, she heaves her body inside the car. She slams the door loudly in my face, making me feel for just a moment as if she has won her war on hearing. Her car roars as she blasts out of our driveway, but she can't hear the sound of her anger coming to life.

CHAPTER 6

Julie Wu

BATTER SPLATTERS ON the counter as I stir dill and pepper into the mix for matzah balls. As I reach for a paper towel, I knock over the challah dough. The bowl makes a crashing sound as it hits the ground.

"Everything okay in there, Mom?" Talia leans her head back and peers at me from the couch in the TV room.

"Fine, I'm just frazzled," I say as I clean up the mess. I'm nervous to tell the kids we're moving in two weeks. I can't believe the offer Eric and I made on the house in Hamilton Beach was accepted. It's a fast turnaround, but Eric and I have been preparing the kids for this moment ever since I got the job at Click Com. I hope tonight's meal, one of Talia and Van's favorites, will soften the blow.

"Smells delicious in here!" Eric strolls in and kisses me warmly on the cheek.

"Thanks! Let's hope Nana Rose's Shabbat dinner helps us out tonight."

"The kids are going to be fine," he says as he scrolls through his phone. "Shoot, I have to jump on a quick call."

"Let me guess, one of your clients requires the counsel of their fiercely conservative lawyer." I regret saying the words as soon as they leave my mouth. Lately, Eric and my differing political views are becoming more and more of an issue. Just last week, we had a big blowout over climate change.

"But you're hopelessly in love with this conservative lawyer," he teases.

My pulse relaxes, relieved he took my words in jest. I smile reassuringly but can't help but wonder how I'm married to a card-carrying Republican. Socially, Eric favors many of the values championed by the Democratic Party, but when it comes time to vote, he cannot escape the lure of lower taxes and less government intervention. He casts his vote for red and tells himself the more extreme parts of the ideology will never come to fruition.

"Ugh, Dad, it kills me you're a conservative," Talia says, overhearing our conversation. She walks toward the refrigerator and gets a glass of water.

Eric throws his hands up in the air and shrugs. "I am who I am," he says.

"But what about social justice issues, the oppression of minorities, women's rights, the environment? Don't those things matter?"

A quick smile overtakes my face as I listen to Talia call out Eric for his political beliefs. I love my little activist daughter.

"Of course, they matter," Eric agrees. "But the financial values of conservatives keep our economy afloat. Someone has to keep fighting for lower taxes."

Talia sticks her tongue out at Eric playfully.

"Talia, I'd be happy to have another one of our political debates after dinner. You know how much I love to hear your point of view, even though you're wrong." He winks at her lovingly as he goes back into his office to make his call.

The kitchen quiets as I finish prepping Nana Rose's recipe. She's the one who taught me how to do a twelve-strand braided challah. The beauty of the finished loaf always evokes oohs and ahhs from my family.

As I cross long gooey pieces of challah dough over one another, my mind wanders back to Friday afternoons spent in Nana's kitchen, kneading dough. I longed to join my peers for the evening football games but couldn't because of the Sabbath. As the only Jewish person in my high school, I never fit in.

Looking over at Talia and Van, I wonder if they feel as excluded as I did. I'm sure it can't be easy being both Jewish and Chinese.

"Unbelievable!" Talia shouts at the TV as I lay the braided challah on a sheet pan.

Placing the pan in the oven, I step toward Talia and see she's captivated by a news story. Unable to hear what the reporter is saying, I walk closer to find out what's angered her. Last year, she demanded we learn how to live off the grid. Best I get a heads-up on what's coming.

Peering into the camera, the reporter speaks. "The new law will make it almost impossible for women in Georgia to get an abortion." The moment the female reporter utters the words, my body jolts up straight, as if I have stepped on a pinhead.

Talia shoots up from the couch. Her eyes are wide with frustration. "How can they do that, Mom? How can they pass a law basically outlawing abortion? What if, one day, I find out I'm pregnant with a baby who has a life-altering disease? What if I get pregnant down the road when I'm not ready to be a mom? What about women who are raped and want to end the pregnancy?" Talia's eyes lock with mine, searching for comfort.

My chest instantly fills with panic. Talia is sixteen. The age I was when I had an abortion. I can't help but think of her life and her right to choose. The blood rushes to my fingers, causing them to burn as if they are hot, even though I know their temperature is unchanged. And, because I had my abortion in Georgia, the new ruling feels like a personal attack.

"When are we having dinner?" Eric appears, unaware of the turmoil both Talia and I are experiencing. Talia points at the TV angrily, and Eric listens as the reporter gives a few more details about the new Georgia law.

"How is it possible to be moving backward?" Talia shouts to no one in particular. "I half expect to see flying cars and robots serving me Starbucks, yet here we are, putting women's rights in reverse." She storms out of the house.

Van runs after her.

"Wow, that was a big reaction," Eric says with surprise.

Suddenly, I feel the weight of fat and forceful tears hitting my cheeks. This is an ugly cry. "How do you not get it?" I snap, bewildered by his ability to disconnect from our personal experience.

"I'm sorry," he says after he realizes I'm crying.

"I'm sorry. That's the best you can come up with? How can you completely detach from how abortion rights have shaped your own life!" My body shakes. Then anger. I am angry. I am so damn angry. I slam my hand hard against the wall several times, demanding to know how he can support conservative politicians. "It's a betrayal of me, and you know exactly why." My chest feels hollow as I think of the child we abandoned. "It's also a betrayal of Talia."

His cheeks sink in for just a moment, and I wonder if he's finally thinking of our past.

"You've benefited from the very laws you vote against. You should be outraged! And don't you understand how these restrictions unfairly impact minorities?" I throw my words at him like arrows, hoping they will cause pain. "You can finish up with dinner and feeding the kids. I'm going upstairs." I don't stay to hear his response.

When I get to my bedroom, I'm desperate for support. I wish I had a close friend to call.

Then I remember the Hamilton Beach Moms' Facebook page. I've been following the page ever since Laura recommended it, wondering if it will help me find a group of women to connect with when we move. I've seen the anonymous posts. They are constant. These moms have no problem discussing their most intimate problems online. Just the other day, a mom posted anonymously because her husband ran off with another man.

Picking up my phone, I create my own anonymous post. My hands tremble as I admit to the abortion. It seems extremely risky to confess this online. The abortion is something Eric and I never discuss. I keep the memory pushed down deep. But, lately, it tears through me with sharp claws when I least expect it. Like on the beach with Laura.

I hit post, and watch my question go live. I feel some relief, knowing the painful truth of it is out there. They say that one in four women has had an abortion. There has to be a mom out there who can offer support.

New Activity

Anonymous Mom Post
Today at 5:23 p.m.

Is anyone else in a marriage of opposing political views? I'm a liberal, and my husband is a conservative. Politics has become such an extreme sport in the last several years. Both parties are so radical. We are both continually outraged by what the other party is plotting. Our political divide is causing problems in our marriage. The worst part is that we ended a pregnancy in high school. I'm outraged that he supports politicians who are not pro-choice. I'm seriously wondering if I can stay married to a man whose beliefs are so different from mine. Has anyone been in a similar situation?

CHAPTER 7

Isabell Whitmore

"**M**ARY?" I CALL into the open air of my enormous kitchen. I need my coffee, stat! Where did she go? My body leans against my gorgeous Calcutta marble island as I scroll through my Instagram posts.

A moment later, Mary shuffles in, holding a basket overflowing with dirty clothing. I notice her white button-down shirt has a yellow stain on the collar. She represents my home when people visit. She must look tidy.

"Sorry, Miss Isabell, I was upstairs getting the laundry." She pushes her red hair away from her freckly face.

"I need my latte." Looking at my phone, I carefully inspect the photo I posted on Insta last week with my tennis team after our lunch at Trendy Greens. I look so fit and fabulous among their soft and pillowy bodies. My body's a temple and will always be my top priority. No apologies.

The lunch with the tennis group was standard, with its passive-aggressive bragging and scandalous gossiping.

"Did you see the post Kate Millar made on the Hamilton Beach Moms' Facebook page?" Nadia looked at us, hoping for more information. Our friend group was swirling with rumors about the Millars.

"The one about helping her son choose between Harvard or Yale?" I couldn't help but share the very juicy piece of information I had. "Everyone knows they used that *side door* to get Harry into both schools," I said assuredly. "The entire family is under investigation." I impressed the group with my intel, and they spent the next twenty minutes peppering me with questions.

We ended lunch by exchanging the information we knew about Liza Braxton's divorce, each one of us trying to sound sad about how her husband ran off with a young stripper.

"Here we go." Mary fills my favorite oversized mug with coffee and steams the milk that goes on top. "And here's your recent issue of *Vogue*." She puts my favorite magazine on the counter next to me, but I'm distracted by the coffee.

"I hope you didn't put cow's milk in my coffee like yesterday. I only drink my lattes with unsweetened almond milk."

Mary's eyes widen at my abrasive tone. She quickly recovers by flashing me a wide fake smile. "Yes, ma'am," she says. "Steamed almond milk."

I know the sweetness of her tone is fake, like her smile, but it doesn't bother me. She's paid to be polite and kiss my ass.

Warm, earthy liquid slides down my throat, instantly kicking up my adrenaline. I need to create a new post for my Insta feed of 250,000 followers. My account, @eightpakcalmom16, has become an obsession. I curate each photo as if it will be displayed at a high-end art gallery. The hours I spend on my posts keep my mind from wandering into my past mistakes.

"Hey, Mary," I say as I take the last sip of my drink. "I need you to stop what you're doing and take a few photos of me." I shove my phone in her hand and pose as if I'm getting ready to be featured on the cover of the *Vogue* issue I'm about to devour.

Mary snaps fifty pictures, until I'm satisfied we have one worth posting. I settle on the photo where my face is partially obscured by the words on my mug—*I'm a ray of fucking sunshine*. The picture looks artsy and still shows the hypnotic blue of my eyes.

As I flip through the thick glossy pages of my magazine, I'm reminded that I once was part of the glamorous world of fashion. My pulse beats with a rush when I look through the stunning magazine photos featuring the latest and greatest collections from the world's top designers.

I grab a pen to make a list of the items I plan to purchase as I inspect the magazine cover to cover. As I squeal over an ad showcasing Chanel's latest soft pink slouchy bucket bag, I gasp. On the opposite page, under the headline, "The Godfather of the Fashion World," is the face of the man that ruined me.

I WAS TWENTY-TWO, living in New York City, working as a low-paid assistant for the one and only Parker T. Boucher, the famous style editor of a glamorous fashion magazine. Hot air tickled my cheek as I steamed dresses in thick, luxurious fabrics and hung them on a clothes rack for an upcoming photoshoot. Mr. Boucher would stop by soon to make his final edit. Hurrying, I set everything up in a small, empty office. Mr. Boucher's choices would determine which dresses would sell out and which would end up on sale racks in high-end department stores.

The photoshoot, pitched as "Fall's Elevated Frocks," showcased a glamorous selection of opulent clothing intended for the rich and famous. My progress stalled as I admired the intricate beadwork on a full-length stunner, whose colors came together like a peacock's impossibly gorgeous feathers. The rich purples, blues, and greens swirled along the one-sleeved, backless dress, allowing the wearer to show off the perfect place where the collarbone met the shoulder. Mr. Boucher walked in just as I held it up to my tall, thin frame.

"It's a size zero, but it should fit you. Of course, we'll have to take it in several inches for the model." He looked at me eagerly.

Flustered by him seeing my unmistakable fascination with the dress, I quickly placed it back on the clothing rack. "It's gorgeous," I stammered.

"Why don't you try it on? I haven't decided if I'm going to include that one."

"Really? Are you sure that's okay?"

He pressed his lips together in a thin smile of amusement. His perfectly gelled hair gleamed from the light streaking through the window. "Of course, Izzy, I'm in charge around here. I'll step out and give you a few minutes to put it on." He turned his tall slim frame and walked out the door.

Instantly, I felt a strange tingle, as if someone suddenly released a jar of captured butterflies to flutter around my body. I took off my black and white plaid blazer and set it neatly over the clothing rack, along with my skirt, cami, and simple pink bra.

As I turned toward the dress, the door opened. Mr. Boucher strode in, holding my naked body in his gaze. I reflexively crossed my arms over my breasts, startled he'd entered the room without even knocking.

"Oh, Izzy, don't be shy. I see naked bodies all day long. It's my job." His words, however, did not diminish the shameless way his eyes lingered over the flesh pouring out from under my hands.

"I'll just turn my back while you finish stepping into the dress." He turned back toward the door.

I swiftly pulled the dress off its hanger and stepped into the center of the glinting fabric, shoving my arm into the one sleeve as fast as I could.

"Are you dressed?" Mr. Boucher called out.

"Yes," I said, as a wave of fleshy bumps spread across my bare arm.

"Let me have a look at you." Mr. Boucher turned and walked toward me. He was an attractive bachelor in his forties. His sex appeal was undeniable. "The dress isn't laying right. Let me see the back. The eye hook probably isn't fastened."

Taking a long stride, Mr. Boucher put his arms on my shoulders and turned me around. I felt his hand as it slowly caressed the length of my bare back, down to where the eye hook sat just on top of my backside.

"Yes, it's not hooked. Here we go."

He stepped back, allowing space for me to turn and face him again, but I stood frozen by the repulsive way his hand had traveled the length of my body.

"Isabell, go ahead, turn around."

CHAPTER 8

Maggie O'Donnell

W AITERS AND WAITRESSES buzz around Trendy Greens, carrying trays piled high with enormous bowls of lettuce and fancy toppings. Waiting for Valerie, I'm reminded it was one week ago that I fled from this restaurant, skipping this very meeting.

My stomach rumbles uncomfortably. *Is it hunger or nausea?* For the last week, I haven't been able to eat and feel like I'm stuck in a whirl of swirling water. *Should I approach Doug about the underwear? Am I ready to hear the truth? Is it possible he's having an affair or even gay?* I keep rehearsing what to say in my head but dissolve into tears before coming up with a cohesive thought.

My hand wavers slightly as I scroll the comments on my anonymous post. Eighty-nine moms have provided input, and it's still going. Suddenly, every mom in this town thinks she's Dr. Phil.

Susan Davidson: Why post this online? It seems crazy. Phone a friend.

A surge of dread catches in my chest. Yes, it was crazy for me to post this. If anyone finds out, Doug's career is ruined. My finger hovers over the "delete post" button. Suddenly another comment pops up.

Isabell Whitmore: Find out his favorite brand of women's underwear and buy him a pair!

My insides dissolve into liquid. *How could someone joke about this?* Before I can even grasp the rude comment, I see Valerie walking past the hostess stand wearing a sharp navy suit. She's the editor of the *Hamilton Herald* and has written a few articles for the *LA Times*. She hires me to do freelance pieces.

"Sorry I'm late!" Valerie tosses her briefcase on the table and sits across from me.

"I wouldn't expect anything less," I tease, shoving my concerns about Doug down deep. "You're never on time. But I still love you."

"I may always be late," she says, laughing, "but at least I'm consistent."

"True. You're lucky I put up with your chronic tardiness," I say, trying to keep up with our usual banter despite the desperation buzzing inside me.

"Except, of course, that time in college when I made you late for Doug's fraternity formal. I've never seen you so mad." She pulls a file from her briefcase as she speaks, then takes a sip of water.

"Sorry I had to cancel last week," I say, wanting to change the subject away from Doug.

"That's okay. Are you feeling better?"

I swallow for a moment, considering whether I want to tell Valerie the true reason I canceled our lunch. I'm desperate for the comfort of a good friend. Valerie and I are close. The years we've spent together traversing drunken sorority escapades, marriage, and motherhood have proven I can trust her with this. *But women's underwear?* No, I can't tell a single soul.

"I'm fine. It was just a migraine." I push my lips out into a smile wide enough to fool *myself* into believing everything is okay.

"Glad you're feeling better." She hands me papers from her file. "I hate to cut right to the chase, but I have a meeting at the *Times* later. I need to get on the road before traffic blows up."

"Sure, I get it; the 10's a nightmare."

"So, I'm looking for a feel-good piece about community support organizations in Hamilton Beach. The world is overwhelmed with bad news. My team wants a cheerful story."

"Makes sense," I say.

"Focus the piece on the Hamilton Beach Refugee Center, the Hamilton Beach Food Bank, and the Hamilton Beach Moms' Facebook page."

My stomach ties up in a knot at the mention of the Facebook page.

"Here's the phone number of a woman who volunteers for the refugee center. She's an orthopedist. Her name is Dr. Indira Acharya. Start with her and then reach out to the center itself. They just hired a new executive director who immigrated here when she was a teenager. Could make for an interesting story."

"What a small world," I say, relieved by the distraction of my professional life. "Dr. Acharya did my father's hip replacement last year." I take the paper with Dr. Acharya's number and place it in my file.

"She's supposed to be the best," Valerie says before continuing. "For the food bank, do a cold call. I don't have a contact there."

I nod.

"As far as the Facebook page goes, it's run by a real estate agent named Laura Perry. You can find her by searching for Perry Properties. That Facebook page should be the focus of its own story down the road. Can you believe the things people post?"

Squirming in my chair, heat rushes to my cheeks. I pray Valerie does not sense my discomfort.

"Those anonymous mom posts are too much. So entertaining!" She laughs out loud as the waiter places a bread basket on the table.

"That Facebook page is just a boring waste of time," I say, eager to redirect Valerie's focus.

Valerie leans toward me, as if she's a teenage girl sharing the latest rumor swirling around the head cheerleader. "But did you see that post last week about the husband wearing his wife's underwear? That's not boring. That's gold!"

Suddenly, it feels like the floor is cracking open, about to swallow me whole.

"What's wrong? You look upset." Valerie cocks her head to the side as she peers at me.

"Nothing's wrong. It's just...the moms in this town are too obsessed with the page. And people make insensitive comments, trying to stir up trouble." I sit back in my chair, widening the space between Valerie and me. "I bet that post is fake. Just someone trying to give the moms something to gossip about."

"Huh. I never considered that moms would make up posts just for fun." Valerie looks away for a moment, turning my words over in her mind. "But, oh my god, can you imagine if this post about the underwear is real?"

My stomach twists as I nod again, giving up on trying to convince her otherwise.

"This poor woman! At least you've got a real man's man for a husband. Ever since college, Doug's been all hunk and testosterone." Valerie lifts her phone and pulls up the post I made last week, promoting Doug's soccer story. "Look at the comments the moms are making about him."

I stare at the photo of our family, focusing on Doug's angular face. I've been so preoccupied with my anonymous mom post, I haven't read any of the comments on the soccer story post. My eyes scan the remarks.

> **Lori Cahill:** The best-looking sports anchor in Cali. 😎

> **Amara Johnson:** I find myself watching his stories even though I have no interest in sports.

> **Isabell Whitmore:** Would love to see him do modeling on the side. Maybe underwear modeling? The less clothes, the better!

My lips tremble as I read the word "underwear." I quickly suck them together before Valerie notices.

"Ladies, what can I get for you today?" The waiter returns, and Valerie tosses her phone back in her briefcase and begins to order.

"I'll have a chicken Caesar," I interrupt. "Sorry, I've got to use the ladies' room."

Rushing away, I breathe in every drop of air I can inhale—the word *underwear* pings back and forth across my brain like a ball in a pinball game.

CHAPTER 9

Indira Acharya

N UNKNOWN NUMBER pops up on my phone. *The name Maggie O'Donnell* flashes across the display. I don't know anyone with that name and let it go to voicemail.

Swiping with my finger, I flip back to the Hamilton Beach Moms' Facebook page. My heart is exploding in my chest. I type my inquiry anonymously.

> **Anonymous Mom Post**
> Today at 3:12 p.m.
> It's almost my fifteenth wedding anniversary, but I'm falling in love with someone else. I can no longer deny the energy between us. I'm devastated the love of my life is not my husband. I'm from a traditional background, and leaving my marriage is not an option. We have children, and I am committed to our family life. Has anyone stayed married, knowing they loved someone else? How did you cope? I cannot end my marriage, so please tell me how to continue and let my true love go.

My body quivers as soon as the post goes live. I toss my phone on my closet floor, suddenly afraid of the phone itself. My eyes wander to my full-length mirror. Adjusting my royal blue silk saree, I pick up a safety pin and fasten the wide drape to the fitted top I'm wearing underneath. This saree was my Nani's. My mom passed it on to me when I got married. It's embroidered with intricate gold thread and clear, sparkling beadwork. The bright fabric evokes memories of Nani, my mom, and me, cooking *keri athanu*. My throat burns as soon as the memory of the fiery dish enters my mind.

What would my Nani and mom think about my post? I've spent my life pleasing my parents, my heritage, and the world. But, since attending a volunteer meeting at the refugee center, I find I'm pushing back.

It was just three months ago when my life took this unexpected turn. I arrived at the refugee center for a volunteer orientation, unaware I was about to discover my heart's true desire.

Memories of the project I did for the refugee center in high school bombarded me as I entered the building. I was looking forward to reigniting my passion for helping immigrant families.

As I walked into a small classroom, a tall, slender man was addressing the group. Running late because of traffic, I quickly took an open seat in the front. As soon as I sat down, the man paused and gave me a warm smile.

"Welcome. I was just getting started. My name is Jon Feldman. I'm an immigration attorney and do the pro bono work for the refugee center." He glanced in my direction with an infectious charm.

As I considered whether he was flirting, the door swung open, and an extremely tall woman with skin as black as night burst through the door.

"Hello, everyone," she said with an expansive smile. "I'm so sorry I'm late. Traffic was a nightmare. Jon, thank you for stepping in and getting things started."

Instantly, it felt as if my stomach unhinged from my body and dropped to the floor. My eyes blinked rapidly as if I was adjusting to a burst of light. They narrowed on the woman's face with the intensity of a predator stalking its prey.

The tall woman continued. "I'm the new executive director here at the refugee center. My name is Fatima. My family immigrated from

Ethiopia when I was fifteen years old. In fact, we immigrated right here in Hamilton Beach."

Fatima. It was Fatima. I could hardly believe it. I had heard nothing about her since she moved away during high school. The incident that happened the summer between junior and senior years flew through my mind, making my body burn.

I'd made a handful of attempts over the years to Google her, but I couldn't remember how to spell her last name. Any guesses I made at pushing Ds, Js, and vowels together were always incorrect, and my searches came up empty.

As soon as the meeting ended, she bounded up to me as if we were long-lost relatives. "Oh, Indira, Indira?! This is unbelievable!" Her voice was loud and consumed the whir of softer conversations happening around us. "Indira, it's you! I know you weren't expecting to see me. I just moved back. I was planning to look you up. I've tried searching for you on Google, but I couldn't remember your last name."

The absurdity of our failed search attempts because of our last names released my frozen jaw, and a hideous cackle escaped my lips. It took me a few moments to gain my composure. "I'm sorry I'm laughing, Fatima," I finally said. "I've also tried looking you up but couldn't find you for the same reason. My maiden name was Hathiwala. And yours was something with a D and a J."

"D-i-e-j-o-m-a-o-h," she said as she put my hand in her large, elegant palm.

I immediately felt a jolt.

Ping. My phone's chime jolts me back to the present. Glancing at it on the closet floor, I wonder if someone has left a comment on my anonymous post? My face burns with heat. I see it's a voicemail from Maggie O'Donnell. No time to check it now. I need to finish getting ready for my parents' anniversary party at my brother's house.

Peering at my face, I see Nani in the elongated shape of my eyes. I sweep a decorative jade comb into the left side of my thick, long brown hair and put in a pair of large gold hoop earrings. As I stack bangle bracelets on my wrist, I hear footsteps shuffling toward me.

"Waah," Kabir smiles and lets out a brief demur whistle as he enters our walk-in closet. He kisses the top of my head. "My love, you look beautiful."

Smiling back at him through the mirror, guilt pulses through my body. I do not deserve his adoration. I quickly point to the shoebox overhead, anxious to change the topic of conversation. "Can you get me my shoes? They're up on the top shelf."

Kabir stretches his long arm toward the ceiling and hands me the box. "Here you are."

"Are the girls ready?" I ask as I take my sandals out and drop them on the floor.

"Yes, they're outside, inspecting the latest work on the new pool. It's almost finished. The contractor's coming tomorrow to do the electrical work. I'm hoping they can fill it with water in the next few weeks."

"That's good news, although I'm disappointed we aren't hosting mom and dad's fiftieth anniversary party." Kabir and I have a beautiful backyard, but since we're in the middle of building a pool, our yard is a mess of dirt and concrete. Large pipes are strewn around the grass as if giants are playing a game of pick-up sticks.

"I'll be ready in five minutes," I say as I close my sandal straps around my ankles.

Taking a small step forward toward the full-length mirror, I review my reflection. I've always liked the way my body looks in this particular saree. It hugs my curves in all the right places, while hiding the areas of my body that are less desirable. It's the little black dress of sarees.

"Here, my love. Open this gift." Kabir pulls a small black velvet box out of his pocket and places it in my hands.

The shame I feel as my fingers brush against its soft exterior makes me wish the box was covered in thorns.

"Go ahead, Indira, see what's inside." Kabir looks at me with anticipation.

The box's edges open, and the hinge loosens. Inside is a gorgeous pair of gold chandelier earrings encrusted with sapphires.

"As soon as I saw these, I knew they would be perfect to wear with Nani's saree."

"They're beautiful," I say as I replace the earrings I put in earlier with Kabir's gift. "But it's my parents' anniversary, not ours."

"No worries, my love. Here, let me see how they look."

I turn away from the mirror and face Kabir, jutting my face forward to emphasize his thoughtful gift.

"So lovely." His eyes are bright with satisfaction. "I'll go downstairs and let you finish." He takes a step forward but stumbles over my phone.

"Oh, Kabir, be careful," I say in a tight voice as I watch him catch his balance.

"I'm fine." He winks.

As he walks out of our closet, I pick up my phone. My finger seems to move on its own accord and quickly taps my notifications. *Has anyone responded to my anonymous post?* Slight dread skirts through my chest.

> **Kelsey Graton:** There is a name for this, and it's called an emotional affair. You should be ashamed. You don't deserve your husband.

The muscles in my back tighten, but I can't help but continue to the next comment.

> **Helen Irving:** @Kelsey Graton: Don't be so harsh. Anonymous mom found a type of love most never experience. She needs support, not judgment.

My stiff back relaxes. Yes, Helen is right. This relationship is something rare and special.

"ZOYA! BE CAREFUL!" Kabir calls out to our six-year-old as I step onto our deck, ready to leave for the party.

My three daughters are running around the unfinished pool. The bright pink, purple, and red smears of their lehengas rush by in a whirl.

Ping. I jump out of my skin as my phone alerts me to another comment on my post.

> **Isabell Whitmore:** Marriage is such an antiquated concept. Talk with your husband about having an open relationship.

An open relationship? Isabell Whitmore is out of her mind. My post is not about sex; my post is about love.

> **Simone Gregor:** If you are considering an affair, it means something's missing in your relationship. I have helped many couples through this. Please reach out. This link will take you to my therapy practice web page. www.savemysoutherncalmarriage. com. You can also buy my book, Save my Southern Cal Marriage, on Amazon.

Save my SouthernCal marriage? My post suddenly feels like the plot for a low-brow reality show. I should never have posted. I will not find the advice I need in a Facebook comment.

As I pull up the post to delete it, Kabir steps behind me. I throw my phone into my purse at lightning speed, so he doesn't see it.

"Girls!" I call out as I wave. "We need to leave for Uncle Keshav's house."

Kabir looks at his watch and smiles. "We're early, as usual. Let them play for a few minutes." Kabir lowers his body into one of our plush patio chairs and sighs. "What a shame the pool took longer than we expected," he says as he motions for me to sit.

Walking toward him, I rest my body in the pillowy fabric of the chair next to him. "Don't let me leave without the *mathiya*," I say.

Kabir smiles. "Kate's been overwhelmed hosting with all the cultural expectations. I'm glad you could help. But you know your mom will complain tonight, even if everything's perfect." Kabir purses together his lips, slightly amused.

"Poor Kate, she'll never please her Saasu Maa," I say knowing it hasn't been easy for Kate. But my brother, Keshav, is the one who put her in this position. He married a white, Christian American. My parents were terrified when they learned their son wanted to marry someone outside of the Hindu faith.

"Your mother has high expectations," Kabir says.

His comment makes the hair on my skin bristle. "But you know exactly what it's like being raised by immigrant parents."

My mind wanders to my childhood. I could always sense my parents' anxiety. For them, leaving India and living in Southern California was like walking around with a small pebble stuck in their shoe. It was a tolerable situation, but one filled with a nagging discomfort.

"Yes," Kabir says. "I understand." He's quiet for a moment and looks at me pensively. "I've asked you this so many times, but I can't seem to get a straight answer. Do you think your parents pressured you to be the perfect Indian child?"

Today his question hits me hard. It's one I've been contemplating since I realized I'm in love with a woman. Did I follow the blueprint my parents designed for my life without considering what I truly desired?

"No," I say honestly as I turn my face toward Kabir's, without making eye contact. "It was a pressure I put on myself. My brother certainly lived life as he wanted, without pushing aside his own desires." The ache that has plagued me since reconnecting with Fatima pulses through my body.

"Is that what you think, Indira? Do you feel you haven't pursued your desires or the life you really wanted?"

His tone is thick with hurt, and I can't help but feel caught. His question nestles too close to the truth. *What if I had explored the reason for my behavior that summer day between junior and senior year?*

"I could always sense my parents' unease that Keshav and I would dilute their traditions and abandon them. I guess I carried the weight of making them proud." Heat crawls up my neck as I speak.

Kabir reaches his hand out toward me and strokes my palm. "I understand what you're saying. You wanted to make your parents happy."

Nodding in agreement, I don't share that I've finally come to understand that I carried the weight of my parents' expectations precisely the wrong way. I let it crush my own yearnings until what I wanted for myself was reduced into pulverized, unrecognizable particles.

Kabir leans into me and tucks a piece of my coarse hair behind my ear. "It's hard to understand that you could feel any dissatisfaction, Indira." He locks his eyes on mine. "You're an accomplished surgeon, a wonderful mother, and a loving wife."

Kabir's comment reminds me of his compassionate nature. I'm lucky to have a supportive husband. But I'm far from a loving wife. I'm on the verge of being unfaithful.

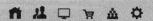

HAMILTON BEACH MOMS
PRIVATE GROUP — 5,329 Members

Laura Perry
Today at 7:21 a.m.

It's Business Thursday. Promote your business in the comments. Let's support the mompreneurs in our community!

Also, over 200 people registered for our fundraising event. There's still space available. Help our community's foodbank. https://www.facebook.com/HBCMomsgiveback.

I'm still looking for a co-moderator. Please message me if interested.

85

Comments

Gabriella Martinez: For those looking for natural cleaning products, check out my Facebook page, GreenCleanHamilton. All the products are chemical-free and created from plant-based ingredients. These cleaning products are powerful while keeping your home free of contaminants. GREENCLEAN!

Dianna Albers: If you're intrigued but haven't tried stick-on gel nail polish, now's your chance. Lush Love Nails are easy to apply and are the same quality you get from the salon. I'll send a free set to the first five people who PM me.

Isabell Whitmore: I'm so over these multi-level marketing companies. They are a scam. Look what happened with that legging business. My friend lost $5,000 and is stuck with a pile of ugly leggings that she'll never sell. I've gone through the heap, and wow, it's hard to understand what the fashion designers were thinking. One pair has hotdogs all over them. One hotdog is placed in the most unfortunate location near the groin area. I'll let your imagination take it from here.

Nicki Flaherty: Yes, If I have one more friend ask me to host a fill-in-the-blank party, I will rage.

Kimberly Larsen: 💯 I don't want in on your Ponzi scheme.

Terri Jordan: Kind of different, but along these same lines, please stop posting on my wall inviting me to join your book exchange, your secret sister gift exchange, and anything else. I'm trying to get rid of the clutter in my house. Not add to it.

Robin Mason: @Terri Jordan When an acquaintance posted on my wall asking me to join her gift exchange, instead of following the instructions, I sent her an envelope filled with a glitter bomb. Safe to say, I don't think she's planning to reach out about her wine exchange. 🌀😂

Lisa Sperber: Bah humbug, you naysayers. When you buy something from a mom, you are helping her gain back financial independence and a feeling of self-worth. These moms deserve credit for putting themselves out there. They face rejection every day but keep pursuing their goals. SELL ON, I say to my mom friends.

Heather Lourie: I agree. Everyone has a side hustle these days.

CHAPTER 10

Laura Perry

TROY WALKS INTO the kitchen, enticed by the smell of fresh pancakes as I finish my Facebook post.

"Did Nora leave for school?" he asks as he peels an overly ripe banana.

I cringe as he bites into the brown spotted piece of fruit. "She did, and she left without her implants. I'm not sure how she's participating. It's not like her teachers know sign language. Nora doesn't even know sign language."

Troy tosses his banana peel in the garbage, helps himself to pancakes, and joins me at the kitchen table. "I never expected Nora to be mad at us for choosing cochlear implants. But it's a phase, and in the end, she'll realize every decision we made was in her best interest." He slices off a thick chunk of his golden brown breakfast treat, unwilling to put too much stock in Nora's behavior.

"Is it a phase?" I ask. "She met those deaf teenagers over six weeks ago. How much longer will this go on?" I recall how she came home equally excited and furious about the encounter.

"Why didn't you let me learn sign language?" Her voice had been gruff.

It was a question I had never anticipated. It took me a few seconds to respond. "The professionals recommended we focus on hearing and speaking. They said exposing you to sign would slow down your progress."

In truth, the recommendation had confused me as well. I wanted Nora to have a way to communicate. But once she received her implants and started talking, her deafness felt like a small object tucked away out of sight. The grief I felt after her diagnosis faded. I never expected it to resurface all these years later.

Troy brings his syrupy plate to the sink, and I shake off my thoughts.

"Have you thought more about letting her learn sign?" he asks. "She's already developed speech and language. It won't interfere with anything." He wipes syrup from his hands as he waits for me to reply.

"I have, but I'm terrified by the thought of her attaching herself to deaf culture. If she stops wearing her implants, she may stop using her voice to communicate. And then the clarity of her speech could suffer. Where will it go from there?" The potent scent of coffee consumes me as I walk to the pot and pour myself another cup. I can't hide the tears gently falling onto my cheeks.

"Come here," Troy says, stepping in close and embracing me in a tight hug.

"Did we fail her?" Suddenly it feels like a boulder is pressing on my lungs, making it hard to inhale. It's the same feeling I had the day of Nora's first hearing test. I can still picture her drifting in and out of light sleep in her baby carrier, as we waited for the audiologist to call us back. I considered making a sudden loud noise to see if Nora would wake up. This was something Troy and I had been doing regularly to calm our nerves.

"See how her arm twitched when I banged that pot?"

"See how her eyes fluttered open when the doorbell rang and the dog barked?"

"If she were deaf, she wouldn't have smiled when I made that silly noise."

"We didn't fail her." Troy strokes my back in gentle waves as he refills my coffee. "We'll get through this. I promise you."

"My heart hurts to see her in pain," I say. "But I'm not sure I want her to explore this." I curl my body further into Troy's broad chest. "Maybe we should have done more to help Nora understand she's deaf, even though she has cochlear implants?"

Troy pulls back and stares at me. "What do you mean?"

"We could have learned sign language. We could have introduced her to the deaf community." My thoughts hang heavily in the air.

"We considered ASL for Nora. We even spent time with that deaf mentor family. There are many positive things about deaf culture, but we wanted Nora to communicate through listening and talking." Troy pulls out of our embrace and faces me. "Nora is thriving and happy." His facial features soften. "I'm confident we made the right decision for our child and our family." He speaks his words confidently, like a drum sure of its beat.

"Yes, you're right. All this is so unexpected." My face scrunches together with tension.

"Try and take it easy, Laura." Troy gently presses his thumb between my eyes, causing me to relax the muscles in my forehead. "Let's not get wound up about this yet."

"Okay," I say. "I'll try. Hey, don't forget I have the closing for the Wu family tonight. They've been staying at Edge of the Water Hotel but are moving into their new home tomorrow. Maybe you can take Nora to dinner at her favorite, Southern Cal Sushi, and score some points?"

"Sure, great idea," he says. "Good luck at the closing. I'll see you later." Troy grabs his wallet off the counter and shoves it into his messenger bag. When he shuts the door behind him, I'm left alone with my memories.

"THEY JUST CALLED Nora. It's time for her hearing test." Troy grabbed the baby carrier's handle and walked to the door leading to the exam rooms. I followed behind, carrying a diaper bag filled with enough items to crowd a small New York City apartment.

"We're doing an auditory brainstem response test, today." Our audiologist, Dr. Melody Flack, was young and fresh, like a shiny red apple just picked from a local orchard. "Once Nora is sleeping, I'll tape a few electrodes on her. I'll also place small inserts in her ears to play sounds. I'll record how her brain responds to these sounds on my computer. This test will not hurt or scare Nora. She'll most likely sleep the entire time. The results will give us a good estimation of what Nora can hear." Dr. Flack paused for a moment to allow us to take in the information.

Immediately, I noticed her expensive glistening white heels and how they accentuated her dark brown skin. And her name, Melody. I found it cruel how it highlighted exactly what was on the line—my daughter's ability to hear the magnificence of sound, words, and music.

Troy stood up, took Nora from my arms, and placed her in the ugly plastic crib beside us. I remember a strange sense of rage overtake me as he lifted Nora out of my arms. How dare he be the one to hold her during what was potentially our last moment of normality?

Dr. Flack began the test. I could see part of her computer screen, although the graphics it displayed made no sense to me. Fluctuating waves in different colors danced across the screen. Would the information in these waveforms crush us or bring us safely to shore?

After a few minutes, I could hear a soft, strange, clicking sound coming from the inserts placed in Nora's ears. Soon, the clicks became glaringly loud, and noise poured out of the tiny inserts, in the same way running water gushes out of a hole. Nora continued to sleep soundly.

"How is that not waking her up?" Troy mouthed silently, as if afraid somehow the sound of his deep throaty voice would cause Nora's deafness.

"I've got the data. I'm going to my office to review the results. Feel free to get Nora out of the crib, or she can continue to sleep." Dr. Flack picked up the laptop computer and left the room.

Troy and I sat in our chairs, watching Nora sleep in the ugly plastic crib. Neither of us said a word. Time is a strange thing. It has no desire to conform to our human constraints. The same span of time can move slow or fast, depending on the circumstances. This particular fifteen minutes was a peculiar paradox. The minutes were interminable, yet Dr. Flack was back in an instant.

She entered the room with Nora's chart and a thick blue folder. Pulling over the chair from the computer desk, she faced Troy and me. She looked at Nora, who was now sleeping soundly in my arms. "She's so peaceful," she said as she pulled out a piece of paper from the blue folder.

It took every fiber of my being to push my lips into a smile. A strange tingle was spreading throughout my body, paralyzing me.

"This graph is called an audiogram of sounds." Dr. Flack began. "It shows the pitch and loudness of sounds. Loud sounds are at the bottom, and soft sounds are at the top. Does that make sense?"

Troy and I nodded as if we understood, but we had zero ability to process the information. We desperately needed to know if Nora could hear before we could grasp an entry-level course on the physics of sound.

"Here, you see the same graph with a plot of Nora's estimated hearing, based on today's results."

I stared at the graph. Red and blue lines were plotted at the bottom, practically on top of each other.

"Nora's hearing is similar for both ears. The red line represents her right ear, and the blue line represents her left ear. Nora can hear the sounds under her lines but does not hear the sounds plotted above her lines."

I again looked at the graph. All the speech sounds, a picture of people talking, a dog barking, a baby crying, and even a car horn, were above Nora's lines.

"I want to make sure I'm understanding." Troy's voice wobbled. "Nora can't hear people talking. She can't hear our dog barking. She can't…" He suddenly stopped and looked at the floor. I could feel his body tremble as he continued. "I'm trying to wrap my head around this. Is Nora deaf?"

Dr. Flack's face sank in on itself as she considered Troy's concern, but her cheeks quickly rose and filled out. I supposed a few years of telling hearing parents that their child was deaf had taught her how to rearrange her facial features to impart optimism rather than dismay. "Technically, Nora's hearing loss is severe to profound in both ears. But, yes, in everyday terms, we consider Nora deaf."

Troy stared ahead blankly as Dr. Flack continued.

"Deaf children can successfully use sign language, total communication, oral communication, hearing aids, and cochlear implants. There are lots of options for us to discuss."

My eyes focused on Nora with a crushing intensity, as if my fervid gaze could fix her condition. She looked adorable with a large pink bow wrapped around her bald head. I noticed the way her tiny chest rose and fell in a slow, rhythmic pattern as she continued to sleep in my arms. I opened my mouth to speak, but suddenly felt an intense wave of nausea.

"I'm going to be sick," I blurted out like a drunk teenager.

I quickly handed Nora to Troy as the coffee and bagel I ate for breakfast splattered all over Dr. Flack's expensive white heels.

CHAPTER 11

Julie Wu

MOVING ACROSS THE country is stressful, and it doesn't help that Eric and I haven't been on good terms since Georgia's new law brought our political differences to a head. Our conversations consist only of details about our move. I have no desire to connect with him. My brain keeps circling the same thoughts, like a shark circling bloody chum. *How did I end up married to someone who could cast a vote that invalidates my free will? How does he go through life, without confronting the decision we made in high school?*

Taking out my phone, I read new comments the moms in Hamilton Beach have made on my post. They've been highly supportive.

> **Riya Kumar:** I'm in your corner anonymous mom

> **Gina Braterlo:** You're one hundred percent right on this anonymous mom.

My confidence swells as my eyes sweep the responses. It's strange to find comfort from something as impersonal as a Facebook page. I understand why people get addicted to social media.

Tina Langer: This is difficult, anonymous mom. My husband and I are perfectly in sync on politics. I couldn't get through these tough times without discussing hard issues with a like-minded partner.

Isabell Whitmore: A wife should abide by her husband's political preference.

Sam Katz: @Isabell Whitmore this "head of household" voting is complete bullshit.

Cara Woods: @Isabell Whitmore 19th Amendment. It's a thing.

Oh my, Isabell Whitmore. Isn't she my new neighbor? She didn't seem like someone to kowtow to her husband's point of view.

I hear a knock and look toward the adjoining door of my hotel room. "Mom, can I come in?"

Looking at the two unmade beds, I hope Talia doesn't realize Eric and I have been sleeping separately. The feel of his body next to mine repulses me. My hand turns the lock on the door between our rooms, and Talia steps inside. Her eyes are red and puffy.

"Are you okay?" I ask as I put my arm around her shoulders. "What's going on?"

Talia shuffles toward the corner of one bed and dramatically lowers herself onto its saggy surface. "Where's Dad?"

"Dad's still keeping East Coast hours with his firm in DC. He went to the lobby at five this morning to take a call."

"Oh," she says as she throws her body back onto the bed.

"So, what's going on?" I say as I lay next to her.

"It's just this move," she says in a grumbly voice. "It's like I said a few weeks ago. I don't think I'm going to fit in."

"I understand how you feel," I say, empathetic to her concerns. My mind suddenly flashes to my hometown of Daisy Springs in 1985. It was a southern version of *Sixteen Candles* and could easily have been the setting for John Hughes-like movies, such as *Pretty in Pink* (Bless Her Heart), or *The Breakfast* (and Biscuit) *Club.*

The isolation I felt growing up bubbles in my gut.

"I know you understand feeling like the odd one out, Mom. But your own experience doesn't change that this move may be awful for me."

I turn my face toward Talia's. She's a combination of all the people and cultures I love. She has my mom's nose, Eric's eyes, and the passionate nature of my dad. She is unique and gorgeous, inside and out.

"Here's what I think. You're assuming things are going to be difficult. Can you stay neutral? Can you be curious about what's going to happen, rather than assume it will be bad?"

Talia looks at me as she inhales deeply and shrugs. "I don't even know where to start. I don't know a single person at my new school other than Van. And people act so weird when they meet me. They get stuck trying to figure out my background."

"Right." I nod. I think about how the girls in my high school never invited me to sleepovers. Memories of my awkward teenage years bombard me—my love of reading, time spent alone making mixtapes, and my obsession with the John Hughes movie *Sixteen Candles*.

Suddenly, I realize the best advice for Talia is to start by finding one friend. "Why don't you find one person you connect with? Maybe a girl on Hamilton High's track team?" I look at Talia, curious to hear her response.

But before she says anything, Eric comes bounding through the door. He's running his hands through his graying hair. A sure sign he's stressed.

"Do you know where I put my flash drive? It's royal blue. It has a bunch of documents I need for my next call." He scours our hotel room's countertops, searching for the flash drive.

"I think Van may have it," Talia says as she gets up to look in their adjoining room. A moment later, she returns with the flash drive in hand.

Van shuffles behind her. "Sorry, Dad, my flash drive looks similar. It has my fantasy football stuff on it."

"Damn it, Van." Eric's nostrils flare.

Talia hands the flash drive to Eric, who puts it in his pocket.

"Thanks, Talia. Want to come with me to Seaside Coffee across the street? My treat for finding the flash drive. I've got fifteen minutes before my next call."

"Sure," Talia says. She exits the room sluggishly, still weighed down with concerns about life in California.

A moment later, Talia and Eric are on their way to coffee as Van goes back into his room to play video games.

I crawl into one of the beds and curl around a pillow. My tears are unexpected and stream furiously down my face. It's hard to hear Talia's concerns about finding her place. They hit a nerve and stir up memories of the struggles I had while growing up.

JUST LIKE EVERY teen-centric movie of the eighties, Daisy Springs was whitewashed. I longed to be Molly Ringwald and find my Jake Ryan. But Daisy Springs didn't know what to make of me. I didn't celebrate Christmas or Easter, and I could never make social plans on Friday nights.

By the time I reached my teen years, I was shy and awkward. I felt desperate to be part of a group. But my saving grace was my brain. I knew I was smart and found confidence in my intelligence. I'll never forget how excited my dad was after I took a series of academic tests and was accepted into the honors program.

I delighted in the praise from my dad, but even in the condensed group of future Mensa members, I felt my otherness. No one in small-town Georgia knew what to make of a Jewish girl living in a city that flew the confederate flag.

I longed for my dad to sit down with me for one of those legendary father-daughter talks I saw in my favorite movies. I'd picture us sitting on my bed, like Andie and her dad did in *Pretty in Pink*. But the focus of our conversation would be the antisemitism I would encounter throughout my life.

But my dad was the quiet type and avoided talking about difficult issues unless they crashed through the fortress he built to protect himself. And there was no avoiding how ugly the world could be. Sometimes prejudice bulldozed right through the brick-and-mortar he surrounded himself with.

It was after our town's Christmas tree lighting. My family had forgotten about the festivities and found ourselves caught in throngs of people on Main Street, outfitted in red and green.

"Let's get home," my dad said as drunk, rowdy men turned the corner.

As the unruly group pushed past us, one man grumbled something to my dad that I couldn't make out.

"Pardon me, but I could not hear what you said." My dad's face tightened as he spoke. I suppose he knew where this was headed.

"I said, go home. No one wants to see you Jews."

My stomach clenched up, and a strange sensation surged through my body.

"*Christ killer,*" the man continued under his breath.

I looked at my dad. He pushed his shoulders back and puffed out his chest, filling the surrounding space.

My mom quickly stepped up and pulled on his left elbow. "He's not worth it," she interjected in a rush. The pause was exactly what my dad needed.

We continued walking toward our car and never talked about the incident again.

As I grew up, the antisemitism I experienced was less overt but no less damaging. I could feel other people's intolerance in how I was marginalized at school and excluded from social events.

A sharp breath escapes my lips as I realize, just like Talia, that I'm anxious to find my place in Hamilton Beach.

I grasp my phone from the nightstand. Pushing through vulnerable feelings, I make a post under my name on the Hamilton Beach Moms' Facebook page. I'm putting myself out there.

Julie Wu
Today at 9:07 a.m.

Hi, my name is Julie. My family and I are new to Hamilton Beach. I have two children, who will attend Hamilton High School. My son will play on the school soccer team, and my daughter will run track. I'd love suggestions on book clubs and social groups I can join to meet new people. Looking forward to our new adventure.

CHAPTER 12

Isabell Whitmore

M Y FRESHLY MANICURED nails tap against my steering wheel as a Lizzo song blares on my radio. Suddenly, my wrist buzzes. It's a text from Laura.

> **Laura:** My client Julie moved in next door. Stop by and welcome her to Hamilton Beach. Also, loop me in on your b-day plans.

Ugh, I rev my SUV's engine and pull around some gray-haired lady going much too slow to be driving in the left lane.

Do I have to invite Laura to my birthday dinner? Her request that I visit Julie compounds my annoyance. I hate making small talk with people of no significance to my life.

"Mary," I call out as soon as I get home. "I need help with my shopping bags." I spent the hour before my nail appointment at Manhattan Threads and bought out the store.

Standing by my car, I wait for Mary, then remember she has the day off. She's only been working for me for a few weeks. It surprised me when she asked for a vacation day. That's a red flag. I should start looking for a replacement now and stay one step ahead.

My bags rustle against each other as I carry them upstairs and dump them on my bed. I'll put everything away later. I need to do this annoying welcome visit for Julie.

Looking through a stash of crappy gifts people have given me, I gawk. Budget brand wines. No, it's not trendy to gift someone with "Two Buck Chuck" from Trader Joe's. Inexpensive no-name jewelry and horrible-smelling candles from some awful place called the Candle Barn! I should teach a course on presenting yourself with class and decorum.

Shuffling through the contents, I settle on a bottle of cheap cabernet. It probably tastes like toilet water, but who cares? I grab my family's bio sheet and stick it with the bottle of wine in a bright pink gift bag.

Getting back into my car, I drive the half mile over to Julie's house. I'll leave this on her front step—no need to socialize.

Fuck. As I pull up, I see Julie outside, signing off on a furniture delivery. I can't get out of chatting.

Parking my car, I make my way toward her. "Welcome, welcome," I coo as I approach her. I force my voice to sound effortless, like the slight breeze brushing against my skin. "I'm Isabell. We met on the beach the day you were house hunting with Laura."

Julie adjusts the messy bun of curls on top of her head and smiles. "Yes, of course. How nice of you to stop by."

"Congratulations. I hope you and your family are getting settled." I do my best to seem like I care.

Julie shrugs. "I guess," she says.

I notice how tired she looks. She needs a facial.

"Do you want to come in for coffee?" Julie asks. "I just brewed a fresh pot. Caffeine is the only thing getting me through this move."

No, I don't want to come in for coffee, I think, as I agree to Julie's request. We step inside her entryway, and I follow her into a small kitchen.

"Here," she says, after as she fills a mug. "I'm exhausted. I've got one more day to get things arranged before I start my job."

"Busy, busy," I say, not caring to hear more about her job or the challenges of moving. "So, I can only stay for a moment, but I brought you wine." I push the gift bag toward her.

"Thanks. Exactly what I need. It's overwhelming to restart our lives in a new town. From small things, like where to find my favorite shampoo, to big things, like which pediatrician to use." Julie stares out into the space between us, momentarily overwhelmed.

"Oh, I've got a simple answer for that—the Hamilton Beach Moms' Facebook page." I pull out my phone and bring up the page to show Julie.

She starts to talk, but I cut her off. "The page is also a great source of entertainment." I snicker. "People post crazy things, and a new catfight breaks out in the comments daily." I grin, thinking of the firestorm I started the other day when I made a snide comment about head of household voting.

Julie moves back, distancing herself from me. She's probably one of those self-righteous moms who thinks she's the moral compass for everyone else.

I press on to see how she reacts when I read a post from the page out loud. "Oh, here," I say, my excitement building. "The anonymous mom posts are always the best! *I'm from a very traditional background, and leaving my marriage is not an option. We have children, and I am committed to our family life.*" I roll my eyes as I finish reading. "If your marriage is falling apart, don't post it on Facebook!" I laugh at the ridiculousness of the page as I take a sip of this bitter liquid Julie calls coffee.

"Oh, yes, the Facebook page. Good idea." Julie shifts in her chair uncomfortably.

We sit for a moment in silence. Yes, she's definitely one of those goody two-shoes moms. How boring. I fill the silence with the only question that comes to mind. "So, where are you working?"

"I'm going to be working for Click Com as an attorney. It's a great position. I'm excited about the opportunity. Do you work?"

I hate this question. I don't work. Anyone who spent one minute with me would know that. An image of Mr. Boucher's face, my boss

from New York floods my mind. Blood shoots through me like a bolt
of electricity as I wonder how I ended up in bed with both him and
his associate Rex Montgomery after a dinner that was supposed to
launch my career.

Images of the two men, as they ravaged each other, and then me,
play in my head. *Did they slip me some type of substance?*

Suddenly, I feel Julie staring, waiting for me to answer her question.
"Nope, I don't work," I say, needing to toss the sinister image of Mr.
Boucher's face far away. "I put years in, raising my three children as a
stay-at-home mom. It was brutal. Young children need you to be open
and emotional every minute of every day. It drained me." Suddenly,
I need to escape. "Glad we got to do this," I say. I stand and take a
step toward Julie's front door. "See you around the neighborhood."

A few moments later, as I pull into my garage, I'm overwhelmed
with memories of my attempt at a career and life in New York. Ever
since I saw Mr. Boucher's picture in *Vogue*, I've been having nightmares. It was my experience with Mr. Boucher that permanently and
irrevocably changed me, making me who I am today. I went through
a complete metamorphosis, like a worm turning into a butterfly.

But in my case, I went from a vibrant winged beauty to a slimy slug.

"I'LL BE GETTING approval for that new position soon," Rex often said after he'd roll his body off mine and then move on to Mr.
Boucher. They kept conversations surrounding a potential new job
at Rex's design house front and center, making me think I was only
moments away from receiving the official offer.

But hushed questions kept running through my mind. *Am I a
victim or a willing participant? Was I drugged and sexually assaulted
when this began?*

I realized my choices were simple—confront my shame about the
three-way relationship, or cast it away like a child's outgrown toy.

What I failed to realize was, when you disconnect from one emotion, you disconnect from them all. You can't feel pleasure without pain. I kept going, but as the outline of a girl. My insides were hollow.

Soon, my ability to feel anything withered away like the plant I neglected to water on the windowsill in my apartment. My soul went missing, and my best friend, Laura, was the only person involved in the search-and-rescue mission. She tried to figure out what was happening, but I was too ashamed to tell her how it all began. That's when I moved out of our New York apartment.

And then, suddenly, out of nowhere, Mr. Boucher called me into his office one day, promptly at eight in the morning. "Izzy, have a seat." He gestured to the wing-backed chairs that faced his desk, indicating I should sit down.

Instantly, I knew something was wrong. For the last year, he would come out from behind his desk and sit right next to me, often letting his hands roam under my skirt until I moaned. Now, he stayed seated behind his desk as if it could provide him protection.

"I don't want this to be awkward, Izzy, but I need to separate myself from our little entanglement. Both Rex and I need to move on."

A wave of relief washed over me. It was over.

Before I could speak, though, he picked up a stack of papers on his desk and moved them toward me.

"It would be better if you found a new job. Unfortunately, the design house position is no longer an option. These papers detail the excellent severance package I have arranged for you. You would be crazy not to sign them this minute."

My shoulders slumped inward. After everything, there was no job at the design house, and he fired me.

"Rex and I will write you glowing references and speak to our contacts about any leads. I'm sure you'll land somewhere great. Consider this a tiny bump in the road." He lifted his hand as he spoke, gently straightening out the green silk ascot surrounding his throat.

If I could go back in time, I would certainly choke him with his silky accessory.

CHAPTER 13
Maggie O'Donnell

S ITTING AT MY desk in our spare bedroom, I dial Dr. Acharya's number. I'm certain my call will land in voicemail. All the attempts I've made to contact her have been a bust. *Ping.* I hear my phone alert me before I can leave a message. My chest tightens. Is it a comment on my anonymous mom post or comment on the soccer story?

> **Alice Martin:** Your husband is wearing your underwear? A secret like this is a betrayal. I think your marriage is over.

> **Elham Dubraska:** I agree. If he's hiding this, what else is he hiding? Cut him loose and move on.

Before I can continue reading the comments, I'm alerted to new comments on the soccer story post.

> **Stephanie Brown:** Hottie Alert! 😍

> **Kathy Kalmon:** Are we sure he's married? I hope his wife realizes what a catch he is!

Ali Cheung: I appreciate the man is good looking, but he's married. His wife is the one who made this post! Everyone needs to tone down their comments.

Tyra Jackson: Yes, I agree. His wife is a lucky lady, but she should keep an eye on him because the vultures are circling.

My brain expands and contracts in rapid beats. The comments on both my posts are a tangle of words with contrasting messages. The delete button on my anonymous post glares, warning me to take it down. Doug's career, my marriage, and the privacy of my family are on the line. But my eyes can't help but move down the page and read the continuing stream of comments.

Leslie Stein: I provide therapy and specialize in issues related to sexuality and gender. Cross-dressing is more common than people think.

Darci Young: @Leslie Stein is excellent. Helped my transgender child through a rough time.

Jen Shamp: Do you think he left them for you to find? As a way to out himself?

Tension winds tightly through my core. My body feels dense like stone. I glance at the photo of Doug and me from his fraternity's formal sitting on my desk and then notice the photo of my Grandma Mable beside it. My name, Maggie, is in honor of Maybelline. Our close relationship foretold by the matching first letters of our names.

I know what she would say. *Be like water, settle into the cracks instead of fighting against them.* Grandma Mable was a woman with a solid backbone surrounded by a liquid soul. She likened herself to water, explaining her peaceful nature resulted from her ability to flow around obstacles instead of trying to change them. She proudly displayed the Ansel Adams photograph, *Fragile Waters*, in the room at the memory care center where she lived.

Shifting my gaze back to the photo from Doug's formal, I wonder if I can flow around this obstacle. The thought only increases my anger.

Suddenly furious, I fling my hand sharply toward the framed photo of Doug and me. It flies into the air and crashes against the window, falling onto the carpet. A discordant sob escapes my lips as I hunch down, afraid the glass has shattered.

Staring at the intact image, I consider what Valerie said at our meeting. She was right when she said Doug was all testosterone freshman year. He was a conceited playboy. I couldn't stand him. But during junior year, he changed. His muscle tanks gave way to shirts with sewn together sides and sleeves. His backward hat disappeared, revealing a thick head of dark hair that curved down to the left, highlighting the intense jade color of his eyes. And I can clearly remember the day he arrived at Ethics in Journalism wearing a collared shirt, khaki shorts, and white Chuck Taylors, properly laced and tied.

It was during this class that our teacher paired us to complete a project examining whether Truman Capote's book, *In Cold Blood*, was a journalist's account of a family brutally murdered or a sensationalized nonfiction novel meant for entertainment.

I was less than enthusiastic about being matched with Doug but forged ahead without complaint. I knew that, during my career, I would have to work with people I didn't like. It would be good training.

Midway through junior year, a few hours before Doug and I were meeting at Powell Library, my mom called to tell me that Mable had passed.

As I finished packing my bag for Grandma Mable's funeral, Doug called.

"Where are you? I thought we were meeting at the library."

Immediately, I burst into tears. "My grandmother passed away."

Twenty minutes later, Doug showed up at my apartment, bringing over my favorite frozen yogurt from the ice cream shop on Tenth Street.

"This was thoughtful of you, Doug. Thanks again," I said as we sat on my apartment's back patio in two cheap plastic lawn chairs.

"Sure," Doug replied. A sheepish grin formed on his lips. We sat in silence for a few moments too long, but it wasn't uncomfortable.

Doug finished his last bite and pushed his empty ice cream container over toward the edge of the table.

"Tell me something about your grandmother, something funny, something serious, anything at all."

My mind suddenly went blank. I squinted as if I was trying to recall the capital of South Dakota on a fourth-grade geography test.

"Mable," I said after another moment. "Her name was Mable. We were close. She took care of me after school and taught me to bake the most amazing treats."

"Wow, you were lucky to have her in your day-to-day life."

"Yes, I was."

"What was your favorite thing to make?"

"Lemon squares," I blurted out. The memory of the bright yellow batter caused my chest to tighten. "The last time I saw her was over Christmas Break."

"Loss is hard," Doug interjected, sensing the emotion in my voice. "I don't talk much about it, but I lost my dad when I was fourteen."

"I'm sorry," I said, surprised this had never come up in all the hours we'd spent together working on our project.

"Yeah, I'll talk with you about my dad another time. Tonight isn't about my grief. It's about yours. I just wanted you to know I understand." He slid his hand over mine, squeezed, and then quickly moved it back to his lap.

It was then, in that brief moment of hand overlapping hand, that I first felt a pull toward Doug. A desire to know him more deeply.

CHAPTER 14
Indira Acharya

THE OCEAN BREEZE tickles my face as I exit my Uber and step inside the upscale restaurant, Ocean Club One. I can't help but think of the last comment I read before I deleted my post.

> **Nia Bak:** Genuine physical and emotional connection has a heartbeat of its own. I'm not sure you can let this go, anonymous mom.

The post pushed me to plan this evening with Fatima. Now, as I walk inside, apprehension mixes with excitement making me feel like I might float away. Where will tonight lead? But first, I need Fatima to open up. She keeps dancing around the edge of her personal life, as if she doesn't want to fall into a gaping hole.

"Hi, I'm running a bit late," I say to the host. "My friend is already here. She's tall with long black braids."

"Yes, ma'am. You must be Indira. You're just as beautiful as she described. Right this way."

My body tingles with delight at the thought of Fatima describing me as beautiful.

"Sorry, I'm late," I say as I look to my left, soaking in the deep blue ocean. "Wow, this view is gorgeous!"

"Yes, it's lovely, isn't it? I hope you don't mind, but I ordered champagne. We need to celebrate." Fatima gestures toward a bottle chilling in a bucket of ice.

Moments later, we hold up delicate, fluted glasses together.

Fatima leads the toast. "To reconnecting with old friends."

"Yes!" I say. "If it wasn't for the dreaded Civic Engagement Project Ms. Timmons assigned in my social studies class junior year, we never would have met."

"Ah, yes, the project that taught students about the role citizens can play toward improving society. We owe Ms. Timmons!" Fatima fills my glass with more bubbly liquid and smiles.

"Cheers to that," I echo back, recalling the care I took choosing a blue throw blanket for the family immigrating from Ethiopia. As well as the hours I agonized over what sneakers to recommend for the teenage girl starting her life over in America.

"I'm glad we were able to make plans tonight." My hand taps my leg nervously under the table. I want to broach the subject of Fatima's mother. She's alluded to a falling out. I think it's about Fatima's sexuality. I'm desperate to find out, considering how I feel. "So, tell me more about your mom," I say.

"My mom? There's not much to tell. Just picture her twenty-five years ago. She hasn't changed." Fatima waves her hand back and forth dismissively.

I picture the short, round woman who welcomed me into her apartment all those years ago. Walking in, I saw the blue throw blanket I had chosen folded neatly over the couch's cushions.

"Fati," she called out sputtering a string of syllables I couldn't understand. A few awkward moments passed, and she yelled again, "Fati!" But this time, her tone was sharp, and even though I couldn't understand her words, I knew exactly the message Fatima's mother was conveying. *Get out here right now.*

Moments later, I heard footsteps, slow and heavy, dragging across the carpet. My eyes hit the ground as if the sound itself was a lure, pulling my focus downward. Then, there against the plain beige carpet, I saw the hot pink and green high-top LA Gear sneakers I had chosen for Fatima.

As I moved my gaze upward, I was astounded by the girl glaring back at me. Fatima took my breath away. She was at least six feet tall with a lean but muscular body. Her hair was styled in tiny rows of long braids that brushed against her waist. Her mouth was large. Almost too large for her face. She peered at me with deep brown eyes that sent a jolt of electricity down my spine. And her skin. Her skin swallowed me. It was the color of a deep, dark starless night. And despite the endless black, I felt a bright white light flood my body.

Looking intently at Fatima now, I'm consumed by the same white light. "You sound angry when you talk about your mom. What happened?" Sweat trickles down my back.

Fatima's face suddenly changes into a serious expression. "We had a falling out. We haven't spoken in months." Tears bunch in her eyes for a moment, and she wipes them away.

I swiftly reach my hand out and weave her fingers in between mine. The feel of her skin is thrilling. "I'm sorry," I say. "Do you want to talk about it?"

She swallows hard and hesitates for a moment. "My mom has never accepted the fact that I'm a lesbian." Her eyes rise and meet mine, dead on. "This isn't a surprise to you, Indira? I'm fairly certain you caught on to this?"

My heart swells in my chest as I nod my head yes. I am both terrified and exhilarated by Fatima's confirmation. The feelings I am developing for her suddenly feel legitimate. It's as if a world of possibilities lies before me.

Fatima continues, "I was in a long-term relationship, and then it fell apart. My mom jumped on the opportunity to denounce the fact that I'm gay." The delicate lines sweeping across Fatima's forehead deepen in anger.

"That sounds hard," I say, knowing full well I have lived my entire life avoiding disapproval from my parents.

"It's not so much that it's hard. It's just that I refuse to live my life for anyone else. I hid my true self from my mom for too long. I felt split in two. You can't feel whole if broken in half."

The ache hits my heart again. It slows its pace, making it seem like I'm not getting enough air. Anxious, I clasp the charm on the chain around my neck and turn it in my free hand.

Fatima speaks again. "I will not let anyone, even my mother, make me conform to something I'm not. I refuse to abandon myself." Her shoulders spread out as she sits up tall in her chair. She knows her own power, and it's the most gorgeous thing I have ever seen.

Sinking back, I turn my gaze toward the water. I finally understand that living one's truth is only for the brave-hearted. Most people are like me, living a half-truth of themselves that leaves them feeling restless and alone. Fatima is strength. Fatima is loyal to herself. Fatima is cut from a lion's heart.

"So that's why you moved?" I ask. My words are a mere pittance after the declaration Fatima has made. Frustrated by feelings of inadequacy, I pull at my charm necklace again.

"It's just easier, for now, to put space between my mom and me." She looks toward the water, and I can tell she's hurting.

Releasing my hand from hers, I caress her cheek, but then instantly snap my hand back, embarrassed. My body burns with heat.

Fatima jumps in her chair, startled by my sudden movement. "Is everything okay, Indira?" She looks at me with a puzzled expression.

I gather myself, pushing my swirling emotions away. "Yes, fine." My free hand travels back up to my necklace and pulls at it again. "Oh, no!" Looking down, the necklace lays in front of me on the table. Tension has caused me to break the delicate chain in half.

Fatima slides her hand across the table, picking it up. She turns the necklace's charm over in her hand, and I wonder if the image of the ocean pressed into metal will evoke memories of our summer.

"The beach." She smiles widely. "This reminds me of our summer."

My heart explodes in my chest. Yes, it means something to her.

"What a shame your necklace broke." She moves the chain through her fingers. "Are you sure you're, okay?" She looks at me, trying to determine what's at the core of my restlessness.

"Everything's fine," I say again, even though the truth is kicking at my throat. *Tell her*, it says. *Tell her*. But I am terrified. I'm not ready to speak my truth. My marriage, my family, and my entire way of life are on the line.

"Here, let me put that in my bag so I don't lose it," I say instead. My hands quiver as Fatima gives me the chain. Opening my bag, I start to drop the chain and charm inside, but miss. My necklace falls away through a crack in the floor and disappears into the sand below the restaurant's deck.

"Oh no, your necklace!" Fatima lets out a low gasp.

My body freezes and my breath stops. *Is there meaning here?* Is losing the necklace a sign I should let my feelings for Fatima fall away as well?

HAMILTON BEACH MOMS
PRIVATE GROUP — 5,335 Members

Laura Perry
Today at 8:24 a.m.

Well, Ladies! I'm officially making Wednesdays the "Dog Day" of the Hamilton Beach Moms' Facebook page. If your house is like mine, your dog is the most important family member! Please post photos of your adorable dogs on Wednesdays. Let's light up the feed with our precious pups!

Also, don't forget to register for our in-person fundraiser to help our community food bank. Follow this link https://www.facebook.com/HBCMomsgiveback right now! 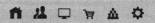. Also, still looking for a co-moderator. Please message me if interested.

Comments

Tina Carlson: Love this so much. 🐾 🖤

Heather Carlin: Yes, great idea! Where can I buy a birthday "cake" for my Lilly. I can't believe she's turning one!

Stephanie Tavani: @Heather Carlin Check out Pet Patisserie on Ivy Road. I did a big party for Rocky. They have everything you need. Even cute bandannas and hats your dog can wear for posting the pics on Insta.

Carly Wong: You dog people are insane!

Heidi Adams: I need a recommendation for someone who can make a shirt for my Yorkie? We're doing family pictures soon, and I want my dog Buttercup to match our outfits.

Chareese Banks: This is perfect! We are getting a mini Goldendoodle. I'm so excited!

Kelly Powell: @Chareese Banks Why buy a designer dog? There are literally at least a hundred dogs at our local shelter up for adoption.

Sandra Clavert: 👍 Exactly @Kelly Powell. Shelter dogs will be euthanized. Buying a designer dog is deplorable when so many loving dogs need a home.

Chareese Banks: @Kelly Powell @Sandra Clavert Not that it's any of your business, but my son has a severe allergy, so we need a dog that doesn't shed.

Sandra Clavert: The allergy excuse is typically BS!

Carrie Rosenstein: What about cats?

CHAPTER 15

Laura Perry

"THAT'S WONDERFUL!" I say. "Yes, we'll name your business as a sponsor, and it will be spotlighted at our upcoming event. We have over five thousand members. I'll circle back with you soon with more details." I hang up from my call and see Troy standing in the hallway next to the kitchen.

"She shoots, she scores!" Troy pretends to toss a basketball into a hoop. "Sounds like you got another sponsor for the mom event."

Troy and I slap our hands together in a high-five. "I'm killing it! California Clean Cans has agreed to donate five hundred dollars. We should start using them. They come twice a month to clean out city garbage cans." The thought of our smelly cans makes my nose wrinkle.

"Sure," Troy says. "I'm willing to pay for that." He pulls me in for a hug.

"Did you see Nora this morning before school?" I ask as our bodies pull away from each other.

"I did. She wouldn't talk to me. She wouldn't even look at me." He sighs in frustration. "She still refuses to wear her implants." Troy's eyes narrow with concern.

"I'm having lunch with Gabriella today. Maybe she can give us guidance." I bite my lip pensively. "She's a great therapist. She won't take Nora as a client since we're good friends. But she can recommend someone."

"Good idea," Troy says as his face relaxes. "Well, I'm off to work. See you tonight."

"Love you," I say, suddenly concerned Gabriella won't have the fix for this problem.

A FEW HOURS later, I pull my car up to the valet at Trendy Greens. Gabriella, or Gabby, as I call her, is probably already here. She's one of those early people. We became friendly years ago when I sold her and her husband Ricardo their single-family home in the Park Town neighborhood.

"Laura," Gabby calls out as we embrace in a quick hug. "It's been months. Where does the time go?" Gabby's hand lingers on my shoulder.

"Right?" I say as the hostess sits us at a table. "I've missed seeing you in person." I can't help but smile at the sight of Gabby's welcoming face. "And I have no idea what's going on in your life because you never post on Facebook."

"I'm a lurker on Facebook," she says. "I sometimes scroll at night when I'm bored, but I just don't see the point in posting." Gabby shrugs indifferently. "Anyway, my cousin three times removed and my friend from that one summer I spent at a college prep program don't need to know the brief moments that make up my life."

"Preach!" I say mockingly.

Gabby giggles. "I'm glad you picked Trendy Greens."

"Yes, I know you're committed to eating organic, non-GMO food. I knew it was the perfect place. I ate Froot Loops for breakfast. Don't judge!"

"Ay! I would never judge. To each their own." Gabby tosses her loose brown waves over her shoulder.

We place our orders and fall into conversation.

"How's Lucas?" I ask. "Is he in third grade now?"

"Hmm. Lucas. Lately, he's been trying to assert his independence. He wants to show us he's his own person, separate from his parents." Her voice wavers with emotion.

"What do you mean?" I say as I take a bite of my chicken salad sandwich.

"Oh, I don't know. For example, last week, we had a family movie night. You know we always watch a *Star Wars* movie. He insisted on watching *Harry Potter*." Gabby throws her hands up in the air, exasperated.

I can't help but laugh. "Oh, my!" I say teasingly. "Lucas, named after the one and only George Lucas, and son of the biggest *Star Wars* fans on the planet, asked to watch *Harry Potter*. It's the end of the world!"

Gabby laughs as she takes a delicate bite of her Tofurky sandwich.

"And how's your mom settling in?" Gabby's mom Carlita recently moved to Hamilton Beach. I sold her a townhouse in the Sunny Cove retirement community off Lomak Road.

"*¡Dios Mío!* Carlita is driving me insane." Gabby shakes her head back and forth, irritated. "She's dating, she doesn't understand boundaries, and she sneaks Lucas candy." Gabby huffs in frustration and continues. "Carlita is just so extra. It's hard for me, since I'm an introvert. But enough about me. How are things with you?" The features on Gabby's face spread out warmly.

"I actually asked you to lunch for two reasons." Looking away from the table, my stomach drops, thinking about Nora's recent rebellion.

"Cue ominous music." Gabby laughs as she puts down her sandwich.

"The first reason is an amazing opportunity. I don't want you to answer me right now. Just think on it and get back to me." My stomach flutters with nervous energy.

"Well, you've certainly piqued my interest. Go ahead." Gabby leans forward in anticipation.

"I desperately need a co-moderator for the Hamilton Beach Moms' Facebook page. I think you'd be perfect! You're levelheaded. You're a skilled therapist, who knows how to approach people and manage conflict. Plus, it will help build your therapy practice. Thousands of women in the area will know your name." I bounce around in my seat as I speak, enthused by the prospect of Gabby being my co-moderator.

"That was quite the sales pitch," Gabby says. "It's not the worst idea I've ever heard. But I'm not a Facebook person. I find it superficial." Her eyes suddenly look tentative. "And the moms are often mean and over-the-top."

"That's exactly why I need you," I sputter. "Lately, the feed has been giving off an unpleasant vibe. It's frustrating because, no matter how often I remind these moms about the page rules, they just can't help themselves from being rude." My body stiffens as I think of a recent mom's post. She was looking for someone who could help her son learn to ride his bike. But, instead of suggestions, several moms blasted her for wanting to outsource this milestone.

"Not following the rules. Ay! That's your number one pet peeve." Gabby chuckles before continuing. "But I understand what you're saying, and it's a shame the page is devolving into the social norms of a middle school." Her lips round in disappointment.

"Exactly!" I say, reassured by her dissatisfaction. "You have the skill set to help me manage the moms who are catty and spiteful. Please," I plead, "will you help?" My eyes bulge like saucers, hoping she'll agree.

"Let me think about it. What's the time commitment?"

"I'd need you to post as a moderator a few times a week with routine business. Oh, and I need help planning the upcoming in-person fundraising lunch. You can market your therapy services at the event." I sit up tall, buoyed with hope Gabby will agree.

"I'll sleep on it," she says, pushing around the mixed fruit on her plate. "It sounds interesting. What else did you want to talk about?"

"It's Nora." I notice how my voice shakes as I say Nora's name. "It's about her identity as a deaf person." Instantly, I recall the turmoil I felt after Nora's diagnosis.

"Tell me more." Gabby's voice is suddenly measured. She's in therapy mode. "What's going on?"

"Nora wants to explore deaf culture and learn sign language. She's angry I didn't incorporate deaf culture into her upbringing."

"Teenagers are *supposed* to grapple with identity issues. It's part of the maturation process. But I understand why this feels intense."

I let out an exhale, thankful for Gabby's understanding. "She hasn't been wearing her implants for weeks."

"I can tell this frightens you." Gabby looks at me empathetically. "Why are you afraid?"

My breath catches. "In those early years, the doctors and therapists said it was important to limit Nora's use of sign language."

Gabby stills for a moment, considering my words. "It's been sixteen years since you were given that advice. Have you reached out about current best practices? Recommendations for children with special needs constantly evolve based on the latest research."

It's a good point, I think. "No, I guess I haven't."

"Start there. But also consider that maybe you're holding on to an old rule that no longer applies." Gabby's not mocking my dedication to the rules. "Honestly, Laura." She hesitates. "I can't be this direct with patients, but as a friend, I think you should let Nora explore this. In fact, consider helping her and being a part of the process."

LATER, MY CAR hums along the coastal highway as I drive away from lunch. I feel a glimmer of hope as the bright blue ocean races beside me. Gabby recommended a therapist. She thinks it's best we work through this as a family.

Her suggestion to fully support Nora's exploration of deafness is harder to reconcile.

Making my way to Julie's to drop off a housewarming gift, I dig deeper into why I'm struggling against this. Is it as simple as Gabby explained? *Am I wedded to a rule that's no longer necessary? Is my thinking outdated?*

My mind races with ways Troy and I can help Nora gently explore deafness. It can be a tricky subject. Some people who are part of deaf culture oppose cochlear implants. It's possible they could reject Nora because she has one. I recall the websites I stumbled upon sixteen years ago that said implanting a deaf child was wrong. I wonder if the perspective of the deaf community has changed.

Thinking for a few minutes, my mind suddenly bursts with an idea. It's so obvious I laugh out loud. As soon as I park my car in front of Julie's house, I pull out my phone.

New Activity

Anonymous Mom Post
Today at 1:27 p.m.
My daughter wants to connect with deaf teenagers who use sign language to communicate. My daughter is deaf, although she uses cochlear implants and communicates through speech. She doesn't know sign language. She wants to learn about deaf culture.

Collecting my things, I make my way to Julie's front door. *Ping.* A comment on my post already? That was fast. I pull out my phone and read.

Teresa Huff: Try contacting Southern California Deaf Services.

Meredith Kurtz: How could you put your child through cochlear implant surgery? Both my parents are deaf, although I was born hearing. Deaf is beautiful. You robbed your daughter.

Katie Harper: I'm deaf and this mom had the right to decide between oral deaf and deaf culture.

Meredith Kurtz: DISAGREE

My hands shake, causing my phone to bobble back and forth. *Am I the cause of a blowup on my Facebook page?* My phone slips out of my grip and crashes onto the concrete just as Julie opens her door.

"Oh, Laura, everything okay?" Julie's clearly confused about why I'm on my hands and knees in front of her door.

I look up at her as I pick up my device. "I dropped my phone." Flipping it around, we both gasp. The screen's completely shattered.

CHAPTER 16

Gabriella Martinez

"**O**H, DARTH, YOU'RE insatiable. How did we end up in your personal quarters on the Death Star?" I cower on the bed as if I am afraid.

"My sweet, sweet Padmé. I have lured you here using the powers of the dark side. You are the most beautiful girl in the galaxy, and now you are mine." Ricardo takes off the elaborate horned headdress affixed to my hair and slowly moves his hand to the zipper of the heavy red robe that covers my naked body.

Our eyes meet as he pulls the zipper toward my feet. His black Darth Vader helmet bobs back and forth as laughter causes his diaphragm to contract. He has broken character, and I can't help but snicker as our bodies move closer together.

Suddenly, we hear the roaring of our garage door opening, followed by the creak of the door into the house. I hear my mom's voice call out.

"Gabriella? Ricardo? *¿Hay alguien en casa?*" she calls, to see if we're home.

Ricardo and I jump apart like two magnets repelled by force. I feel like a teenager busted for hooking up in a dark basement. Ricardo bolts out of bed and starts throwing on his clothes. As he steps into his pants, he trips on the long black robe of his Darth Vader costume and goes flying headfirst into the corner of our solid wood dresser.

"*¡Ay, mi cabeza!*" He yelps and grabs his head as I quickly pull on my denim skirt, top, and clogs.

I step over to where Ricardo is standing and inspect the slash over his left eyebrow.

"Oh, Ricardo, it looks pretty nasty. Grab a washcloth from the bathroom and clean it up. I'll bring up ice."

"Gabriella? Ricardo?" My mom calls again.

"*Un momento*, Mom!" I scream in a voice inflamed with irritation. I'm still not used to her living just 3.2 miles away.

"Not cool," Ricardo says as he walks toward our bathroom. "It's two o'clock on a Wednesday."

"*¡Estoy de acuerdo!*" I nod my head vigorously in agreement. Carlita's move from St. Louis has thrown me off balance. I'm perturbed by her sudden presence in my daily life. She has a way of stirring up minor feelings of aggravation that quickly mushroom into an enormous dust cloud of fury.

"And why does your mom think she can just stop by unannounced?" Ricardo growls.

I look at him to see if my easygoing husband is angry.

"Oh, and Padmé," he continues, jumping back into the role-play we were engaged in before, "bring up my lightsaber with the ice. Its magic will heal this gash in seconds." He turns his face upward and grins. His humor and good nature remind me how lucky I am to be married to a man like Ricardo.

"Yes, of course, my dark lord." I wink.

My hand grasps the railing to the stairs as I stomp down to confront my mom about her unannounced visit. My insides burn hot and fast, like a comet blasting through space. *Why has this transition been so difficult?* I think about the day I left my childhood home to start college at UC Berkeley. I haven't interacted with Carlita beyond a few phone calls a week and a three-night visit to St. Louis over Thanksgiving since I was eighteen. Our relationship is in a new phase. I need to figure out my boundaries.

"*Hola*, Gabby," my mom says as I walk into my kitchen. "I was driving home, and since I pass your house, I thought I'd stop by."

She pushes aside the ceramic fermentation Crockpot sitting on my kitchen counter and plops her large designer handbag in its place.

"*¡Esto huele muy mal!*" she says, crinkling her nose in displeasure. "Whatever you're making in that thing stinks to high heaven!"

"Mom, please keep your opinions about my homemade sauerkraut to yourself," I snap. Earlier this morning, I spent an hour thinly slicing cabbage, pounding it out, and combining it with Celtic Sea salt and caraway seeds before placing it into the slow cooker. I make Lucas eat a little of my fermented sauerkraut daily to keep his digestive system running smoothly.

"I can't believe Lucas eats that hippie-dippy food," she says, knowing Lucas and I have been at odds lately about his desire for Cool Ranch Doritos over my rich probiotic concoction.

My brow furrows. "Just stay out of it, Mom."

"Oh, Gabby, relax," she replies as I contemplate Lucas's new zeal to establish his individuality.

I want him to be his own person, of course. But I want us to enjoy the same things and have a similar outlook on life. God knows my relationship with Carlita would be better if we were more alike.

"I don't understand your obsession with raw, vegan foods," she continues in a sing-song voice. "When you were growing up, I opened a can of SpaghettiOs with franks, and voilà, dinner was served." She moves her hand as if she has a magic wand in her palm and gestures toward the imaginary bowl of processed pasta and meat.

My shoulders immediately scrunch up, and my frame stiffens. My core and limbs are attempting to solidify into a rock to protect myself from the erupting emotions coursing through my body.

Before I can reply to her SpaghettiOs proclamation, her phone dings, dings again, and then dings again, and again, and again. Her phone is constantly ringing, dinging, chiming, and emitting all kinds of sounds, alerting her to various emails, text messages, Silver Single alerts, and God knows what else.

She rifles through her bag in a frenzy, as if she's an emergency room doctor who must drop everything after hearing the call for a code blue. She's so furiously searching for her phone that she barely notices as the contents of her oversized bag fall around her.

A moment later, she's on her phone. Her voice is loud and exaggerated. She has the full attention of her friend, Harriett, and is soaking it up for all it's worth. I can hear both sides of the conversation because they are screaming into the phone like cheerleaders at a high school pep rally.

Carlita: "I was invited to the key exchange."

My ears rise like soldiers who have been told to stand at attention. A key exchange?

Harriett: "I thought that was a myth. People in Sunny Cove would never do that!"

Carlita: "No, it's real. Fred asked me to come to the next gathering on Friday night. It's at his house."

Harriett: "Razz my berries! Are you going? How does it work?"

This can't be what I think. My mom only divorced my straitlaced Midwestern dad one year ago.

Carlita: "The men drop their keys in a bucket. The women pick a set of keys and that's it. That's your person. You spend one night together. Anything goes. Married, single, it doesn't matter. No questions asked."

¡Increíble! It's precisely what I suspected. I bob my head back and forth to shake out my building anger.

Harriett: "Carlita, you're asking for trouble if you get involved in this."

Carlita: "Oh please, behaving is boring! I'll see if I can get you an invite."

Harriett: "Please don't bother. I'm alre—"

Carlita: "Listen, Harriett, I'll call you later. I'm at my daughter's house. I need to go. Adios."

My mom hangs up and looks at me. She's grinning like a child caught stealing a cookie from the cookie jar. She knows I've heard her conversation and thinks it's funny.

I want to say something, but my throat is closing on itself, almost as if I'm choking on said cookie.

"Oh, Gabby, don't be shocked," she says before I can get a word out. Your dad and I divorced, and I've moved to California for a new start."

My eyeballs feel like heavy weights about to drop out of my eye sockets as she tries to justify her reckless sexual behavior.

"Stop staring at me like that. I'm an adult. I can do as like."

"Yes, Mom, you always have and always will." I feel an intense need to make sure she knows the seriousness of her exploits. "You know STD cases are out of control for the sixty-five and over population. You need to be careful."

"Oh, Gabby, I know you're a therapist, but stay out of it. I'm a big girl and can take care of myself." She bends down to pick up the items that fell out of her bag, wiggling her keys in my face as she stands. She's laughing as if choosing sexual partners via a key exchange is a big game.

It's the perfect opening for a conversation about the lubricant and lingerie she's been buying on my Amazon account, but I don't have the bandwidth for it. We need to talk about why the "pop-in" is unacceptable. I ignore the silver and gold keys jingling in my face and move on.

"Mom, listen. I know Ricardo and I are home during the day, but you can't pop in unannounced. We're busy. These hours are not leisure time. Ricardo is often working on new menu ideas. Ever since he was made executive chef at Ocean Club One, he's been under pressure to take their menu to the next level."

"And you?" she says, with an air of condescension. I've hurt her feelings by expressing my displeasure.

"Yes, Mom. And me. I'm starting own my therapy practice and seeing patients in the small office in our basement."

"Oh, okay, fine," she huffs. "I just stopped by to say hi. I'll get out of your hair. *Que tengas un buen día*, and have Lucas call me later."

"I will," I say as I walk toward our front door and open it wide, signaling that it's time for her to leave.

As soon as I shut the door, Ricardo appears. "You never came back with my ice."

"Yes, sorry. Carlita is going to be the end of me. How's your forehead?"

"It's not too bad," he says as he grabs my hand and leads me to the couch in our den. "Come sit. Let me rub your feet."

My body hums into a relaxing lull as his firm hands push against my stiff joints.

"So, what was that about?" he asks.

"*Ah mi amor*, let's not talk about Carlita. I'm finally relaxing."

Ricardo continues pushing his palms against my calves. "Okay, then tell me about your lunch with Laura."

"It was interesting. She asked me to co-moderate her crazy Hamilton Beach Moms' Facebook page. I'm thinking of doing it."

"*¿En serio?* Why in the world would you do that? You've read me the craziest posts from that page."

"Yes, I know. But, often, people need help. The other day, a woman posted wondering if she should divorce her husband because of their different political views. I started my therapy practice to help people like her. The page will get my name out there."

"That makes sense," Ricardo says as his hands slowly trace the inside of my thighs.

"But I'm conflicted," I say. "My experience as a therapist has shown me over and over that social media leads to isolation rather than connection. Do I want to be part of that?"

"Well, what about changing it, then?" Ricardo says as he leans in close to me. "You are the perfect person to help move the page from something exclusively virtual to something authentic."

"Maybe, but that's a lot to take on." My body tingles from the kisses Ricardo is planting up and down my neck.

"*¿Qué estás haciendo?*" I playfully ask what he's doing as his lips brush against my skin.

He winks. "We've got an hour until Lucas comes home from school, my sweet Padmé."

CHAPTER 17

Julie Wu

P ING. MY PHONE lights up on the kitchen counter as I smear cream cheese on a bagel.

> **Amber Bray:** Hi Julie. PM me! My daughter also runs track for Hamilton High. Let's plan for coffee.

My heart skips happily in my chest. Several moms responded to my post about starting our new life in Hamilton Beach. I've become a believer in the positive power of social media. I send Amber a private message and then notice the time. Why isn't Talia downstairs?

Walking into her room, I push open the curtains. Her windows face the ocean, and I gasp at the beauty of the crystal blue water in the distance.

"It's time to wake up," I bend over Talia's bed and brush the hair from her eyes.

She curls into her body and sinks under the edge of her covers.

"Come on, Talia. I know it's getting harder to wake up now that you're not on East Coast time, but you need to get ready for school."

She makes a sound that's somewhere between a moan and a sigh.

"Don't make me pull the covers off your bed. I just did that to Van. He may never talk to me again."

"Don't you dare. That's the worst."

"Oh, I guess you're awake," I say playfully.

Talia sits up and leans her back against her bed's headboard rubbing the sleep from her eyes. "Can I just skip school today?"

Sitting on her bed, I look at her face to gauge her mood. She said she met a friend she liked the other day. What was her name? Brooke, Brooklyn? "What about the friend you made? It just takes one to get started. How's that going?"

"Blair? It's going okay. She has a boyfriend, so she's kind of busy."

"Right. Have you met our Realtor's daughter, Nora Perry?"

Talia looks at me. "Is she deaf? I think she's in my debate class, but she's shy and isn't participating because she's not wearing her hearing aids or something."

"Yes, that's her. Why don't you introduce yourself? Her mom's very friendly."

"It's just not that easy," Talia says. "And, of course, everyone loves Van. He's already the center of attention at Hamilton High."

Just like Eric, I think. I picture him being introduced as a new student during my sophomore year in high school by Lorilee Wethersfield. She walked into Mr. Rifkin's math class glowing in a fluorescent pink skirt and top. Her teased blond hair defied every law of gravity. Mr. Rifkin motioned toward Eric, pointing him to an empty seat.

Eric stepped toward him. However, he didn't slouch away to the empty desk as most self-conscious new students would have. Instead, he positioned himself front and center in our classroom with the confidence of a United States President speaking from the podium on Inauguration Day.

"Hi, my name is Eric Wu. I'm from New York. I thought I'd take a moment to introduce myself. I have a passion for economics, am obsessed with Wall Street, and am a staunch supporter of Reaganomics. I plan to be the student government president of Daisy Springs High School and then attend Harvard. Looking forward to connecting with you over the next few weeks."

He was Alex P. Keaton, from *Family Ties*, come to life. He shifted the knot of the red tie lying under his navy sweater vest, sure of himself in a way that was foreign to me. His eyes entranced me. They glowed golden brown.

The memory infuriates me. Our marriage is falling apart. We had another blowout yesterday about the Georgia law.

"Lower taxes over a woman's right to choose," I screamed as I grabbed my pillow and went to sleep in our guest room. If the kids have caught on, they haven't said anything.

As I go downstairs to finish making breakfast, I picture the day Eric and I met at our school's library to work on an *Animal Farm* character analysis. My stomach fluttered with nervous energy.

We were discussing the white pig, Snowball, and his representation of Leon Trotsky. My nerves settled as soon as we started a spirited conversation. My brain was bigger than my crush.

Two hours later, as we finished our assignment and placed our worn copies of *Animal Farm* into our backpacks, Eric broached a topic most people avoided.

"Do you hate it when people ask about your background?"

I had just adjusted the bright yellow banana clip in my hair. Startled by his intrusive question, my eyes bulged.

"Oh, I only ask because, ever since I moved here, people ask me strange questions about being Asian."

"Huh," I said, ever so eloquently.

He looked at me curiously. "Well, people seem to treat you differently because you're Jewish. The same way they treat me because I'm Asian."

"Oh," I blurted, suddenly feeling like I was in a John Hughes movie. *Was Eric my Jake Ryan?*

CHAPTER 18

Isabell Whitmore

M Y ESCALADE SCREECHES as I turn onto CoCoplum
Way. I'm going way too fast. The wind tousles my long
blond ponytail as Missy Elliott blasts my ears. I just spent a
steamy afternoon with my hot young tech whiz. My body shudders
as I replay our moments together. Let's just say he gave me quite a
gift for my upcoming birthday. Too bad he's getting skittish about
Harris finding out.

What my hot tech piece of ass doesn't realize is that Harris and I
built our relationship on a tacit agreement, never to find out the truth
about each other's lives. We always focus on present tense, frivolous
actions, like whether to buy the designer leather or microfiber couch,
or if we should visit the Ritz in Aruba or the Bahamas for a family
vacation.

It was clear from the beginning that Harris wasn't interested in
forging an emotional connection. He was heartbroken after his previous two-year marriage ended in divorce. He just wanted someone
who checked all the boxes. She had to be beautiful and impress the
venture capitalists he relied upon to fund his startups.

"So, why did you and Celeste get divorced?" I asked one Sunday,
as Harris and I sipped coffee at our usual deli on the Upper East Side.
I was curious about why his first marriage ended.

"She cheated," he said, without looking up from the newspaper's financial section. He pressed his lips together tightly when I pushed for more details, exhaling forcefully. "It's in the past, and that's where it stays."

I respected his stance, given I had secrets I didn't want to reveal. It had been six months since Mr. Boucher fired me.

It was a relief to be in a relationship where both parties valued their emotional privacy. He did not attempt to unlock the mysteries of my past, and I did not attempt to unlock his. We focused on protecting ourselves over creating a deep connection.

My thoughts about Harris unravel as soon as I pull into one of the five garage parking spaces that encircle our home's large roundabout. *Why is Grace's convertible Mercedes parked here?* Grace and Lola rarely bother coming home until ten at night during the week.

A moment later, Warren swings into the driveway in his Range Rover. Then *BOOM!* The entire garage rattles and shakes.

"*What the actual fuck!*" I scream as I look into my rearview mirror.

And then I see exactly what's happened. My dim-witted son has crashed his brand new car into the corner of the garage door.

I leap out of my car. Warren sits in a trance. His mouth hangs open.

"What the hell, Warren? What happened?"

He stays frozen for a moment before rapidly blinking his eyes. "I don't know. I think I pulled in before the door was up high enough?"

"Seriously? How could you be so careless?" I can feel my long ponytail bobbing as I shake my head in anger.

"Is everything okay? I heard a loud noise." Mary suddenly appears wearing the new housekeeper's uniform I purchased for her. She looks ridiculous in the puritan black dress and white apron. But at least she won't show up to work in a stained white shirt.

"We're fine. Warren's fine. He made a stupid mistake," I snap.

Warren shuts off the ignition to his car and steps out to survey the damage. "Dad's going to kill me. There's a huge dent over the front bumper." His voice is unsteady. It sounds like it did when he was a toddler and got caught eating candy.

"And don't forget the garage door," I snarl. "Look at it. The metal's all twisted." I walk closer and point to the damage.

"I can see it from here!" Warren snaps.

"Is there anything I can do to help, Ms. Isabell?" Mary shifts around in her uncomfortable uniform.

"Yes, call a garage repair company. I need someone to fix this immediately. I'll pay extra to bump the line or whatever."

Mary nods, adjusts her wide Peter Pan collar, and turns back toward the house to make the call.

"I suggest you call Dad now to break the news," I tell Warren. "I'm going inside to shower."

Turning away from the scene of destruction, I enter my house through the grand front staircase. The smell of garlic and Italian spices overwhelms me. *That's strange.* I told Mary to make grilled tilapia. The displeasing odor leads me straight to the kitchen.

"Yes, I need to schedule someone to repair a garage door."

Mary's on the phone, but I need to know what's happening with dinner. I hold my finger up in front of her face, cueing her to pause her conversation.

"Can you hold on one minute?" she stammers into the phone.

"What's for dinner tonight? It smells like a cheap chain restaurant in here."

Mary's face scrunches together as if she's trying to solve a hard math problem. "Mr. Harris saw me this morning and asked me to make spaghetti and meatballs," she says sheepishly.

"Spaghetti and meatballs?" I repeat. "What the hell? This isn't a freaking Olive Garden! You know I'm a pescatarian, and I absolutely never eat carbs with my dinner."

Suddenly, we both shift our eyes to the phone in Mary's hand.

"Anyone there? Ma'am?" A man's voice shouts.

Waving my hand at Mary, I signal for her to return to the call.

"Worst day ever," I huff as I stomp upstairs to take a shower.

As soon as I walk into my bedroom, my blood boils. Lola, Grace, and one of their blond pixy friends are sitting on the floor, surrounded by piles of my expensive shoes and clothes.

"Are you kidding me?" I growl. "What are you doing?"

Grace laughs as Lola hugs my favorite pair of bright yellow Manolo Blahnik shoes.

"Give those shoes to me right this second!" I take a step toward Lola…then smell it. They are high. Even the friend is unruffled by my loud, angry voice.

"Oh, Mom, relax. We're just looking at your beautiful things."

"Relax? You want me to relax? You've violated my privacy. And let's hope you haven't ruined anything! Dad's coming home for dinner tonight. Just wait until I tell him what you girls have done."

"Wait," Lola says with a smirk. "You're going to *talk* to Dad. You're going to sit at our dining table, have dinner together, and have a conversation. That's hilarious. You're really on fire."

Grace cackles in laughter as she wraps my bright red, limited-edition Gucci scarf around her neck. "Yeah, Mom. You and Dad are such a joke. You hate each other. It's so obvious. You're not fooling anyone."

My mind races back to the moment I agreed to marry Harris, when we had everyone fooled. The crowd at the top of the Empire State Building went wild when he proposed. I remember the wave of relief that washed over me. I'd never worry about money, and more importantly, I'd never need to confront my pesky emotions.

As Harris slipped the six-carat, round-shaped diamond onto my finger, the onlookers gasped in excitement. Neither of us felt true joy. We fed off the euphoria of those around us, who believed we were perfect and in love.

All of a sudden, my voice explodes with rage. "Get the hell out now. All of you. All of you pathetic, spoiled girls. Stand up and get out of my room."

The girls look at me but don't move. Out of ideas, I inhale deeply and unleash the highest-pitched, piercing scream this world has ever heard. The girls instantly sober and run out.

I look around at the mess. I'll get Mary to put everything away later. Collapsing into my California King-size bed, I picture Harris and I after we were engaged.

We moved back to the West Coast and started planning our wedding. We focused on superficial details, while continuing to perfect the protective armor that kept us from forming a deep emotional connection. Should we have the nuptials at a glamorous private estate or in an opulent ballroom? Should we release doves or set off fireworks after the ceremony?

I realized I was practically bulletproof the day I mistakenly opened a letter addressed to Harris and found out his divorce wasn't final. I simply steamed the envelope shut and assumed he'd do what was necessary to move forward with our marriage. We quickly adopted a don't ask, don't tell policy.

For many years, it worked. By this point, I had given up on a career in fashion and stayed busy with my endless tasks. I picked up tennis, joined volunteer committees at the country club, and worked out daily. I was continually moving to distract myself from my past, but I was running a race with no finish line.

It was after the birth of Lola and Grace that Harris had an emotional awakening.

"The birth of our daughters has changed me," he said one evening as he cradled a twin in each arm, lulling them to sleep.

I put down my latest issue of *Vogue* and looked at him blank-faced.

"It's like I'm finally seeing all the beautiful things in the world. The sky at dusk, the way the sun comes into the windows in Lola and Grace's bedroom."

There was a swell of tears in his eyes. I felt embarrassed for him. He seemed weak and vulnerable.

Suddenly, Harris yearned for a deeper connection. He begged me to go to couples' counseling. He left books on my pillow with titles like *How to Build a Happy Marriage* and *How to Love Fully*.

I'll never forget the day he came home from work and forced me to talk.

"We don't really know each other, Isabell. We're a family now. We need to open ourselves emotionally for the benefit of our daughters."

"I'm not sure what you mean? You sound like a free-thinking bohemian," I said, irritated.

"Isabell, listen to me. I can't live like this anymore. I need a deeper relationship with the mother of my children."

Before I could blow off Harris's request, Grace woke from her nap, crying.

"I need to go get Grace. We can talk more later." I rushed away, knowing I wouldn't re-visit the conversation. It had been too long. Emotional isolation was embedded in our relationship. I didn't want to look inward and feel my life's pain and regret.

This is when I started swirling drama around myself. I found that bitching out the maître d' at a restaurant for making me wait for a table, or calling the manager at a boutique to complain about poor service, were ways to avoid the crisis brewing inside. The petty arguments and my arrogant attitude were a new type of armor. They distracted me from confronting the questions that flitted through my mind. *Was I drugged? Was I raped? Was I a willing participant or a victim?*

Suddenly, I shoot up in my bed. I know precisely what to do to push away the miserable feelings Lola and Grace have stirred up.

"Mary!" I scream as I fly down the stairs to the kitchen. "You need to stop what you're doing and go to the grocery store. I told you to make tilapia and grilled asparagus for dinner. Spaghetti and meatballs are unacceptable."

Mary looks at me. Tears prick her eyes. "Yes, ma'am," she says as she collects her keys.

"And Mary, don't bother coming back tomorrow if you can't follow simple instructions."

There, I think to myself. *I'm feeling better already.*

CHAPTER 19

Maggie O'Donnell

"I THINK SOPHIA'S FINALLY asleep," I say.

"I wonder why she had such a hard time tonight?" Doug shifts in our bed.

Before I can answer, we hear Sophia's voice. "I need water."

"I'll get it." Doug tosses his phone onto the comforter and walks downstairs to the kitchen.

My heart beats heavily. Desperate for clues about what the underwear means, I grab his phone. *Will his Google search history reveal if Doug has a strange sexual fetish, if he's cheating, or if he's gay?*

I pick it up and hit the home button, but the phone has already secured its secrets and asks me to input a passcode. I've tried a million combinations over the past weeks. His birthday, my birthday, our anniversary, and the kids' birthdays, but none of the number sequences are correct.

I put his phone down where he left it and accept defeat.

"She said she's stressed about her math test."

"Oh," I say as Doug walks toward our bed. He's wearing blue plaid boxer shorts. I can't help but picture him wearing my red lacey underwear. The thought makes me shudder.

"Are you cold?" he asks, getting under the covers.

"No, I'm okay. I'm turning off the light now."

"Wait for just a second." He grabs his phone from the bed and plugs it into the charger on his nightstand.

As we lie in the darkness, my brain explodes with fear. It's been almost three weeks, and I still can't find the courage to talk with Doug. I'm frozen by dread and find obsessively reading the comments on my anonymous post is the only way to deal with my overwhelming emotions. I think back to one comment someone made.

> **Aviva Omer:** Kick things up in the bedroom. If he's not interested, then you have a problem.

Moving my body against Doug's back, I circle my arms around his waist. I stroke his chest. Slowly, I move my hand further and further down. I slip my fingers under the band of his boxer shorts, making my intentions clear.

But before I can go any further, Doug gently grasps my hand in his. "I'm sorry, Maggie. You're catching me on a bad night. I'm tired, and I've had a sore throat all day. Can I give you a rain check?"

Suddenly, my face is burning hot, although Doug can't see how it has turned crimson in the dark. "Okay," I say meekly, turning my back to him. The tears come quickly. *He can't know I'm crying. He must not know I'm crying.*

"Maggie, oh my god. I didn't mean to upset you. I'm tired. It's just sex one night. It's not that big of a deal."

But it is a big deal, I think to myself. It's not just this *one* night. Our sex life has practically disappeared over the past year. My head pounds with the Facebook comment: *if he's not interested, you have a problem*.

I clamp my hands around my pillow, fearful that the life I've built for myself is on the verge of imploding.

Why are you wearing my underwear, and how long has this been going on? The words come together in my mind, pushing against my lips. My body quivers as I open my mouth to speak, but at the last second, I decide to go with something more neutral.

"I feel like things are off. Is there anything you need to tell me?" I pray this is enough to make Doug speak his truth.

Doug lets out a frustrated sigh. "No, Maggie, there's nothing we need to talk about. It's just life. It's busy with work, and the kids. I think it's normal for a couple who's been together for half their lives."

I want to believe him, but his explanation does nothing to address the red lacy elephant in the room.

Sitting up and facing him, I continue. "Remember what it used to be like? "Remember how you used to play a song for me every morning, and we'd cuddle and laugh."

"Yes, of course, I remember. I loved our routine."

We lay in silence for a few moments too long.

"It's just, I miss *us*," I finally say.

"What do you mean you miss us?" Doug sits up, turning toward me.

"I don't know. In college, we did everything together. You were my best friend. You always asked questions about Maybelline, and I loved hearing stories about your dad. I felt really close to you." I can't help but think of the long talks we used to have. When Doug spoke about his dad, his words sounded heavy, as if they were laying the foundation for a house where the memories could reside.

"Yes, of course, I remember. I especially remember how you'd show up at my frat house buzzed. We'd drink a few beers, and then you'd pass out in my bed."

"Yes! Exactly. We were best friends. Somehow, we slept in the same bed for months without hooking up."

Doug groans playfully. "Ugh, those nights were torture. Every time you slept over, I wanted to wrap my arms around you and tell you I was in love with you."

My heart swells as he recalls how he longed to be with me. "And then, finally, that one night, when we had the impromptu seventies' karaoke party."

I picture Doug plodding down the stairs of his frat house, where I sat waiting for him on a beat-up gray couch. It smelled like stale beer and dirty socks. He had recently redecorated his cramped room and was excited for me to see it. His full-sized bed was now propped up off the floor, as a top bunk loft, and his Papasan chair sat pushed against the wall, flanked by a *Pulp Fiction* poster. Several CD towers sat next to the closet. Extra CDs lay haphazardly on the tower's top, in a pile that could fall to the ground at any moment.

"That was the best night," Doug says. "Tell you what. Let's get tickets to see that Yacht Rock cover band. We'll have a real-deal date night."

"I'd like that." I lay my head back and sink into my pillow. Nothing's resolved, but maybe if we spend time alone, I'll work up the courage to talk with him.

"Great. I love you, Maggie May," he says as he quickly drifts to sleep.

Closing my eyes, I try to let my worries melt away. I toss and turn for a while, but sleep doesn't come. Instead, my mind floods with memories of our impromptu seventies' karaoke party. I couldn't have known it, but that night was the first time I saw evidence that Doug liked to wear women's underwear.

"YOU MUST HAVE over a thousand CDs," I said as my eyes ran over his collection.

"Well, I love music," he replied with a prideful look in his eye. "My dad loved music too."

"Duh!" I responded with a sarcastic smirk. "Your Discman is your number one accessory."

"Ha! Yes. I know. Music helped me through my dad's death." He paused for a moment, swallowing the sadness on his face. "Here, I'll play you one of his favorite songs. He was a huge fan of seventies' music, yacht-type rock, in particular. Listen and tell me what you think."

He walked over to one of the many CD towers filled from top to bottom, and hunched over. Reading the spines of each one, he pulled out a case with a pink flamingo centered over a dark green background. I liked music, too, but I didn't recognize the jewel case.

I stepped up the short ladder resting by his bed and laid down as he put the CD in his stereo. He pressed play and laid down beside me. The room was silent, and then suddenly, the hum of nothingness filled with the harmony of soothing sounds, followed by a man's voice.

Lyrics about sailing to paradise and finding tranquility echoed in my ears.

The song was familiar, although I didn't know the artist. As the notes crested, the lyric came bounding into my mind. Facing each other, Doug and I belted out the chorus in unison.

My heart floated in my chest. We grasped hands, giggling.

"I love Christopher Cross!" Doug's eyes twinkled with pleasure. "I have an idea!" He stepped down from the bed and pulled a blue plastic milk crate from the closet.

"Here, come down and see." He began digging through the miscellaneous items in the crate. There were a few scarves, a UCLA Bruins felt blanket, and more CDs. He grabbed an item I couldn't see and hid it behind his back. He looked at me as if he'd just found a winning lottery ticket.

"What is it?" I asked, impatient and giddy. His excitement was contagious.

"Close your eyes."

Making a face of mock displeasure, I held my hands loosely over my eyes. A few moments later, when I uncovered them, Doug was standing before me wearing a sea captain's hat. A large yellow anchor embellished the hat's center.

It was a moment of pure, drunken, heavenly happiness. I broke apart laughing and rummaged through the milk crate to see what other items I could find to add to our impromptu costume party. As I pushed my fingers through the various items, I saw several pairs of women's underwear.

"What's all this?" I blurted out in amusement.

Doug's lips collapsed from a wide, toothy grin into a thin line. "Oh, that stuff. Just gag gifts. It's stupid fraternity prank stuff." He kicked the beat-up crate aside and grasped my hand.

"And now, ladies and gentlemen, it's time to sing more yacht rock." His voice bellowed like a radio announcer. He stepped over to his CD tower and began pulling out CD after CD, queuing up the tunes for our very own karaoke party.

The night became a blur of mishmashed soft rock melodies that made us feel we were beachside, enjoying a summer breeze.

"This is so fun," I said. "It's the most fun I've had since…" My voice trailed off. I don't know why, but the tears came fast and frantic.

Doug leaned in and gave me a tight hug. "At first, it's hard to feel joy without feeling pain right behind it. Grief is weird like that."

I nodded my head into his shoulder.

"Here. I want to play you another song." He pulled away from our embrace. A line of sweat appeared on his forehead. "I need you to really listen."

My stomach flipped over itself.

He took out a CD and placed it in his stereo, forwarding it to the correct track. "It's REO Speedwagon."

He inched toward me as the song crooned with lyrics about friendship that has turned into something more.

"Do you understand?" he asked, a slight shakiness to his voice. "I can't fight this feeling," he said.

I didn't reply. Instead, I moved close to him, and we kissed.

CHAPTER 20

Indira Acharya

"THIS NEW FAMILY is from Syria. A mom and five children. I'm not sure what happened to the dad." Fatima's long tie-dyed skirt swings as she flits around the refugee center's supply closet, gathering pots, pans, and dishes.

She stops and hands me a stack of crisp white sheets. Her deep, woody scent overwhelms me as I take linens and put them in the cardboard box we're bringing over to the family's temporary home.

"Does Kabir mind you've been spending every extra moment with me?"

Kabir. When I hear his name, my body fills with regret. Not for what I've done, but for what I want to do.

"No, he knows I wanted to major in social work, but I was afraid to pursue anything other than being a doctor. He's glad I'm doing something I'm passionate about."

"And what an amazing doctor you are. The very best orthopedist this side of Los Angeles." Fatima looks at me with bright eyes.

"Thanks. I know I'm good at it, and I have a pleasant bedside manner, but I just don't find replacing the hips of the elderly satisfying."

"It's great how Kabir supports you. You have a great marriage."

I nod my head weakly. *Tell her*, the voice kicks at me again.

"Is something wrong?" Fatima's eyes squint with concern.

"No, just tired," I say, knowing the reason for my exhaustion is my emotional turmoil.

Fatima doesn't know how I feel. She believes I'm happily married. And it's not that my marriage is unhappy. It's just that it's more like a friendship. It lacks passion. If my relationship with Fatima is going to move forward, it will depend on me. She doesn't know about the desire simmering below the surface.

Fatima grabs a box and exits the supply closet. "Let's load this stuff into my car. Why don't we stop at Seaside Coffee for the largest caffeinated beverage they have? Maybe that will help."

SEASIDE COFFEE IS bustling. Fatima and I sit at a small table crammed near the barista. A mom herds three children, who are dripping wet from the ocean across the street, to the bathroom. A young couple in their twenties places their coffee order from behind dark and stylish sunglasses.

"Order for Jax and Clementine," the barista shouts.

The trendy couple picks up their drinks and leaves.

My tongue feels like a dead weight in my mouth. The kicking in my throat is relentless. I have to tell Fatima how I feel, yet I cannot get my jaw to move.

"Order for Maverick," the teenage barista calls, interrupting us again.

"Maverick?" Fatima locks her eyes on mine.

Could it be? My gaze follows the gorgeous man approaching the counter. He's got white blond hair, bronzed skin, and wears brightly colored surfing shorts and flip-flops.

"Oh, wow. Maverick. Is that you?" I blurt. "Haven't seen you since high school."

Fatima cranks her head around as her jaw drops. "Oh my god!

Maverick. It is you. Come have a seat. Let's catch up." Fatima jumps out of her chair and scoots it closer to mine as Maverick pulls one over.

"Epic!" Maverick says as he takes a seat at our small table. "My long-lost compadres." He hunches his tall, muscular body toward us and smiles. The skin on his face is deep bronze from spending every day at the beach. He appears to be the same person he was in high school. A piece of the California coast come to life.

"Looks like you're still surfing every day," Fatima says with her radiant smile as she pushes her long braids over her shoulder. The sight of her bare collarbone makes my body pulse.

"Right on, ladies. I spend all day, every day, surfing, like the old days."

"So, you're retired?" I ask, envious.

"I got lucky and created something for surfboards that slows them down, helps newbies. It caught on like wildfire." He leans back in his chair, spreading out his broad shoulders.

"Wow! An inventor," Fatima says with excitement.

"It was just simple math," he says humbly.

"You were always good in math." Back during high school, he floated above everyone, as if he were a supernatural god. When around him, I felt like the world was his, and I just existed in it. The most gorgeous girls in school tried constantly to get his attention, but he stayed above the fray. Everything about him was effortless and cool. We had every class together because, on top of his good looks and captivating presence, he was brilliant.

"You still don't own real shoes," I joke, glancing at his flip-flops.

"Nah, nothing better than feeling sand between my toes." He smirks.

"We made quite the threesome back in the day," Fatima says.

Nodding in agreement, my mind's eye pictures the day our friendship bloomed. Fatima and I were at the library. She was new to Hamilton Beach. I was busy working on a set of challenging math theorems. Fatima was excitedly devouring a stack of American magazines.

As I sat, struggling to prove the product of two even integers is an even integer, I heard a voice break through the web of math concepts swirling in my mind.

"Any luck, Indira?" Maverick stared at me.

"No luck at all," I said, glad I wasn't the only one having difficulty solving the problems. "I'm getting nowhere with these." I lifted my hands in front of my face and shrugged my shoulders.

"Who's your friend?" he said in gravelly voice as he looked toward the ebony goddess sitting across from me.

"This is Fatima. She just moved here from Ethiopia."

"Rad," he said as he pushed his hand through the wisps of white-hot hair hanging over his eyes.

Fatima smiled at him but quickly went back to reading an article in *Cosmo.*

"These problems are a real bummer," he continued. "Paul and Mike are planted by the biography section. Let's see if they're conquering."

Fatima looked at Maverick, confused. She was fluent in English, having attended a top school in Ethiopia, but Maverick's California surf dialect took getting used to.

"Sure, maybe Paul and Mike can help." Lifting my body out of the chair, I turned to Fatima. "Be back in a few minutes," I said as I followed Maverick to the other side of the library.

"Dudes," Maverick said as we approached Paul and Mike's table. "Making any headway on these problems?"

Suddenly, I realized I'd left my worksheet at the table with Fatima. "I'll be right back," I stammered, taking a shortcut through an aisle filled with books about space.

When I burst through the narrow shelves stacked with publications describing star systems and asteroids, I saw Fatima hunched over my worksheet, pencil in hand.

"Here," she said. "I finished."

Looking down at the worksheet, my eyes widened in surprise. Fatima had solved the theorems.

MY BODY BOUNCES forward as Kabir gently hits the brakes. His car creeps through traffic as we drive to my parents' house.

Ping. Pulling my phone out of my bag, I see another voicemail from Maggie O'Donnell. She's tried calling me several times for a story she's doing on the refugee center. I wish she'd get the hint. I'm not interested. My time at the center is much more than a volunteer opportunity. It's the place that makes my heart feel like fire and my body tingle with anticipation.

"Who was that?" Kabir asks as the car slinks along.

"It was the reporter who wants to interview me about the refugee center." My throat tightens with guilt.

Before Kabir can respond, Ahana, our thirteen-year-old, yells out, "I hate this stupid Punjabi suit. Lisa Clark still calls me Jasmine after seeing me dressed like this when we were in preschool."

"Ahana, we talked about this. Your grandmother gave you these beautiful clothes for Diwali last year, and she'll be happy to see you wearing them on her birthday." I turn toward the back seat and drink in the image of my three beautiful daughters. The garments they wear momentarily disrupt time, bridging the gap between my Nani, my mom, and my daughters.

Ahana clicks her tongue in annoyance and shifts her gaze toward the window.

I ignore her salty attitude. "Who wants to come into the grocery store with me? I'm getting chai for Grandmother."

Navya, my ten-year-old, who idolizes her older sister, rolls her eyes. "No way. I hate the way people stare at me when I'm wearing these clothes."

Zoya, my six-year-old, is busy fiddling with the beads on her bright pink Punjabi suit and ignores my request.

"Zoya, why don't you go in with Mommy? You can help get the chai." Kabir looks at Zoya through the rearview mirror, raising his eyebrows.

She stops pulling at the beads, looks up, and sticks her tongue out. "Oh, Zoya, you're silly." I don't let minor behavioral infractions rattle me. "Okay, I'll go in by myself," I say, with no air of disappointment.

Kabir pulls our car to the entrance of Ackerman's Grocery, and I unsnap my seat belt.

"Be right back." I gather the red fabric of my saree and exit the car. As I walk into the store, I feel every set of eyes following me, as if I'm a model walking the catwalk at Paris Fashion Week. You can't disappear into the background in an American grocery store when wearing these clothes.

I pick up a large box of chai and walk to the checkout line. It's six deep, and the person at the register is paying by check. This is going to take longer than expected. Pulling out my phone, I text Kabir to let him know.

As I'm placing my phone back into my purse, it vibrates. Looking down, I expect to see a reply from Kabir, but the text is from Fatima.

Fatima: Please volunteer tomorrow. I miss you.

As soon as I read it, my face burns bright, probably matching the blood-like color of my saree. It's only been two days since our run-in with Maverick, and she already misses me. Reading into the meaning of her text like a schoolgirl, I suddenly feel a sharp tug on my saree.

"Emma, no!"

I turn around and see a mom with young twins and a baby.

"I'm so sorry," she says as she pulls her young daughter away from my flowing garment.

The little girl looks at me with awe. "So pretty." She reaches out and runs her hand over the red fabric.

"Emma, stop it now!" the mom yells, as she tries to wrestle a candy bar from her other twin's hand. I can tell she's overwhelmed.

I crouch down to get eye level with the girl. "Do you like my clothes?"

"Yes, pretty." Emma grins, and I notice the adorable dimple on her left cheek.

"This is called a saree. You can touch it." I hold a piece of the fabric away from my body, and the girl glides her tiny hand back and forth over the soft material.

"Thank you for being so understanding," the mom says as I stand up to pay.

Before I can respond, my phone buzzes again.

Fatima: Why haven't you responded? Please come tomorrow. XO

HAMILTON BEACH MOMS
PRIVATE GROUP — 5,349 Members

Gabriella Martinez
Today at 9:17 a.m.

Hello Moms! My name is Gabriella, and I have agreed to help Laura co-moderate this page. I'm a therapist and believe in living my life with gratitude. I thought it would be fun for everyone to comment about things we are grateful for. Share the first thing that comes to your mind, even the small stuff.

Also, have you registered for our first-ever in-person fundraiser to help our community food bank? Stop what you are doing and register right now. There are only twenty tickets left! Follow this link to the event page https://www.facebook.com/HBCMomsgiveback 😊

117 👍

Comments:

Deb Pristach: I am grateful for my mom.

Amy Rosen: Grateful for my preschool mom friends.

Robyn Klugman: Grateful for my husband. 🖤

Emily Smith: Grateful that I am divorced. 😆

Awaidia Bukhari: Grateful for my kids.

Diane Rose: Grateful for the hot dad I see running every morning on Lomack.

Jodi Pila: Yes! He is gorgeous!

Jia Xu: OMG, I'm not the only one who times my commute to get a look?

Latisha Williams: I just want to know who the lucky wife is?

Tara Goldstein: 🔥🔥🔥🚚

Susan Knapp: Grateful for my tennis ladies. Go Hamilton Country Club!

Patti Wasserman: With the amount of online shopping I do, can I just say I'm grateful for free shipping!

Michele Blondheim: Grateful for romance novels!

Jill Wong: Grateful for my SUV. I don't know how I'd get myself and my three baseball playing boys around town without it. With all the baseball bats, helmets, and other gear, it's a lifesaver. I consider it part of the family 🚗.

Jennifer Boxt: Honestly, you should get a minivan next time. Best mom vehicle on the planet!

Lisa Malkin: Yes, I agree. A minivan is the most convenient way to get your kids and their stuff around town!

Claire Doyle: Getting to the third row in a minivan is also much easier than in an SUV.

Jill Wong: My SUV has captain's chairs, and it's just as easy.

Gen Katz: It's easier to park my SUV than a minivan. The van is just so huge.

Hailey Chen: If I see one more minivan with a bumper sticker that says, "I used to be cool," I am going to lose it.

Sara Bier: #Minivanmamas

Hailey Chen: #SUVsoccermoms

Jill Wong: Boy, I didn't mean to start a controversy about SUVs vs. minivans. This is ridiculous!

CHAPTER 21

Gabriella Martinez

RICARDO SPINS ME around as the *Star Wars* theme song, "Across the Stars," plays. It's the first song we danced to at our wedding. His Han Solo cape brushes against my Princess Leia buns as our bodies glide around the kitchen. Our outfits should make for some exciting role-play later.

"Nine years, *mi alma*," he says as he dips me toward the floor.

"Nine wonderful years," I say back.

We've taken the day off to celebrate our anniversary and all things *Star Wars*. Carlita's picking up Lucas from school, and he's spending the night.

"Are you sure you want to watch the movies in number order?" I ask, curling up next to Ricardo in front of the TV. Of all the debates around the *Star Wars* series, which order to watch the films in is the most heated. We typically watch the movies by release date.

"*Si, mi alma.* Let's try something different. I read a blog post about how watching in number order helps you understand Anakin's transformation from Jedi to ruthless villain Darth Vader. You witness the complex tragedies that lead him to the dark side." Ricardo's tone is assured, as if the information was taken from the Bible itself.

"I get that," I say. "But I've always loved the simplicity of knowing Darth Vader's the villain. I don't feel bad for him. It's black and white. It's without complication."

"Ay, Gabby, but people are complicated. You, as a therapist, know this better than anyone."

"*Cierto.* You're right. People are complicated." I think of Carlita. Maybe I've simplified every interaction into her being wrong and me being right. But, certainly, she's just as complex as an eighties' movie villain. "Okay, you win. Cue up *Phantom Menace.*"

I'M PUSHING MY fork into the last bit of the GMO-free veggie loaf I made for lunch when Ricardo stands.

"I need thirty minutes before we start *Revenge of the Sith.*" He brings his plate to the sink. "I have to call the restaurant. There was some screw-up with our tomato order."

"Take your time," I say as I clear my dish and then lay on the couch.

Pulling out my phone, I scroll Facebook as I wait for Ricardo's return. I'm trying to get more familiar with the Hamilton Beach Moms' Facebook page since I agreed to be a moderator. I'm hoping to ground this page to reality and make it a community that thrives off genuine connection rather than snarky comments.

Laura has uploaded a photo of her and a client with the caption *SOLD! Perry Properties does it again!* Angela Pinker is hiking in Colorado. Melissa Constantine is humble bragging about her kid getting into an Ivy League school. She's posted a photo of her son wearing a Yale sweatshirt with the caption, *They must be letting anyone in these days!*

And then, as I continue scrolling, I see an alert pop up on my screen, *New post from Carlita Anderson.* I go to my mom's Facebook page and see she has posted a link to something titled "Medicare, Men, and Marilyn." Marilyn, who's that?

I click on the words, and it takes me to a blog site. I read through the opening paragraph.

> *About me:* I'm a sassy lady in her 70s, who began her online dating adventure a year ago. As I joined the ranks of digital silver singles, I found I needed advice and encouragement. I

was astonished to find little information that caters to fabulous women dating in their twilight years. I created this blog to chronicle my escapades and provide advice. I'm going by my pseudonym here, Marilyn, to keep things private. All hail to the original fem fatale and my alter ego, Marilyn Monroe!

"*¡Mierda!*" I gasp. What is she doing? And how is this private if she posted it to her Facebook page? It's hard to believe she's my mother. We are different in the way we think, the way we move our bodies, and the way we look. I'm tall and willowy, with curly brown hair and brown eyes. My looks are average, like the pasta dish served at a chain Italian restaurant in a suburban strip mall. Carlita's petite, slim, and stylish, with a platinum blond pixie cut, flawless tanned skin, and bright green eyes. She's the nightly special at the fancy exclusive brasserie downtown.

Here are a few of my personal rules for online dating.
- Don't be afraid to date younger men!
- He should pay, always, every time.
- Texting and emailing are not a substitute for calling.
- Use a private investigator to do a minimal background check if things get serious.
- Don't let 1950s rules about sex hold you back.
- One last word, my daughter would be appalled if I did not include any of the traditional safety rules for online dating, but I know you are intelligent enough to seek out that information elsewhere.

Yes, accurate statement, Carlita, I think before scrolling further. I see there are ten entries. I start at the beginning.

January 18th

I walked into The Mad Meatball, the Italian restaurant my date chose for our first meeting. The smell of heavy garlic wafted through the air. The crowd was elderly chic.

As I walked to the bar, I saw a paunchy man dressed in his best bright orange Hawaiian shirt. I realized this was Ted. But he looked to be well into his eighties. His dating profile, *I'mMrRight*, said he was seventy-six, and the photos posted to his page were of a man with hair, twenty pounds lighter. It's not that I require the most handsome silver fox. It's just that I expected to meet the Ted portrayed online.

I introduced myself and was assaulted with the odor of mothballs. Ten minutes into a boring conversation, my phone rang. I took it out of my purse and looked at the screen, acting surprised.

"Oh, that's strange. It's my neighbor, Harriett. She's supposed to be seeing *Jersey Boys* right now." Harriett had agreed to call me in case I needed an excuse to get out of my date.

I answered the call, making dramatic ooh and ahh sounds. "Yes, I will, of course. I'm here for you," I said as I hung up. "She's in the emergency room. She fell and hit her head while walking into the show."

"Oh, that's terrible," Ted replied.

I could tell Ted knew I was lying. What did he expect? He so grossly misrepresented himself.

"And let me guess," Ted continued. "You need to leave to help her." He smirked as if he was in on my scheme.

"Well, actually, yes."

Ted didn't look the least bit shocked.

"Well then, Marilyn, it was nice meeting you. I'll tell you, the best part about dating at this age is that tomorrow I won't even remember meeting you or the way you so rudely blew me off."

I put my phone down and cackle in laughter at Ted's clever comment. Okay, maybe Carlita can handle herself better than I thought. Perhaps I need to give her more credit. I scroll a bit and land randomly on entry four.

February 10th

Last night was my long-awaited date with *CoolCatCarl*. We'd been talking on the phone and texting non-stop since we connected on Willyougosteady.com. I was a smitten kitten the moment I laid eyes on him. He had a real Humphrey Bogart vibe, and our chemistry was undeniable.

We each ordered a dry martini. And then another and another. Before I knew it, we were ordering dinner. We were as drunk as skunks. The night was leading somewhere fulfilling, if you know what I mean.

Ay! Yes, I do know what you mean, Mom. I stop reading and look up at the paused image of Obi-Wan Kenobi on the television screen. I know I should go back to mindlessly scrolling on Facebook. Nothing good will come from reading this, but I can't help myself.

> "So, what's in that small shopping bag you have with you?" I asked CoolCatCarl between drunken sips of my fourth dry martini.
> "Oh, in here? This is a gift for you, my beautiful Marilyn. I had to make sure you were worthy."
> "Well," I shot back coyly, as if I was Marilyn Monroe in the movie *Some Like It Hot.* "I was born worthy. So, let's see it."
> He handed me the bag and told me to open it. Inside was a pair of black thong underwear.
> "There's nothing sexier than a woman wearing a black thong. Why don't you go in the bathroom and put it on?"

I stare at the words "black thong underwear" for a solid three minutes until they lift from my phone's screen and begin swirling around me. I toss my phone on the couch as if it's burning my skin.

¡Hijo de puta! I curse in my head as I picture my mother going into the bathroom at a restaurant and changing into skimpy underwear for a man she only met thirty minutes earlier. *¡Hijo de puta!* I think again as I pull off the iconic Princess Leia wig that makes it look like I have huge hair buns.

I curl desperately into the safety of my comfortable couch. But a moment later, I find myself posting to the Hamilton Beach Moms' Facebook page.

Anonymous Mom Post
Today at 1:21 p.m.

Desperate for advice. My seventy-year-old mom uses my Amazon account. She doesn't realize I can see what she orders, and lately, she has placed orders for vibrators, scandalous thong underwear, trampy negligees, and lubricant. So much lubricant. The brand she prefers is called LubriCAN, but this daughter just CAN'T! I'm not sure how to tell her I can see what she's ordering. But, more importantly, I am genuinely concerned about her dating life. She's recently divorced. How do I talk to her about dating safety? I'm afraid for her health and safety. Please advise!

A few minutes go by, and my phone explodes with advice.

Isabell Whitmore: Your mom is my hero!

Janice Smith: I'm envious of her active dating life.

Julie Furney: You are missing the point of anonymous mom's post. Sit your mother down and talk to her like she's your teenage daughter. The world has changed since the last time she was out there.

Hilary Schubert: That silver hair dating scene is intense. My mom's been a part of it for a few years. I try and stay out of it.

Brandi Russel: Anonymous mom should get over her self-righteous attitude! Let your mom live it up and have fun.

My arm hairs bristle at Brandi Russel's mean comment. If she only knew this post was made by her therapist. At least I know Brandi believes she's morally superior to *everyone*. Posting this online was a huge mistake. It's hard to believe that I would rely on a public forum for help. I've gone temporarily insane.

I quickly delete my anonymous post and pledge to have a face-to-face conversation with Carlita the next time I see her.

HAMILTON BEACH MOMS
PRIVATE GROUP — 5,349 Members

Laura Perry
Today at 12:21 p.m.

Hi friends. Some of you have been using this page as an outlet to shame people and area businesses. A member of our online community recently posted about a situation involving a teenager that was misconstrued. Unfortunately, the poster did not hide the teenager's identity. Although I took the post down immediately, the damage was done. This teen and his family are now dealing with the fallout. This page is not to be used as a pulpit to defame others. Please think carefully before you post. Thanks for your cooperation!

On to a more exciting topic. Don't forget to register for our first-ever in-person fundraiser to help our community food bank. Follow this link to the event page https://www.facebook.com/HBCMomsgiveback and register right now! 😆.

83 👍

Comments

Tina Liu: This post is about my son. Last week, someone posted a photo of his car and license plate. He parked illegally. I find this deplorable! Many friends texted me to share the photo and rant that went along with the post. My son is a good kid. He made a mistake. To the mom who posted about my son's regrettable parking mishap—get over yourself! Sorry, you weren't able to pull your Hummer into the handicapped spot you're illegally using anyway!

22 👍

Marcia Fleishman: Personally, I want to know if my teenager is driving like a maniac. I always tell my son the moms of Hamilton Beach are watching. ●●

Alicia Carlson: There's no reason to blast businesses around town. I hate when people do this.

Ayesha Thomas: I'm sick of cancel culture. Just mind your own business.

Isabell Whitmore: I'd like to know if a business provides poor service so I can avoid it like the plague.

Dale Atkins: Everyone, just stop being a Karen. Plain and simple!

Karen Holden: As someone named Karen, can I just say that using my name as a catch-all for bad behavior is extremely offensive.

Cecily Lopez: I run a public relations firm specializing in online reputation management. Check out my company's website www.reputationdoctors.com. I will do a free consult for anyone who mentions seeing this post on the HBC Mom's web page.

Gennye Krasner: This post by our administrators is important. There are always two sides to a story. I try to keep this in mind whenever I read these shaming posts.

Jennifer Mann: Yes, everyone should remember the stupid things they did when growing up. We were lucky no one was taking pictures and videos of the mistakes we made.

CHAPTER 22

Laura Perry

"THIS HAS NOTHING to do with Jolie moving and Lorna having a boyfriend!" Nora is livid that I asked if her interest in deaf culture is linked to her dwindling friend group. "Anyway, it's too late!" she screams.

"But I don't understand." I look at Nora, startled by her reaction. "I have contact information for deaf teenagers. I thought you'd be happy."

"You already stole my deaf identity. There's no going back." Her voice pulses with rage.

"Hold on right there, Nora. You can't talk to your mother that way. Apologize right now." Troy looks sternly at Nora, but she turns her head away from him.

"What? I can't hear you!" She points at the empty areas on her head where her cochlear implants should be.

I instinctively step toward her, wanting to soothe her anger. As soon as I do, she jumps backward.

"All those hours you made me spend in therapy, forcing hearing on me…" Her lower lip wobbles, and then her voice bursts. "And putting me through a surgery when I was only twelve months old!" She flies out the door, consumed by rage, and leaves for school.

Feeling breathless, I collapse onto the living room couch. Troy nestles next to me as my eyes spill tears. "That day…the surgery. I can remember every detail." I lean into his solid body.

"I know," he agrees. "It's almost as if it happened yesterday."

I rest my head on his shoulder, remembering Nora's surgery day. My feelings of fear, mixed with dread and hope, creating an emotional cocktail as complex as a hipster bartender's latest libation. The preop room was sterile-looking, except for the wallpaper splattered with bright red hearts. The image of the hearts danced in my mind as I disconnected from reality and held Nora in my arms—hearts exploding, hearts beating, hearts twirling and spinning, surrounding Nora in love.

Nora had never heard the word "love." I had told her I loved her countless times—a hundred times a day, a thousand times a week—but the truth was, she had never heard the word. Despite this, I knew she felt the emotion. The image of the hearts continued to dance in my mind—hearts exploding, hearts beating, hearts twirling and spinning.

As soon as the nurse wheeled Nora away, blood rushed through my veins as if it were launching a rocket into outer space. I left Troy in the surgical waiting area and paced the hospital's lobby. Restless, I entered the hospital's sundries shop.

As I stepped toward an aisle of food, I felt sure someone was watching me. Turning around, I glanced to my right. Sitting on a shelf under a sign that read *Fifty Percent Off* was a football-sized red plush heart with two eyes.

My arms trembled slightly as I reached out and grabbed it from its resting place. Two white arms flopped down, revealing the words "I love you" sewn neatly across the middle. It reminded me of the preop room. I bought the heart, along with a few protein bars and returned to the surgical unit.

"Nora's a teenager," Troy says, bringing me back to the present. "She's going through a hard time. But we got through the surgery, and we'll get through this too." Troy's words are edged with sorrow.

I nod hesitantly.

"I need to leave for work. Are you sure you're okay?" I can tell by Troy's expression he's apprehensive about going.

"Yes. Thanks for staying," I say. Squeezing his shoulder, I gently edge him forward off the couch.

He hesitates for a moment before standing. "When's Nora starting therapy?"

"The appointment is next week. The therapist wants to meet with all of us." My body flutters with sorrow.

"Okay, whatever we can do to help Nora and our family figure this out." Troy holds my gaze, and I feel thankful for his partnership. "I'll check in with you at lunch, when I have a break." He collects his things and leaves.

LATER, AS I melt into a warm bath, my mind shifts back to Nora's surgery day again. Three hours and twenty-two minutes after the procedure began, Nora's surgeon appeared in the waiting area wearing a surgical gown and hat. She pulled the paper cap off her head and approached Troy and me. "I have great news. Nora's heading to recovery. Everything went well. Keep busy, and before you know it, you'll be seeing Melody for activation."

"I can't wait to start Nora's hearing journey," I said as I grasped the red plush heart to my chest.

A few moments later, a nurse called Troy and me to the recovery room, where Nora was slowly coming out of the anesthesia.

Hunching over the crib, I took in the sight of the thick bandages wrapped firmly around Nora's head. A bulge of white fabric covered both her ears. I was desperate to engulf her in my arms and hold her close. Suddenly, I remembered the plush heart. I took it out of my bag and placed it next to her.

"I love you," I said as I tucked it over her right shoulder. "I love you, Nora, and I can't wait for the day when you will hear me say these words."

As I step out of the bath, my cell phone rings and my memories fade.

"Laura, it's Mr. Bronstein, from Hamilton High."

My pulse shoots through my body. *Why is the school counselor calling?* "Is everything okay? Is Nora, okay?"

"Well, that's why I'm calling. She was here first hour, but didn't show up for her second class. Normally, I wouldn't reach out so quickly, but since Nora's been coming to school without her implants, I thought I should call."

Suddenly, I'm on the edge of panic. "She should be there," I say frantically. "Please let me know if you hear anything. I've got to go." I end the call before Mr. Bronstein can say more.

I send a frantic text to Nora, but she doesn't respond.

"Call me right away! Nora's missing!" I screech into my phone, leaving a voicemail for Troy.

Flying up the stairs, I burst through the door to her bedroom. I open her computer and type in her password. Thank God I have a rule about knowing her passwords. The screen displays a chat from someone I've never heard of—Heidi.

> **Heidi:** The pier 10 tomorrow. U in?

> **Nora:** School?

> **Heidi:** Teacher's workday. Meet us. You can wear your implants

> **Nora:** I'm done with those implants. I'm DEAF

> **Heidi:** Bad a**

For a moment, I'm confused. Heidi must be one of the deaf teenagers Nora met at the mall. It's the only thing that makes sense. Nora didn't tell me she exchanged information with them. I scroll back in the conversation, looking for clues, and realize Nora's been communicating with Heidi for several months. *How did I miss this?*

Looking at my watch, I see it's just after ten.

My car skids as I pull into the parking lot surrounding the pier a few minutes later. Leaning my weight into the door, I push it open with too much force. I tumble out, scraping my cheek against the pavement. It stings, but I ignore it and quickly stand.

As soon as I steady myself, my phone rings.

"Laura, it's Mr. Bronstein again."

My heart thuds heavily.

"I'm here with Nora," he says.

My chest expands, finally letting in air. "Oh my god. Thank God. Can I talk to her?"

"I asked if she wanted to talk to you, but because she's not wearing her implants, she said she can't hear."

Frustration mixes with anger as I realize Nora's right. She won't be able to hear me on the phone.

Mr. Bronstein continues. "She has her phone if you want to text."

"Yes, I'll text her after we hang up. Did she say anything about where she was?"

"She just said she thought she had to be somewhere but then realized she didn't."

My mind jumps around, trying to interpret her cryptic response. "What does that even mean?" I say, not expecting an answer.

"I'm not sure, but she's back now. Do you want me to send her to class?"

"Yes, send her to class. Tell her I'll be expecting her home immediately after school."

As soon as we hang up, I send Nora a text.

Me: I'm so glad you're safe. I love you.

I wait for a few minutes, but she doesn't respond.

Driving home, I can't help but wonder how long Nora's been interacting with Heidi? As soon as I arrive, I climb the stairs two at a time and log back into her computer. There's a new thread on the chat.

Heidi: Where R U?

Nora: My sign isn't good enough.

Heidi: nah just come

Nora: sry I'm out

My heart breaks as I realize maybe I've hurt Nora, by not acknowledging her deafness.

CHAPTER 23
Julie Wu

"WHEN WILL WE move past this, Julie?" Eric peers at me as I gather pillows for another night in the guest room. His jaw tightens. "I don't understand how we ended up here. It's not fair to hurl your resentment about Georgia's law at me. We don't even live in Georgia anymore!"

"But you still support the people who support these policies." My voice simmers.

Eric lets out a low sigh. "You're everything to me. I want us to do whatever it takes to work through this. Maybe we should go to counseling?"

I can tell by the way his eyes dart around that he's seriously concerned about our marriage, but I can't help myself from lashing out. "This could be over and done if you agree to vote blue. Other people should have the right to make the same choice you made all those years ago!"

The angles of his face sharpen. It reminds me of how he looked the day he drove me to Planned Parenthood all those years ago. When we arrived at the nondescript, faded building just west of downtown Atlanta, I was thankful there wasn't a crowd of protestors.

"I'll drop you here," he said as he pulled his car up to the door.

I sat in the front seat, frozen with fear. "No, I can't walk inside alone." I closed my eyes, inhaling deeply. Air filled my chest, but it was hard to breathe.

The memory increases my anger tenfold. I lower my voice to a furious whisper. "We never talk about it. It's as if it never happened."

Eric freezes and stares at me blankly. His lips move, but then collapse together.

"We paid with crumbled up cash we pooled together," I blurt. "The dog-eared bills made me feel like the whole thing was a dirty backroom mob deal!" I rush to the guest room before he can respond.

Pacing the floor, I inhale deeply, trying to relax. I need to read more comments on my anonymous mom post. The supportive responses continue to roll in. Cradling my phone in my lap, I sink into the guest bed.

> **Dawn Keim:** Your husband sounds like a self-absorbed, selfish narcissist who's only concerned about himself. Makes me sick.

Really? I think. I wouldn't describe Eric like that. The comment scratches at my throat.

> **Marta Patterson:** I can understand why you feel the way you do, anonymous mom. But think about your relationship as a whole. Is he a good husband, a good dad? Is he a caring person? Is this issue more proof of his flawed character, or is it an outlier?

Eric's a great father and a caring person. He's loyal and trustworthy. I reflect on Marta's comment for a moment before I read more.

> **Amber Bray:** You have committed a sin. The political divide in your marriage is the least of your problems.

Oh my god. Amber Bray. She's the mom that reached out to me after I posted about my family's move to Hamilton Beach. We just made a coffee date.

Shame consumes me, making my entire body vibrate. Jumping off the bed, I rush to the bathroom and splash cold water on my face.

Ping. My phone rings out in the silence. I lunge toward it and press my finger down. The screen unlocks, and I see a rash of comments under my post.

> **Deena Murphy:** I'm so glad someone called out anonymous mom for having an abortion. Unforgivable.

> **Tara Goldner:** Her body her choice!

> **Simone Tyler:** Anonymous mom should have had the baby and given it up for adoption.

> **Diya Patel:** Where do men come in? How come they're never held responsible?

> **Anadia Syed:** There's never a reason to end a human life

My pulse throbs in my neck as the comments continue. I was foolish to think any good could come from social media.

Flinging myself back onto the bed, I curl up like a cat. Recollections push through my consciousness. I can't stop my mind from picturing the nurse who led me back to a small, clean room that smelled like bleach. She asked me a few questions and told me what to expect.

"I'll need to do a quick ultrasound." She made brief eye contact and pursed her lips together in what was supposed to be a smile. "I'm going to put gel on your stomach. It's going to be cold." She squirted a thick clear slime onto her hands and rubbed it on my belly. My body did not register the coolness of the gel; I was burning inside.

"You're eight weeks. Would you like to see?"

Her words conjured up the image of a baby with Eric's golden brown eyes. My body tensed. I assumed the nurse was instructed to ask patients if they wanted to see the ultrasound image. To think any person could be that cruel is beyond reason.

I shook my head no, just as the doctor entered the exam room.

I stared at the ceiling, my eyes firmly focused on a poster of a snowy mountain scene pinned above the surgical table. To this day, I cannot look at an image of a majestic snow-capped peak without my throat constricting.

When Eric and I walked out a few hours later, I was no longer the same girl who had walked in. My own story had veered far from the scripts of my favorite teen movies, starring characters who were simple and wholesome. I longed to have my innocence restored. Eric and I stayed the night in a Holiday Inn. My body was not in pain. Instead, the pain pooled in my heart.

CHAPTER 24

Isabell Whitmore

STROLLING IN THE accessory department at Saks, I'm desperate to find a replacement for my Gucci scarf. After going downstairs and unleashing my fury on Mary, Grace and Lola went back into my room and cut my limited-edition scarf into shreds.

Those girls have gone off the rails. They're grounded for the next month—no socializing, no driving, no shopping, no computers, and no phones. They go to school and then come home. Harris masterminded the punishment. But it's more of a punishment for me. I hate seeing their mopey faces around the house.

My eyes settle on a brown and beige wool scarf with Gucci's signature pattern. It's nice, but I want something with more personality. *Ugh*, that limited-edition scarf was a unicorn.

As I sort through other options, my wrist buzzes.

> **Laura:** Having a hard time with Nora. Meet up for wine later?

My eyes roll as I read the text from Laura. My favorite boutique is having a trunk show. I don't have time for Laura and her drama. I debate calling her to break the news, but I don't want to end up in an hour-long conversation. Laura has a way of droning on and on.

Her insistence on being my "best friend" is juvenile. When we lost touch in New York, I thought that was the end. But then she moved home, and we randomly ran into each other when pregnant. Suddenly, we were spending all our time together. We'd meet at upscale baby stores and buy the most adorable matching onesies. We'd spend hours over coffee, looking through books on pregnancy, parenting, and baby names. We kept our focus on superficial details in the same way Harris and I did.

I text back.

> **Me:** Sorry! I'm busy. Send me other options.

Laura's notoriously bad about getting back to me with dates. I smile, knowing I've gotten out of having to make plans. She texts back.

> **Laura:** Okay. I'll check my calendar. Still waiting on the date for your birthday dinner. Send me the info!

I angrily pound in the details for my birthday dinner and hit send. She's oblivious to the fact that I keep blowing her off. But getting the hint is not her forte. It reminds me of why I had to resurrect the walls between us all those years ago.

OUR BELLIES JUTTED out, barely leaving room for us to sit in the narrow booth of our favorite ice cream shop.

"It's been great spending time together," Laura said as she licked up an enormous chunk of cookies and cream ice cream.

"Yes," I said before changing the topic to the luxury double stroller Harris and I had just purchased. "It cost as much as a small used car!" I said as I tried to catch drips of ice cream with a napkin before they got onto my favorite designer maternity jeans.

Laura quickly wiped the dribbles off my leg before I had a chance.

"Wow, you've already got mom skills. Impressive."

She looked at me intently and let her hand linger on my thigh. "You never told me what happened when we lived in New York. I have my suspicions about your boss. I wanted to help you. I tried to help you, but you shut me out."

I pushed her hand from my leg as if her touch could somehow penetrate the truth.

"Who cares now? It was a different life."

"I care. You're my friend, and whatever happened in New York changed you. It's hard to know what you're really thinking." Drops of her ice cream splattered on the ground below her hand.

"You know, I love those tiny pink Uggs we just bought for the girls," I said, hoping my sarcasm would push her off topic.

"Really, Isabell? You know that is not what I mean." She bolted up, frustrated, tossed her ice cream into the garbage, and left me sitting by myself.

Her lame attempt to connect made me queasy. No thank you.

As we continued to spend time together, she kept pressing me on topics I did not want to discuss. *Did I miss the world of fashion? How did Harris and I meet?* And over and over, *What happened in New York?* Soon, her endless attempts to dig into my emotional core had my head swimming in despair. She was forcing me to confront my inner turmoil. *Was I drugged? Was I raped? Was I a willing participant or a victim?*

I began having nightmares that still plague me. Each nightmare was a variation on the same theme. I'd walk into Lola and Grace's nursery and find a man standing over their cribs. I'd rush forward to protect them as the strange man turned and smiled, revealing himself as Mr. Boucher.

I had to break away from Laura. I had to put distance between us. *But how?* It wasn't until Nora's diagnosis that I found a way to slip away.

"Would you like to try that one on? It would look great with your coloring." The saleswoman at the Saks counter pulls me away from my memories.

"Yes, I would."

"Wonderful, let me take it off the hanger for you."

As I wait for the saleswoman to hand me the scarf, my wrist buzzes with another text from Laura.

> **Laura:** How about Tuesday the 10th, Thursday the 12th, or Saturday the 14th?

Fuck, I think as I take the scarf and wrap it around my shoulders. How am I going to get out of this?

CHAPTER 25

Indira Acharya

I GRAB ZOYA'S HAND, and we run toward the crashing waves. We're at the beach, making an offering on behalf of Nani. My mom brought a coconut, considered the fruit of the gods. She places it in the water and watches as it floats away. Water is where all life begins, and the yearly ritual provides a moment for us to think of Nani. She passed right after the birth of Ahana. If only she had the chance to meet all my daughters.

I watch as Kabir carefully escorts my aging mother through the sand. He's kind and caring. I love the life we've built. But it's a love constructed around a shared background and friendly camaraderie. I agreed to marry Kabir when we were in medical school. It was the next right step. He was my ideal match and treated me with respect. I never considered grasping for something more. I never considered the person I married should make my heart skip inside my chest and my body burn with desire.

As the cold water hits my feet, I breathe in the salty air and smile. Anytime I'm near the ocean, my mind fills with memories of Fatima, Maverick, and me, racing down the highway to the beach in his red Jeep Wrangler. I loved sitting shotgun, as my thick hair tossed around in the breeze, wondering if the feelings bubbling up inside of me meant Maverick had a crush on me too.

Looking out into the distance, I can still see an image of Maverick's athletic body crouched under the canopy of a blue wave and the way Fatima's ebony skin glistened against the pale cream sand. I'd rest my hand in her large, pulsing palm, as we pressed our bodies tightly together on a towel, laughing and wondering when Maverick would kiss me.

After Maverick finished surfing, the three of us would walk along the beach, talking loudly over the noise of crashing waves. Maverick and Fatima saw the truth about me as the sun beat down on our heads. It was like they knew something about me I could not understand about myself. We made a strange trifecta, a boy with hair as white as snow, a girl with skin as black as night, and me a mixture of both those colors combined.

"Is everything okay?" Kabir asks now. "You seem distracted." Water splashes around his legs as he joins me a few feet from shore.

I snap back to the present moment. "Fine, just thinking of Nani." My words are a lie, but what else can I say? *I'm in love with someone else? I'm thinking of ending our marriage.*

"Your mom's more upset than usual. She's tired. We should go soon." He places his hand on my shoulder and squeezes. "I'll get Zoya and meet you back on the beach." My eyes follow Kabir as he playfully scoops Zoya out of the water. She squeals with delight.

Moving my gaze back to the horizon, my mind lands on the summer day buried deep within myself. Fatima and I were meeting at Maverick's house to drive to a small surf shop he liked. I arrived thirty minutes early and knocked on the front door, but there was no response. Since the three of us usually hung out in Maverick's pool garage, I walked around back to the detached structure and approached the door. I noticed the lights were dim but put my hand on the doorknob anyway. It was warm from the thick heat of summer.

I turned the knob and pushed the door open. In front of me lay Fatima and Maverick, half undressed and tangled together on a few pool rafts that were pushed together into a makeshift bed.

"Oh my god!" I blurted. Startled, I bobbed my head upward toward the ceiling and gulped the air around me as if I was going to drown in betrayal.

"Indira, wait! Let us explain." Maverick's voice trailed behind me as I ran to my car.

A moment later, I heard the smacking of flip-flops on concrete. I turned around, expecting to see Maverick, ready to explain that he liked Fatima. He didn't mean for it to happen, he'd say. But when I turned toward the slapping sound, it was Fatima I saw running after me. She had slipped on Maverick's shoes.

"I'm sorry," she said.

Suddenly I was overcome with a longing I had never felt. I was jealous, but not because I had feelings for Maverick. I moved in close to Fatima.

When my lips brushed hers, she pulled me closer. Our kiss vibrated throughout my body. She pulled away as soon as we heard Maverick running toward us.

I stepped back, humiliated and confused. I've never been able to remember the words she said as Maverick grabbed her hand and pulled her away. The only recollection I have is how her black skin reflected the darkness I felt consuming my heart.

As Fatima and Maverick disappeared inside the pool garage, a sharp realization fell in my lap. I was in love with Fatima, not Maverick. This love pushed against everything I believed about who I was and what my life should be.

I quickly buried my feelings and let dusty layers entomb my true desires.

A month later, after school began, I opened my locker and found a scrunched-up note from Maverick. My name was written in his sprawling handwriting. Each letter stretched and curvy as if they were the waves he hoped to surf on later. I took the note and quickly peered to my left and right, hoping Maverick and Fatima were not spying on me. I did my best to keep my distance from them.

> *Indira,*
> *Fatima moved to Florida. Her aunt's family immigrated to*
> *Miami. I miss her…and you too.*

"Mom! Mom!" My body jolts toward the shore at the sound of Zoya's high-pitched screams.

Rushing out of the water, I kneel in the sand next to my mom. She's sitting up but disorientated.

"She fainted." Kabir removes his hand from her wrist. "Her pulse is fine. I think she's just tired and upset."

"Let's get you home," I say as I stroke my mom's back.

Her eyes focus on Kabir and flicker back to life. "Kabir," she sputters. "Such a good man."

HAMILTON BEACH MOMS
PRIVATE GROUP — 5,352 Members

Laura Perry
Today at 1:21 p.m.

Just a quick note about posts pertaining to medical questions.

1. This page is not to be used in place of professional medical care.

2. If you or a family member have a health issue, please consult your doctor.

3. If you're looking for recommendations, be aware that recommendations made on this page are only the opinions of other Hamilton Beach moms and not a professional referral.

4. Do not, under any circumstances, take screenshots and/or share anyone's medical posts.

5. The page administrators are not responsible for any misinformation communicated on this page.

Also, there are only five spots left for our in-person fundraiser to help our community food bank. 😀😀😀. Follow this link to register https://www.facebook.com/HBCMomsgiveback

Comments

Candice Armstrong: Please stop posting photos of your children's gross rashes, cuts, and pus-filled ears. I almost threw up my lunch as I innocently scrolled through the feed yesterday.

Faye Carter: Just a shout out to Dr. Susanne Kish. She's a pediatric ENT. She contacted me yesterday after I made a frantic post about my three-year-old shoving a corn kernel up his nose. She fit us in her busy schedule and removed the kernel. I will never allow popcorn to be eaten in my home again! 🍿🍿

Isabell Whitmore: Keep in mind, none of us need to hear updates on your second cousin's great-aunt's knee surgery.

Holly Ramirez: Whoever posted the video footage of their child coming out of anesthesia after wisdom tooth removal should be ashamed of themselves! Your child will forever be the kid who woke up mooing like a cow.

Amira Najjar: Someone recommended Dr. R. Smith for Botox and now it looks like my face is frozen. I'm livid. Research your own medical providers. You have been warned!

CHAPTER 26
Laura Perry

THE GRAY CLOUDS gathering in the distance reflect my mood as I walk along the gravel path at Hamilton Beach Gardens. This is where I came during the first year of Nora's life when struggling with her diagnosis. And here I find myself again, struggling with Nora's desire to embrace the deaf community.

It's astonishing, but I don't remember thinking our decision to get implants for Nora would deny her of her deafness. Troy and I felt certain that giving Nora the ability to hear was the only choice. It felt wholly like the right decision.

As I walk under a steel arbor covered with jade vines, my head replays the conversation Troy and I had with Nora last week after the incident at school. She refused to tell us anything. If it weren't for finding her chat, I wouldn't have a clue about what happened. Troy and I agreed to wait and discuss everything at the therapy appointment we have scheduled later this week.

What I need right now is a friend. I reached out to Isabell, since she knows the history, but she blew me off. Was I surprised? No. I'm not sure why I bothered. She refuses to engage with her own emotions, so there was zero chance of her supporting me. Gabby is another option, but I never want her to feel like I'm taking advantage of her therapy background.

Looking ahead, I see the rose gardens are just around the path. I'm instantly dazzled by the deep reds, soft pinks, and bright yellows. But a moment later, my heart sinks. Yellow roses are the quintessential friendship flower. Where are my friends now? Why isn't there anyone I can lean on? I have fifteen hundred friends on Facebook. Surely, there's someone.

Finding a bench, I take a seat and scroll through my friends list considering the pros and cons of reaching out to the perfectly curated photos that stare back at me. Each person is wrong for a different reason. Kathy Leiter and I only discuss happy news. Ayesha Brooks has been avoiding me ever since I had to ask her to stop trying to sell her essential oils daily on the Hamilton Beach Moms' Facebook page. Erin Woods is kind, but always turns the conversation around to her own life.

As I continue to scroll, I see the faces of all the women I distanced myself from after Nora's diagnosis. Maybe it's not surprising I have no one to reach out to after all.

Although I tried to travel alongside my mom friends as we marched down the new baby path, I had to separate myself. My chest pounded each time I'd meet for playdates and listen as they bemoaned diaper explosions and sleepless nights. Theirs was a flat, paved road with occasional potholes. They could not grasp the fears that kept me up at night.

And, as soon as Nora was fitted with hearing aids, I discovered a deep dark truth about new mothers. Nothing terrified them more than seeing a baby who existed outside the realm of typical. The first time I realized this, I was at the grocery store. I had just parked my shopping cart next to a bin of apples. Nora was sleeping soundly in her baby carrier, docked safely in the cart. As I sorted through the fruit, tossing aside any that were bruised or discolored, I heard a voice.

"I think you dropped this."

I turned. A petite woman in workout wear held out a small fuzzy lavender blanket monogrammed with a huge white "N."

"Oh, thanks," I replied as I took the blanket. "It's hard to keep track of everything."

"Totally understand." She stepped to the side, revealing a baby carrier like mine.

"How old is your baby?" she asked.

"Ten weeks," I said. "What about yours?"

"Charlie's twelve weeks, so just a little older." She gazed lovingly at the big bald baby squirming around in his carrier before she looked back at me. "What's your baby's name?"

"Nora," I said, holding the blanket and pointing to the mono-grammed "N," as if it were evidence in a legal case.

"Oh, what a lovely name." She moved forward toward my cart and peered at Nora asleep in her carrier. Her eyes bulged when she saw Nora's hearing aids.

In the next moment, I noticed her transform from chatty and unguarded to panicked. Her lips collapsed from a wide, natural smile into a thin line. She spun away from Nora and shifted her gaze downward. Her eyes darted around, finally landing back on the lavender blanket.

"She's a beautiful baby," she said, but her voice sounded hollow. "Well, nice meeting you. I've got to get Charlie home for his nap."

By the time Nora was five months old, I had completely withdrawn from my circle of friends. They infuriated me. I felt alone—the end-less therapy sessions, learning how to manage Nora's hearing aids, the ongoing evaluations, the upcoming surgery. I wanted to pull my mom friends off their smooth paved road and make them take just one step onto my path coated in thick sludge.

And then, when Nora was six months old, I finally broke and unleashed all my fury on Isabell. I was recounting a story to her about how overwhelmed I was with Nora's diagnosis.

"As I got Nora's bottle from my diaper bag, her hearing therapist, Jackie, hurried over and looked at me like I was crazy. I was soaking wet. I didn't even realize it until Jackie told me. It must have been pouring outside. How could I not realize it was raining? I'm so com-pletely overwhelmed, I'm so lost in thought, I didn't even realize Nora and I were dripping wet."

Isabell's nose wrinkled as she considered my words. "Were you wearing those adorable Tory Burch rain boots I told you about? Those things would have at least kept your feet dry." She winked playfully.

As usual, she avoided any real engagement about Nora's diagnosis. "So, did you read that article I sent you comparing homemade baby food to store-bought organic? I'm struggling with what direction to go." She paused, waiting for me to weigh in.

I felt a pulsating wave of anger jolt through my body. A scream was forming in my mouth. "Homemade or organic?! Tory Burch rain boots?!" The volume of my voice increased with each syllable. "Why can't you talk about Nora's deafness? Why do you constantly change the subject? Lola and Grace are fine. Your twins can hear. Deafness is not contagious!"

I shot up off her expensive couch, scooped up Nora, grabbed my diaper bag, and stomped out the door.

I look up from the bench where I'm seated. My head swirls with all the decisions Troy and I have made after Nora's diagnosis. *Is she grieving who she might have been if we made different choices?* Still, I don't regret our decision to have Nora implanted. But maybe I should have helped her appreciate her deafness rather than bury it.

Suddenly I feel the stab of rain on my skin. *Is it raining?* The bright and lush roses scattered around me are wilting in the downpour. I brush water from my hair and realize my clothes are soaked. I quickly recognize I'm back to where I started. I'm completely overwhelmed. I'm so lost in thought I didn't even realize it started to rain.

HAMILTON BEACH MOMS
PRIVATE GROUP — 5,344 Members

Gabriella Martinez
Today at 8:24 a.m.

Hi ladies. This is a gentle reminder about how to post for-sale items. Lately, we've noticed people posting on random days. We don't want this page to be one of those online "garage sale" pages. Please post for-sale items on Fridays only. I have listed the rules again below, just in case anyone needs a refresher. Thank you for your understanding and cooperation. 😊

1. Only post items for sale on "For Sale Fridays."

2. Posts should categorize the item, e.g., furniture, clothing, toys, housing, vehicles.

3. Posts should clearly state the condition of the item using these abbreviations: NWT (new with tags), NWOT (new without tags), EUC (excellent used condition), VGUC (very good used condition) GUC (good used condition), or U (used).

4. You must sell the item to the first person to comment "sold," unless that person backs out. (We have had lots of complaints about people selling to their friends after another group member had already commented "sold").

5. The page administrators are not responsible for any misrepresentation of items bought or sold.

Also, don't forget to register for our in-person fundraiser to help our community food bank. It looks like this event will sell out! Follow this link to the event page https://www.facebook.com/HBCMomsgiveback and register right now! 😊

108 👍

Comments

Stacey Hernandez: Just some food for thought, but no one wants to buy your son's old socks, your used vegan clothing, or your dilapidated basement couch.

Lauren Davenport: Also, be honest and post photos of any irregularities. Meaning, if it has holes or stains, be upfront. I bought a used Gucci bag as a starter purse for my sixteen-year-old daughter, and the inside lining had several nasty stains. The seller would not take it back. 😒

Mallory Wilson: I'm not sure people are completely clear about what Never Been Worn means.

Talya Rozio: My friend made five figures last year selling items on this page!

Wanda Harrison: I have a bunch of lacrosse gear for sale. It's appropriate for someone age twelve. My son is not as athletic as I hoped 😣 😩 PM if interested.

Gabriella Martinez: @Wanda Harrison This is not the place to post for-sale items. Please see above and post your son's lacrosse gear this Friday.

CHAPTER 27

Gabriella Martinez

MY BODY PUMPS with adrenaline as I set up our backyard for Lucas's birthday party. How is my baby ten years old? I'm trying my best to look past the *Harry Potter* theme he chose, but it's difficult. Lucas has had a *Star Wars*-themed birthday party since his birth.

It's not that I don't like *Harry Potter*. I do. I've spent hours reading each of the seven books out loud to Lucas before bed. It's just that I'm upset he's abandoning our family's holy grail of *Star Wars*. While I know he's only trying to assert his independence, this awareness doesn't diminish the slight pang in my chest as I lay out Gryffindor paper plates and cups atop a Hogwarts tablecloth.

"*Hola,* I'm here to help." Carlita bursts through our back gate just as I'm hanging the Voldemort piñata from our wood pergola.

It's only been a week since I discovered my mom's dating blog. I need to talk to her about it. I've been avoiding her.

"It's my *muchachito's* birthday!" she says, dropping another one of her designer bags onto the table. "I guess you've been busy planning the fiesta. I haven't seen you since last Friday."

"There's a reason you haven't seen me." I run my hand through my hair, pushing my fingers through the resistance of my curls. It's a tell-tale sign I'm nervous. "Listen, Mom, I read your dating blog. I'm terrified about how careless you're being. And, quite frankly, I'm shocked by the way you flaunt your escapades for anyone to read."

Carlita smirks. "Oh, Gabby! Don't be such a prude!" Her tone is mocking, as if each word she speaks is a small child sticking their tongue out at me.

"What if something happens to you?! What if you go on a date with some crazy man and he hurts you or murders you?"

"Oh, *por favor*, my dear Gabby! I know how to be safe. And don't worry, I've told Harriett where I keep all my vibrators so she can get rid of them before you have to clean out your dead mother's condo!"

"Ugh!" I scream in frustration. It's clear Carlita has zero ability to take my concerns seriously.

"And by the way," she continues, "people enjoy reading about my escapades. A woman named Maggie O'Donnell, from the *Hamilton Herald*, called. She wants to do an article on my blog and the senior dating scene."

"Sounds right," I say, annoyed Carlita's receiving encouragement to continue chronicling her crazy dating life.

"So, *Harry Potter* this year," Carlita says, changing the subject.

"Yup." I continue laying out bags of carrots and organic juice boxes. I'd rather drop our discussion than get into a fight right before Lucas's birthday party.

"I love that Lucas isn't afraid to tell you what he likes. He's had enough of *Star Wars*. He's a *Harry Potter* fan now."

"I don't want to talk about it."

A moment later, Lucas appears.

"*Abuela!*" he yelps as he throws his arms around Carlita, hugging her tightly. When he pulls away, he notices the neat row of carrot sticks I have put out as a snack for his friends.

"Carrots?" he says with a look of disappointment. "I told you I wanted Doritos and Oreos."

"But, Lucas," I say, feeling a twinge of regret about my commitment to healthy eating, "we will have candy from the piñata, and everyone will have cake before they leave."

"Mom!" he screeches. "You always embarrass me. Why can't we give everyone Doritos? My friends are going to make fun of me!" He storms back inside the house, slamming the door behind him.

My eyes prick with tears. *Lucas is embarrassed by me.* The same way Carlita embarrasses me.

"*¡Está muy enojado!*" Carlita says with a twinkle in her eyes, pointing out my son's anger like I might not have noticed. She steps close and whispers, as if she's about to tell me the secret to life. "You know I wasn't going to say anything, but Lucas told me something you may want to know. It may be why he's done with *Star Wars*."

I look at Carlita's face. She's amused, as if she's in on a comedian's punch line the rest of the audience has missed.

"Oh really, what's that?"

"Lucas told me he saw you and Ricardo dressed up for *Star Wars*, doing gymnastics in your bedroom. Can you blame that *muchachito!*" She chortles in laughter. "He caught his parents in the act, as Rey and some evil character, I can't remember the name he said. Sithiodious, or something?" Carlita bends over, grasping her side, laughing hysterically.

My mind skips back to a few weekends ago when Ricardo and I were role playing. *Did Lucas catch us?*

I stand there feeling equal parts humiliation and anger. But, before I can even respond, Lucas comes bursting through our patio door crying. He runs toward the carrots and juice boxes and smacks his body into the table. Everything flies up into the air and drops to the ground in a crash. He looks at me with tear-stained cheeks.

"Lucas! What's gotten into you?" But before he can answer, guilt pulses through my body. "I didn't mean to upset you. I should have bought Doritos and Oreos. I'll go to the store so you can have the food you want at your party. I wasn't trying to embarrass you."

After a brief hesitation, Lucas steps toward me and puts his hand in mine. My words have loosened his tightly wound emotions. I pull him in tight for a hug.

Driving to Ackerman's, my head replays the confrontation with Carlita and Lucas's outburst. There's a common thread weaving itself between the way I feel about my mom and the way Lucas feels about me. *I'm not intentionally doing things to upset Lucas, and Carlita is not intentionally doing things to upset me.*

The realization takes my breath away.

CHAPTER 28
Julie Wu

I HEAR THE *SWISH* of a door opening. "Mr. and Mrs. Wu, I'm Dr. Gabriella Martinez. Why don't you follow me, and we can get started?"

Eric glances at me from across the room. We sat as far away from each other as we could when we entered Dr. Martinez's office.

Now, as we follow her down the hallway, I wonder if therapy can solve the impasse in our marriage. We made a choice together, all those years ago. The fact that Eric votes for a party that wants to take that choice away makes me feel like he's a fraud.

"So, after the abortion, and high school graduation, did you stay together?" Dr. Martinez adds a few notes to the paper on her lap. She's spent the last thirty minutes listening to Eric and me recount our history.

"Yes," Eric says. "I left for Harvard, and Julie left for Yale. We broke up only once during the spring semester of junior year."

"Tell me why?" Dr. Martinez presses for more information.

"I'll let Julie answer that," Eric says. I notice the tone of his voice sounds shaky. The same way it sounded after I broke up with him all those years ago.

"I got involved with the Jewish Student Alliance. It was the first time I was surrounded by people who shared my background. It made me want to separate myself from everything familiar. Including my relationship with Eric."

As I watch Dr. Martinez write, I remember the intense emotions I experienced during that time. It felt like a tornado ripped through and threw me onto a path I could no longer ignore. I was obsessed with claiming my Jewish identity. But I found the Jewish friends I made were confused by my southern roots. I didn't think and act the same way they did. Soon, I experienced that familiar feeling of needing to fade into the background.

"So, what led you back to Eric?"

"Most of my friends were from strong Jewish communities in the Northeast. They'd never experienced antisemitism. They weren't marginalized their entire life. Eric understands this part of my experience. Eric understands why I try to blend in."

"That's important." Dr. Martinez nods her head once for emphasis. "Can you speak more about that?"

I shift in my chair, confused by her question. "More about Eric understanding me?"

"I'm trying to understand if you're saying you've stayed in the background, hiding for most of your life?"

"Well, yes, in a way," I say. "Not professionally, but personally. Especially because I was raised in a small southern town. People needed Eric and me to disappear. They didn't want to understand what made us different. They didn't want to connect with us." I slump in my chair, overwhelmed by my heavy emotions.

"It must be hard, having to fade away or dampen aspects of yourself to make relationships work."

"Yes, it is hard." My voice wavers. "I've spent a lot of my life accommodating this need of other people so I can feel accepted."

Dr. Martinez leans forward in her chair. "But are you truly accepted if you're ignoring part of yourself?"

"No," I sputter through tears, as Eric reaches over and hands me a tissue. "I guess that's what always leaves me feeling hollow in friendships. I'm not one hundred percent my authentic self."

"And, with Eric, are you saying you can be? That you feel completely accepted and known by him?"

"Yes, I guess I am," I say softly.

"Well, that's a huge realization, Julie. It's not uncommon for patients to tell me they don't feel accepted or truly known by others. It's a feeling many people struggle with. What's uncommon is that you've found a partner who understands how your past has shaped you and truly connects with you."

Eric reaches his hand toward me as my eyes spill with tears from a lifetime of feeling marginalized by others. Dr. Martinez has shifted my perspective about my marriage ever so slightly. He's the person who understands what it was like for me growing up. Suddenly, my feelings for Eric feel like a crazy ball of knotted-up string. How can I be so angry at him but still love him so much?

"Is there anything you want to say, Julie?" Dr. Martinez waits for me to respond.

I shake my head, unable to put a cohesive thought together.

"Okay, before we move on, I want to make sure Eric doesn't have anything he wants to add."

Eric squeezes my hand. "Just that I love you, Julie. And I want us to work this out."

"Thanks, Eric." Dr. Martinez leans back in her chair. "So, let's quickly finish up, and then it will be time to go."

"That sounds good," I say, feeling exhausted and ready to leave.

"So, what happened after you got back together?"

Eric answers. "After graduating from college, we both attended Harvard Law School, then both accepted positions at law firms in DC. We got married right after graduation."

"And tell me more about the work you do, Eric. Julie mentioned earlier your political beliefs have a lot to do with your job."

"Sure. I specialize in counseling lobbyists on issues related to finance. My work centers on supporting policies that ensure less government regulation and lower taxes." Eric speaks confidently.

"Exactly," I say, exasperated, suddenly caught in that web of tangled emotions. "His entire career is based on the foundational principles of the conservative movement."

Dr. Martinez stills. "Give me a moment here. I'm thinking back to how you described Eric the first time you met him in high school."

We sit in silence for a minute before Dr. Martinez continues. "I guess, in a sense, Eric is exactly who you thought he was when he introduced himself to your class in high school, Alex P. Keaton, in the flesh."

She's right, I think. He's the same person he's always been. My head pounds, as distress overwhelms me. *How can I expect Eric to change who he's been all along?*

CHAPTER 29

Indira Acharya

"THE JOB FAIR went well!" Fatima says as she unlocks the door to her townhouse.

"I agree. The mom from Syria is sharp as a knife. Someone will hire her quickly." I follow Fatima inside. A buzzy hum courses through my body. This is my first time at Fatima's house, and I feel electrified.

"This painting is gorgeous," I say as my eyes stare at the colorful image of men dressed in long robes wearing brimless hats. Each one holds an ornate, brightly colored cloth umbrella over their head.

Fatima stands close to me. Her arm brushes mine. The elation my body feels from her touch is overwhelming.

"This is one of my favorites. It depicts a scene from the Timkat Festival." Fatima runs her almond-shaped eyes over the image slowly, taking in each brush stroke. She then looks at me with a bit of sadness. "I've lost touch with these traditions. I have such fond memories from Ethiopia." Her voice catches for a moment. "Sometimes I wonder who I would be if we had stayed."

Placing my hand on her shoulder, I lead her to the couch, and we both sit. "Your sadness reminds me of my parents. They certainly struggled after leaving India. But they passed down traditions that have shaped my life." My voice sounds steadfast, but my feelings waver as I consider if these traditions have shaped me into the wrong version of myself.

"You're lucky you found Kabir and have a partner who shares your background. I would love to be in a relationship with someone who understands my customs." She pauses for a moment before continuing. "But I've found that my romantic partners have had little interest in embracing my traditions."

As she looks back toward the Timkat painting, my mind fights against itself. Yes, there are advantages to having a like-minded partner, but there needs to be more to make a relationship thrive.

"How about some wine?" Fatima rises.

"Sounds great." My eyes trace the sway of Fatima's hips as she walks to her kitchen.

"I picked up that Sauvignon Blanc we've been drinking around town," Fatima calls from the kitchen. "I like to think of it as our signature cocktail." She laughs as she walks toward me, holding the wine and two glasses.

Bringing the glass to my lips, I hope the sweet tropical taste from New Zealand can calm my swirling nerves. Suddenly, I'm aware we're very alone, and I'm not expected home for hours. The truth kicks at my throat again. I desperately need to know if Fatima feels what I'm feeling. Words thrust at my lips. I open my mouth to speak, but Fatima fills the space.

"Can you believe we ran into Maverick Parker? It's brought up so many good memories." Fatima smiles with her large and sultry mouth.

"What are the chances?" I say, agreeing, as my nerves urge me to finish my wine.

"Well, pretty good, considering Seaside Coffee is across the street from the beach." Fatima pours more wine as she chuckles.

I force myself to laugh, although the truth is still pushing at me. "We should go to Santa Barbara, rent wet suits, and have him teach us how to surf," I say instead.

"Ha," Fatima echoes back. "I can picture it now. Two middle-aged women, falling over, flanked by Maverick, who, of course, is still gorgeous." She rises from the couch, a bit unsteady from the wine bottle we've drained. She wobbles around, pretending she's surfing on a wave.

A genuine giggle escapes my lips, heavy with bubbly buzzed breath. I smile and then quiet as an honest question comes to mind. "How come we never tried surfing back then? Why did we always lay on the beach?"

Fatima's facial features tighten. "To be honest, Indira, I wanted you all to myself. I didn't want to share you with Maverick. I think you were my first real crush."

My breath slows as a montage of images from our past flit through my mind's eye. Maverick is there but tucked neatly in the background, where, in truth, he had been the entire time. Fatima, solving the theorems. Fatima, holding my hand as we lay on the beach. Fatima, seeing the truth of me.

And the day my heart broke when I discovered Maverick and Fatima in the pool garage, not because I was in love with Maverick, but because I was in love with Fatima.

My heart skips a few times like a stone thrown by a boy at the edge of a lake, and before I can consider what the world would think, I lean in and kiss Fatima. Moments later our clothes are on the floor as I disappear into her blackness.

CHAPTER 30

Maggie O'Donnell

P *ING. THE COMMENTS* keep coming on my anonymous mom
post. They've mostly died out on the soccer story. I'm relieved.
I hate knowing there are dozens of women who would jump
at the chance to be with Doug.

> **Imani White:** Please, anonymous mom, don't do anything rash. You
> need to have an open conversation. Hear him out, and then take it
> one step at a time.

> **Kim Adams:** Don't leap to conclusions. Some people like to dress
> in the opposite sex's clothes or just experiment with things that
> are taboo. Is he a good husband and father? Do you have a good
> relationship? Yes, it's concerning. I can understand, but let him tell
> his side.

The comments I've received lately are just like these. Most moms
think I should just ask Doug and let him tell his side.

Finally, I'm ready to do that.

Glancing at my watch, I see it's close to seven. Doug will be home
any minute. We're supposed to go to the yacht rock concert. My kids
are staying at my mom's house. Tonight, is the perfect time to ask Doug
about my underwear. I have a feeling we won't make it to the show.

As I pace back and forth in our living room, I try to work out how to bring up the underwear without letting Doug glimpse the terror swirling in my mind. I catch sight of a wedding photo proudly displayed on one of the tall shelving units that reach up to the cathedral-shaped ceiling in the room. *Is my marriage going to end?*

I peer intently at the black and white candid. Doug and I are looking at each other, a trace of laughter on our lips. Doug's best man had just made a joke about how Doug won their fraternity's annual fundraiser for Southern California Children's Hospital. The event, called Queen of the Night, featured a representative from each fraternity dressed in drag. The story seemed so insignificant at the time. But now, the image of Doug as a senior, decked out in a baby blue, tight-fitting dress, blond wig, and pink high heels seems like a critical clue in a mystery I don't want to solve.

Averting my eyes from the photo, I try to pull my mind out of the downward spiral. And then I see Grandma Mable's Ansel Adams water photo. It's only inches from the candid wedding photo. It's as if Mable is here, reminding me to be like water, to flow around, surround, settle into it.

I must stay centered on the facts. Let Doug tell his side. I must suspend judgment. Doug likes to wear women's underwear. This does not mean he's perverse. This does not mean he's gay. This does not mean he's having an affair. This does not mean he's not the man I know him to be. Doug likes to wear women's underwear, I repeat. End of known facts.

I take a deep breath as I hear the garage door open.

"Hey, Maggie, I'm home."

Walking from our living room, I meet Doug in the kitchen.

Doug pecks me on the cheek. "Hey, honey, ready for our date night? You're dressed kind of casual for a concert. Where's your captain's hat?"

Looking at him for a long moment, my heart breaks. This is the last time he can look back, knowing his secret is safe.

"Let's sit on the couch. We need to talk."

"Uh oh," he says in a playful voice. "Nothing good ever happens after the phrase 'we need to talk.'"

Sitting on our plush gray sofa. I take a seat in the corner, leaning against the thick, sturdy arm. I need all the support I can get.

"A few weeks ago, when I was getting clothes together for the dry cleaner, I found a pair of my underwear in your pants."

I purposely do not say they were stretched out, and I purposely do not accuse him of wearing them. My statement is a testament to neutrality, just like water. No color, no smell, no taste. No judgment.

Doug's body immediately slouches forward. He presses his large palms over his face and sits perfectly still.

I move toward him, putting my arm around his shoulders. My innate love for him overpowers my fear about his response.

"It's okay," I say. "Whatever you have to tell me, it's okay."

Moving his hands away from his face, he drops them into his lap with a thud. He looks toward me, but not into my eyes. "I always thought I'd lie. I've played it out in my head a hundred times. You discover my sickness, and I tell you you're wrong. It's a misunderstanding. It's a mistake." He pauses and gulps in air, as if he's having trouble breathing. "I'm so sorry, Maggie. I'm so ashamed." Tears stream down his face.

Water, I think to myself. Water… "We need to talk about this," I say, being careful to embrace the obstacle rather than push it away with ultimatums.

"I know we need to talk about this, but I'm not prepared to do it right now. Can I have a few hours to get my thoughts together?"

"Yes, of course." My words come out before I consider if I can handle a few more hours not understanding what lies ahead. "I'll just go out for a bit. I'll be home in two hours. Will that work?"

"Yes, thank you. You are unbelievable for being so understanding. I know you must be confused. I love you so much."

He leans in and hugs me close. We both break into sobs.

Catching my breath, I pick up my purse and enter our garage. My car rumbles to life, as I wonder, where does a wife go when her husband's trying to work out how to discuss his need to wear women's underwear? The moment is surreal, and the thought causes my heart to constrict.

Pulling my car into the playground near our home, I recall when Doug and I used to bring our children here. My car headlights illuminate the brightly colored slides and swings, shining a spotlight on our past. Sophia, in a bright yellow floral dress, grasping Evan's hand as he toddled around to keep up with her. Two parents, both exhausted, but exhilarated by the family they created. *How could that mom know what was coming? How could that mom's husband keep a secret like this for so long?*

Two hours later, I inhale deeply, steeling myself for what's ahead. It feels as if everything is going in slow motion as I walk inside.

Doug's seated at our kitchen table. He's changed out of his work clothes and is wearing a UCLA t-shirt and athletic shorts. My body feels heavy as I take a seat at our large round kitchen table. There are no corners. No sides to be on.

"I want to be honest with you, Maggie," he says as I settle in my chair.

"Yes, I want you to be honest too," I say.

"You're right. I do wear women's underwear. It's been a thing for me since I was fourteen. I started doing it a few months after my dad passed away." His voice is sluggish.

"Oh." Blood starts speeding through my body in a quick rush. "So, it's something you've been doing most of your life?"

"Yes, it's hard to explain."

I nod, unsure of what to say. "So, in college, when we met, when I hated you for being such a chauvinistic pig, you were wearing women's underwear then?"

"Yes, I was such an asshole freshman and sophomore year. I was compensating for the fear I felt about wearing the underwear." He shrugs, as if helpless, and looks at me.

My mind fills with an image of Doug, dressed in his sleeveless tank tops and ratty gym clothes, with women's underwear underneath all the bravado.

"I actually see a therapist because I wish I could make it stop."

"Oh," I say, surprised. At that moment, I wonder again, in a marriage, *what's private and what's secret?* "Are you still in therapy?" I ask.

"I've been seeing the therapist for a year. To be honest, it's really hard work. I find I'm often exhausted and have little energy left for anything else after my sessions." Doug looks off into the distance.

A year, I think. That's how long I've felt things have been off. I wonder if the work he's doing in therapy is the reason he feels far away. It makes sense. He's concealed his turmoil. Maybe that's the secret I've felt between us all this time. *Or maybe it's something more?*

I swallow hard, trying to ignore the unease coursing through me. "Do you think therapy's helping?"

"It's given me insight, but the behavior has continued." He lowers his head as if he is ashamed.

My mind spins like I've just gotten off the Mad Hatter's tea party ride. I finally have the truth, but is it the whole truth? Are there more details he needs to confess?

"After my dad died," he continues, "I grew extremely attached to my mom. If she was out of my sight, I'd panic. It was debilitating. I experienced panic attacks."

I can tell the memory of his father's death is invading his mind by the way his eyes cloud. "You never told me that. That sounds frightening."

"Yes, my mom pulled me out of school two months before eighth grade ended. My grades were good, and my teachers agreed to let me finish out the year at home." His eyes slowly move away from mine as he gets closer to the heart of things. "I started hoarding everyday items that belonged to my mom. I kept an old shoebox behind a stack of books in my closet with various items. A bracelet she left on the counter, a small scarf from the hallway coat rack, a grocery list with her handwriting. The box was my salvation when she disappeared into the world."

I sense the hurt slicing through him with each word he utters. But it doesn't lessen the betrayal I feel.

"One day, as I was sitting on the couch watching TV, my mom stood beside me, folding laundry. It was the end of the summer, and my anxiety about returning to school was growing exponentially. I watched as she folded our clothing and stacked each like item in small piles on the couch. As she was finishing up, the phone rang, and she rushed to find our cordless. My hand grabbed the first item of hers I could reach—a pair of white cotton underwear. My brain was not involved in the action. The act of snatching the underwear was instinctive, primal even." His voice suddenly breaks, and a small gasp escapes from his lips.

I start to speak, but he puts his hand up, motioning for me to stay quiet.

"Let me just get through this next part," he says, spitting the words out like bullets. He's suddenly agitated and in a frenzy to finish.

"That's when it started. I wore my mother's underwear to soothe my fears about losing her. Each day before school, I'd sneak into her room while she showered and take a pair of underwear. Wearing her underwear was the only way I could get through the day without her." A look of shame engulfs his face. "After several months, my mom caught on. She asked me if I'd put her laundry away in my room by mistake. I couldn't risk being discovered, but I was incapable of giving up my compulsion. This is when I started buying women's underwear—nothing fancy at first. Just plain cotton underwear like my mom wore. Eventually, though, I indulged in all varieties of women's underwear." He glances at the table. His eyes fix on the swirling pattern of the wood.

"I can imagine that was hard to tell me," I say, trying to be empathetic, but my mind suddenly races furiously with the details of his admission. "I need to know if there's anything else going on. If you have anything else to admit to, please do it right now." My stomach churns as I speak.

"What do you mean?" Doug stands up from the table and takes a defensive posture.

"Can you even imagine what it's been like for me these past weeks?" I ask. "I've been terrified that the underwear is the tip of the iceberg." I grab onto the edge of the table, squeezing tightly.

"I'm not sure what you mean, Maggie. I just told you everything."

"I'm sorry, Doug. I need to know. Are you having an affair? Are you attracted to men? I need to hear your answers before I can digest what you've told me." Suddenly my fears are running down a steep hill, unable to stop.

Doug's expression crumbles. "My god, Maggie. No. I wear women's underwear when I'm stressed or anxious. To be honest, it happens several times a month. My therapist explained it's more an obsessive-compulsive disorder than a fetish. I've never cheated on you, and I am not gay." He sits back down and looks me in the eye. "And can you imagine how hard this is for me? If anyone found out, if my need to wear women's underwear was exposed, my entire career would be ruined."

The anonymous post I made on Facebook flashes through my mind. *What have I done?* I've put our entire family at risk. I turn my face away from Doug as regret tears through me.

"I understand why you're upset, Maggie. I've kept it a secret because I was scared you'd leave if you knew. But there's nothing else to it. This is the iceberg." Doug pushes his words out through deep howls. "Say something. Please just say something, anything. I need to know if our marriage is over."

Water, I think to myself. Sitting still for a few seconds, I try and let myself flow and settle into Doug's confession. But, instead of settling in, it's as if I'm being submerged under a forceful wave. I've made this situation a million times worse by posting on the Facebook page. I push my chin upward and gulp at the air.

"Please, Maggie. I need to know. Can we work through this, or is it over?" His face goes pale.

My head bobs. Sucking deeply, I pull as much air into my lungs as possible, but it's no use. I feel like I'm drowning.

CHAPTER 31
Laura Perry

THE MOM EVENT is in two weeks. My to-do list overflows. As I jot down another chore, Nora walks into the kitchen in fluffy flannel pajamas. Today is her hearing birthday. Many children who receive implants celebrate both the day of their birth and the day they were welcomed into the world of sound.

We usually commemorate the occasion by presenting Nora with a fun gift and watching video footage of her activation. Last year, we bought her AirPods. We always purchase something related to hearing. I remember when she had her thirteenth hearing birthday, and we gave her a karaoke machine.

"I'm going to sing for you," she'd squealed with delight.

Troy and I sat on our couch as Nora sang at the top of her lungs. *Frozen* was a favorite for months. "Let it go!" she'd belt out, as if Anna and Elsa were in the room. And while most parents would force their child into a basement, to avoid tuneless droning, Troy and I always sat rapt, with a profound sense of gratefulness.

The memory's a good one, but it's painful to look back right now. Pushing the tune for Disney's hit song out of my head, I glance back at my list. There are a million things to do, like pick up tablecloths and decorations at Party Time and stop by Harmony Spa to get the mani-pedi gift cards.

"I know, I slept so late." Nora glances at the clock, noting it's noon, and looks at me sheepishly. Pulling out a chair, she unexpectedly sits. *Is she making a gesture toward reconciliation?*

Our first therapy session went okay, but I don't want to push her. I'm afraid to engage, but motherhood is an endless series of having to do things, even if they scare you.

"I'm headed out in a bit to do errands. Dad's at the gym. How are you doing today?"

As Nora turns her head toward mine, her hair pulls away from her face. I notice she's wearing her implants.

"I'm meeting up with Heidi. We're going to see that superhero movie. The new theater on Lomak has individual monitors on the back of seats that show captions." Nora's lips spread out wide, and I revel in the first genuine smile I've seen from her since this began.

"Wonderful," I say. "Tell me more about Heidi. Seems like you're getting to be good friends."

"She's a senior at California School for the Deaf. She's going to Gallaudet University in the fall."

"Interesting." I look at her expectantly, trying to keep the conversation going.

"She actually has a cochlear implant but doesn't use her sound processor. It didn't work for her."

My body stiffens, but then I take a deep breath and continue. "Yes, I remember the professionals telling us they don't work for everyone. It depends what age you are when you get it and many other things." Feeling nervous, I shift the conversation to a different topic. "Do you need any money?"

Nora looks at me with a cute, sneaky expression, like when she was a kid wanting candy. "I've got plenty from babysitting, but if you want to give me a few dollars, I won't say no."

I'm no match for the memory. Standing up, I rifle through my purse and take out my wallet. "Here's a twenty."

"Thanks, Mom." Nora places her hand on my shoulder and squeezes lovingly.

"Sure," I say as she stands and walks toward the stairs.

"Oh, and Nora. Happy Hearing Birthday."

She pauses.

Crap. I hope I didn't say the wrong thing. This past moment was our first peaceful interaction in weeks.

"Thanks. I want to understand my deafness. I hope you get that." Her expression is open, and her voice is relaxed.

I nod my head, feeling good about the interaction.

She walks up a step but then pauses again. "I was thinking, maybe we could go out for dinner tomorrow night. Just the two of us."

Ugh. I have Isabell's birthday dinner. But I instantly realize the time with Nora is much more important than celebrating Isabell. "I would love to go dinner," I say, as a hopeful burst of energy surges through my body.

Nora smiles. "I'm going to take a shower." She takes another step. "And thanks for wishing me a Happy Hearing Birthday." She quickly disappears out of view.

As soon as she leaves to meet Heidi, I rummage through the files on my computer. I recently had Nora's activation video cassette converted to an iMovie. I scroll my mouse over the file and hit play.

I sit mesmerized as I watch Dr. Flack lay out the equipment and prepare for Nora's activation. Nora's only thirteen months old. Dr. Flack places the sound processors, which look like large hearing aids, on Nora's small ears. And then she places an extra circular piece on Nora's head directly above her ears. The video jumps a bit as it plays.

"This is called the headpiece, and it has a magnet. The implant inside Nora's head also has a magnet. See how the headpiece snaps into place behind Nora's ear?"

It still amazes me how easily the headpiece attaches to Nora's scalp through the natural attraction of the magnets. I perch closer to my computer screen.

I watch with rapt attention as Dr. Flack leads us through Nora's appointment. "I'm going to connect Nora's sound processor to my computer and start programming her device so she can hear. Just continue playing games with Nora. I'll let you know before I turn it on. Remember," Dr. Flack continues, "adults describe the sound like a bunch of buzzes and beeps. Some have said it sounds like Mickey Mouse."

The video captures Troy leaning down, looking closely at Dr. Flack's computer, trying to understand the software. "So, at best, Nora will hear a bunch of beeps and buzzes today? I can see why that might be scary, but I have to say I've never been more excited for anything in my entire life."

As the memory replays from my computer screen, it continues with one of my favorite parts. Nora, seated happily in a highchair by a table scattered with toys, is curious about what's happening and keeps pointing to her ears.

"I'm going to get started now. Just keep Nora distracted with the toys and any snacks if necessary." Dr. Flack turns her attention to her computer and begins pecking the keyboard.

Troy and I focus on Nora, building a tower out of blocks until she knocks it down with pure delight. We arrange Barbies into a circle, pretending they're having a tea party. We blow bubbles as Nora watches, wide-eyed and giddy.

Twenty-three minutes into the video, just as I'm about to open a huge lollipop, Dr. Flack interrupts. "I'm ready to turn Nora on for sound."

You can see my body stiffen in anticipation as I reach for Troy's hand.

"Keep in mind, children can have various reactions when it's turned on," Dr. Flack continues, to prepare us for what's coming. "Some laugh, some cry, and others don't react at all. Don't be alarmed if Nora doesn't give a strong reaction. It's just the way some children handle this overwhelming experience. I'm going to turn it on at a soft volume and then slowly turn it louder. I will point to you when it's time to say something. I want your voice to be the first sound she hears." Dr. Flack returns her attention to programming.

Looking up from my computer, I inhale deeply. A thin layer of sweat immediately lines my back, making my top stick to my shoulders. It's as if I'm back in that very moment all those years ago. I glance back at the screen and watch as Dr. Flack points, giving Troy and me the go-ahead to speak.

"Hi, Nora," I say, my voice unsteady. "Hi, Nora," I say again. This time a bit surer of myself. "I love you."

As soon as the last three words escape my lips, Nora freezes, and her eyes balloon with worry.

"She's hearing!" Troy pants, exhilarated by Nora's reaction. "Oh my god, she's hearing."

Nora looks over to his lips and then back at me. She points to her cochlear implants and shakes her head back and forth, confused.

I can't help myself from running my finger over her image on my computer screen. I want to comfort her, even now. As I pull my finger away, she scrunches her face tightly and then erupts with a thunderous giggle. A moment later, tears stream from her eyes.

I watch as I console her, telling her it's okay, as I rub her back. "That's Daddy's voice, and he's excited you can hear him. Mommy is excited too. I know you don't understand what we're saying, but you will. Eventually, you will."

Nora cocks her head to the side and scrunches up her forehead in confusion. She's stuck in a bizarre cycle of laughing and crying. I recall how badly I wanted to fix this moment for her. I needed something to calm her. Watching the video play on, it shows as I stand and retrieve the red plush heart I bought on her surgery day. I had stuffed the toy into my diaper bag at the last minute, knowing she had become attached to it, ever since waking up and finding it lying next to her.

"I love you," I say as I hand the toy over to Nora, who is sitting in her highchair, still crying. "Now I know you can hear me. I love you."

I turn my face away from my computer and inhale deeply. "Happy Hearing Birthday," I whisper out into the quiet of my house as I shut off my laptop.

CHAPTER 32

Julie Wu

TAKING MY USUAL spot on the couch in Dr. Martinez's office, I sink into the soft leather.

"Great to see you, Julie. I'm looking forward to another individual session." She smiles warmly. "I'd like us to focus on the feelings you have about the abortion today. Once we examine this, we'll bring Eric into the conversation at another session."

Discomfort overtakes me. I nod but break eye contact, bracing myself for whatever's coming.

"To start, Julie, do you find you're weighed down with thoughts about what life would be like if you had continued with the pregnancy?"

The shame I've experienced since the Facebook attack winds through my core. The comments got out of hand, and the post was deleted. I inhale deeply, conflicted about admitting the truth. "No, I don't dwell on what life would be like if we'd had the baby. But sometimes something happens that makes me recall the choice Eric and I made. And when that happens, I feel sad and very alone."

"Tell me more about feeling alone." Dr. Martinez's voice is soothing and encourages me to continue.

"I guess because Eric and I never talk about it. I often wonder if he even thinks about it. On the day's anniversary, I always shut down. But Eric doesn't even realize why. For him, it's like it never happened."

A bloom of heat creeps up my neck. "And then, when he votes for politicians who want to outlaw abortion, it reinforces this idea that he doesn't remember that *we* ended a pregnancy. I'm so angry I carry the weight of the decision by myself."

Dr. Martinez nods in understanding. "It sounds like you want to share your emotions about the abortion with Eric."

"Yes, but because he's a conservative, I can't. How can I confide in him when he supports politicians who say what we did is wrong?" My hands cut angrily through the space in front of me.

"But Eric has made it clear he supports a woman's right to choose. Does that help?"

"Not really," I say, sinking back into the couch. "While I know that's true, what matters are his actions."

Dr. Martinez cocks her head to the side. "By actions, you mean the way he votes?"

"Yes." I shift uncomfortably.

"Does Eric have to be a Democrat for your marriage to continue?" Dr. Martinez's eyes focus directly on mine.

"I don't know," I say. "I'm trying to figure that out." My words drag.

"I can see you struggling, Julie. Why don't you tell me some of the things you love about Eric?"

I let out an unsteady breath, feeling somewhat pathetic. "This may sound strange," I say, "and maybe you already put it together because you moderate the Facebook page, but I'm the one who made the anonymous post about politics in marriage. Looking back, it was stupid to post. It caused a lot of controversy. But someone called Eric a selfish, self-absorbed narcissist, and it really bothered me. I stewed about the comment for days."

Dr. Martinez brushes the hair out of her face. "That's noteworthy. Why do you think it bothered you?"

"I just kept thinking, if this mom could only meet Eric, she'd know he's a kind and caring husband and father. And more than that, he accepts me for me. All of me."

Dr. Martinez continues. "So, knowing that Eric lets you be exactly who you are, I wonder, given all the good in your relationship, can you stay with Eric and not force him to reject his conservative political views?"

Dr. Martinez's words ring in my ears. "I just don't know," I answer honestly. "There's a part of me that believes divorce is the only solution."

CHAPTER 33
Gabriella Martinez

"I 'LL CALL EDGE of the Water Hotel and give them our final number for the event. Can you go by Hamilton House Athletics and pick up the swag?" Laura stares at her to-do list. We're having lunch at Trendy Greens as we make final preparations.

"Sure," I say. "Hamilton House Athletics is on the way to Party Time. I have to stop by to pick up candy. I've waited until the last minute to get treats to give out for Halloween next week. Lucas will be angry if I come home with Smarties and Dum-Dums. He's demanding Twix and Reese's."

"Reese's is my absolute favorite. I used to steal them from Nora's Halloween stash when she was little." Laura looks up from her notepad and gives me a snarky grin. "It's my right as a parent to take whatever Halloween candy I want."

"Well, you're better than I am. I used to throw away all of Lucas's candy and replace it with homemade natural treats."

"Yuck!" Laura says as she takes a bite of her chicken Caesar salad. "What could you make that could compete with Twix and Kit Kat?"

"Organic juice lollipops, natural peanut butter balls." I screw my eyes together jokingly, knowing my commitment to clean eating is extreme. "But I'm loosening up. And I'd never throw away Lucas's Halloween candy now."

"So which *Star Wars* characters are you dressing up as?" Laura asks with a giggle. She loves to make fun of my family's *Star Wars* obsession.

"Ricardo has to work on Halloween. Carlita's going trick-or-treating with Lucas and me."

"That should be interesting. How's everything going with you and your mom?"

My body tenses as soon as Laura asks about Carlita. "It certainly wasn't easy to see that article in the *Hamilton Herald* that detailed my mom's dating blog," I say.

"Right, I bet. Your mom puts it all out there. Actually, I wanted to ask, but didn't want to overstep. Were you the one who made the anonymous post about the mom ordering lubricant and sexy lingerie on Amazon? I noticed it was deleted quickly after it was posted."

My left leg bobs back and forth under the table. *Does Laura want me to confess to an anonymous post?* Laura and I have spent years laughing, commiserating, and enjoying each other's company. She's intimately familiar with the issues I have with Carlita. My leg stills, and my body relaxes.

"I actually made an anonymous post about Nora." Laura rushes to fill the silence before I can answer. "But I'm sure you saw that." She stares at her salad uncomfortably.

"Yes, I saw your post. I think it's a great way to support Nora. And yes, that was my post about Carlita." I quickly realize I'm relieved to be talking about this with a friend.

"Wow!" Laura says. "Carlita's living her best life."

"She sure is," I say. "But to tell you honestly, I realize now that Lucas often feels about me the way I feel about Carlita."

"What do you mean?" Laura asks, leaning forward.

"Sometimes I make Lucas angry. And sometimes I embarrass him. But I'm not intentionally trying to. I'm just being me. Just like Carlita. She's living her extra, out-loud life. She's not intentionally trying to make me embarrassed or angry."

Laura puts her fork down and looks me straight in the eye. "Gosh, Gabby. Do you know how lucky you are that you can be your own therapist? It would take months of psychoanalysis for anyone else to make that realization. Impressive."

"Thanks." I laugh. "I guess all those years of school had benefits beyond helping my clients." A ripple of pride moves through my chest. "Now, let's get back to planning the event," I say. "Here's a crazy idea. We should do randomly assigned seating, so the moms will meet new people."

Laura flips to a blank page on her pad and jots a few notes. "Love that idea! The moms should get to know new people and not stick with who they already know."

"I'm so glad you like the idea!" I say excitedly. "But if we do randomized seating, we need to prepare for pushback. Some moms may feel awkward and complain."

Laura looks up from her notebook. "Right. Well, you're the therapist. How do we make it comfortable?"

My mind scrambles through the main points of a class I took on fostering connections in groups while getting my PhD. "There's a science behind building comradery," I whisper, feeling like we're starting a revolution against the failings of social media.

"Well, I'd love to hear the science behind making women who don't know each other relax and have fun. Seems more like science fiction to me!" Laura throws her head back and laughs.

The idea for a plan pierces my thinking. "A common goal to better society mixed with friendly competition." My words rush out.

"Umm...care to break that down a bit for a layperson like me, Professor Gabby? Do you have an actual idea for the event?"

"Yes!" I beam back. "Let's have the women sit at randomly assigned tables and then have the tables compete to see which one makes the highest donation to the food bank."

"Brilliant!" Laura says. "This way, the women will have something to talk about and a clear focus."

"Yes!" I say, bouncing in my chair with enthusiasm. "Keep it up, and I'm going to be calling you Professor Laura."

Laura nods her head, grinning. "Professor Laura, I like the sound of that! Anything else we can do to help the moms bond?"

A drum of nervous, yet excited, energy fills my chest. I've been waiting for my chance to be open with Laura about my ideas for the Hamilton Beach Moms' page. "To be honest, I've been thinking about how we can use the fundraiser to persuade the moms of Hamilton Beach to connect in person regularly. This event could be transformative for our community if we play it right."

Laura stares ahead, lost in thought. "Yes, I sometimes think the page is doing a disservice when I read the catty comments and posts. I'm still amazed by the fight that broke out over minivans and SUVs. The thread is still going."

As Laura speaks, my enthusiasm for making the page a launching pad for genuine in-person relationships builds. "Exactly. Most moms would never say in person what they type in a comment. Except for your crazy friend Isabell. But that's a discussion for a different day."

"Yes, I know. Isabell is the queen of insensitive comments." Laura's eyes shift away. I can tell she's irritated by the thought of Isabell.

"But it's not just Isabell. People think a screen gives them some type of exemption from common decency," I say.

"But the page does a lot of good too." Laura's expression changes from annoyed to soft and sympathetic. "I especially love that moms can post delicate questions anonymously. Remember that post from the mom struggling with four small children and an unsupportive husband? She got over a hundred supportive comments. I hope they helped her realize she's not alone."

"I agree," I say. "The page is a double-sided coin. It can be positive and useful in some cases and negative and harmful in others. But the thing about a coin is that you can easily flip it over, if you just remember you're the one holding it. We just need these moms to flip and use the positive aspects of the page, rather than the negative ones."

"Quite profound," Laura teases with heartfelt warmth.

"Ha! Clearly, I'm beginning to sound like Yoda and all the other Jedi characters I idolize."

"I know nothing about *Star Wars* and Jedis," Laura jokes as she vigorously searches through her bag for something. "But I'm glad we're going to make this page more than an online forum. Nothing can stop us now!" She pulls her hand out of her bag and pushes her chair out from our table.

"What are you doing?" I peer at her through squinty eyes, confused.

She beams at me as she throws a quarter toward the sky. "Let's throw this Facebook page into the air and flip it over!"

CHAPTER 34

Indira Acharya

'M RACKED WITH guilt as I watch Kabir complete a crossword puzzle across from me on the couch. I've risked my family and my entire way of life. My head's saddled with confusion since my afternoon with Fatima. One moment I'm euphoric, and the next, I'm panicked that I'm turning my back on my traditions.

"Why are you staring at me?" Kabir asks with a muddled expression.

"Oh," I say, shifting my guilty eyes away from him. He's a good man. He's my best friend. "I meant to thank you for taking care of my mom at the beach when she didn't feel well. She was so upset about Nani." It's strange how my infidelity has brought the things I cherish about Kabir to the forefront. It's as if my mind is fighting against my heart.

"Of course, Indira. I love your parents like my own." Kabir reaches for my hand. The moment stretches, and I find myself torn between this reliable, loving, solid man and my heart's passion. I love the life Kabir and I have created together. I relish our daughters and the culture we are passing down.

I think of a comment someone made on my post right before I deleted it.

Tia Decker: If you stay in the marriage, you must end the relationship. If not, you're teaching your children that infidelity is okay. Kids pick up on everything. I promise you it will come out.

I know I must decide. There's so much at stake.

"I meant to ask, how did your interview about the refugee center go? I'm glad you finally agreed to do it." Kabir squeezes my hand for a second and then gets up and walks toward the kitchen.

"It was fine," I say. My chest constricts at the mention of the refugee center. I agreed to talk with Maggie O'Donnell finally, after Fatima convinced me it would be good publicity for the center. "What should we have for dinner?" I ask, eager to change the subject.

Kabir peers into our refrigerator, searching for something to eat. "I have an idea!" he says. "Let's go out for a nice dinner. Maybe your parents can watch the girls. I feel like we need to reconnect."

Why does Kabir suddenly think we need to reconnect? Does he know about Fatima?

Getting up from the couch, I try to push away the storm of fear stirring inside. At this moment, the thought of spending "quality time" with him rubs me uncomfortably. I want to tell him I'm tired and want to stay home, but guilt pushes at me. "Sure, that sounds nice," I say as Kabir picks up the phone and calls my mom.

"All set." Kabir smiles and hangs up his phone. "Your parents said we could drop off the girls. I'll see if we can get a reservation at Ocean Club One."

Nausea makes my stomach cramp. I just spent a lovely dinner at Ocean Club One with Fatima. "How about California Coastal?" I suggest, unnerved by the way things are colliding.

"THIS WAS PERFECT," Kabir says as we look at the dessert choices.

I nod, trying to keep my face neutral. Inside, my feelings of guilt, uncertainty, distress, and sadness are churning, as if in a high-speed blender.

"Is that your phone ringing?" Kabir looks at my small clutch on the table.

"Yes, but I'm sure it's not important." The thought of seeing a missed call from Fatima is terrifying. I'm certain my face would betray me.

"So, I'm thinking of ordering the flourless—" Before Kabir can finish speaking, his phone rings. "That's odd, I'm not on call tonight. We should make sure it's not your parents." He slips his hand into his pocket, pulls out his phone, and flips the screen so I can see the call is from my dad.

"Hi, yes." Suddenly Kabir's face goes ashen. "Yes, we are coming right away."

Before I can even ask what's happening, Kabir is next to me, leading me out of my chair. "Your mom, she had a heart attack. We need to get to the hospital immediately."

CHAPTER 35

Isabell Whitmore

HOPPING OFF MY Peloton, I wipe sweat from my forehead. I got my birthday shout-out from Jenn. And she congratulated me for 7,500 rides. As far as ride stats go, is it considered cheating if you do four ten-minute classes a day? *Asking for a friend.*

After taking a long hot shower, I walk downstairs, expecting to see flowers, balloons, and cards. But when I step into the kitchen, it looks as it does every day. There's not a gift, a sign, or anything at all wishing me a Happy Birthday. My family better have something big in store for me later.

It's hard to believe I'm forty-eight. I'd easily pass for mid-thirties. And believe it or not, I've only had garden-variety Botox. My strict gluten-free and pescatarian diet, intense exercise regimen, and excellent gene pool are the keys to my beauty.

"Here you go, Ms. Isabell. Happy Birthday." Mary puts a steaming latte in front of me. "I did a tutorial and learned to make the whipped milk into a heart. What do you think?"

"Wait," I say, "is it milk or almond milk?"

Mary's face falls. "It's almond milk."

"Perfect." I take a large sip. "Let's walk to the beach to take some photos. I need something fabulous to post on Insta for my birthday."

Twenty minutes later, Mary and I are standing on the sand, doing a full-on photoshoot. I'm wearing cherry red workout tights and a cropped tight t-shirt that says "It's My Birthday" in all the colors of the rainbow.

"Here, let me take a peek." Mary hands over my phone, and I scroll through fifty shots. "I think this one's a winner. I love how my hair is blowing in the wind. Plus, the way I'm standing takes off five pounds. Not that I need it." I walk back to my house, and Mary follows. I notice she's sweating in her thick, black cotton uniform.

Back inside, I post the photo to my Insta. I create a caption, so everyone knows it's my big day.

> *My B-Day is off to a great start! I have the house to myself. No husband or kids to deal with. Dinner celebration tonight at Ocean Club One with family and BF Laura!*

As I finish the post, my phone buzzes with a text from Harris.

Harris: Haven't had time to order the cake. Can you do it? Sorry.

Last night, Harris told me he was overseeing the merger of two fitness companies' software systems. I guess he's busy, but so am I. I have a massage and a nail appointment, and Brody is coming over at five to do my hair and makeup. How am I supposed to fit in getting this cake?

Harris better throw me the bash I deserve in a few years for my fiftieth birthday. I'm thinking upscale water-view restaurant, caviar, sushi, and eighties cover band, The Cabbage Patch Dolls. My friends and I lost our minds when they played "Careless Whisper" and "Always Something There to Remind Me" last time we saw them. We did edibles, and I made out with the saxophone player. I squirm thinking about his hot breath on my neck, but then remember I need to order my cake.

Where can I find a gluten-free and vegan cake at the last minute? I absolutely refuse to use Breaking Free Bakers. I've been meaning to

warn others about their sub-par service on the Hamilton Beach Moms'
Facebook page. Now's my chance. I'll post anonymously since those
posts get the most attention.

New Activity

Anonymous Mom Post
Today at 9:38 a.m.
Looking for recommendations on where to buy a gluten-free,
vegan cake that's edible. I had a terrible experience with Breaking
Free Bakers, so please don't bother suggesting them. PSA:
Breaking Free is overpriced, and their cakes are dry and tasteless.
I had a war with the owner when I tried to get my money back for a
full-size sheet cake. The owner was unresponsive to my multiple
calls and emails, and I eventually had to go into the store and raise
hell. Stay away from Breaking Free. I need to order this cake ASAP
as I'm late with my plans. Hamilton Beach moms, I'm counting on
you! Stop scrolling and give me your recs.

Immediately, I get two comments.

Lorna Golder: Gluten-Free Goddess on Ponce is really good. They
usually need specialty cake orders a week ahead of time, but give
them a try.

Amy Patrick: My son has celiac's, and I can't say enough good
things about Wheatless Wonder! You'll need to drive thirty minutes
as it's on El Rancino, but believe me, it's worth it. They made
a gorgeous Spider-Man cake for my son's birthday. Everyone
gobbled it up. Not just the gluten-free peeps.
8 👍

As I Google the phone number for Wheatless Wonder, I realize
I won't have time to pick up the cake. I'll send Mary and have her
drop it off at Ocean Club One.

"Wheatless Wonder. This is Katie. How may I help you?"

The cadence of Katie's voice reminds me of an irritating Spice Girls' song. I'm immediately annoyed. "Yes, I'm in a bind, and I need a cake for tonight. It must be gluten-free and vegan."

"A cake for tonight...for how many?"

"Enough for six people."

Silence, silence...

"Hello, Katie, are you there?" My words are sharp, but time's ticking. I'm already running late for my massage with Victor.

"Yes, ma'am. Sorry about that. I was helping a customer with—"

"I don't need to hear the details, Katie. Let's just get back to my order."

Katie doesn't respond, clearly rattled by my rude tone. I don't mean to be such a bitch or, I don't know, maybe I do.

"Hello, Katie, are you still there?" She better pipe up quickly or I'm going to flip out.

"For six, that's not a problem. We keep a selection of six-inch round cakes on hand for last-minute requests. I'd be happy to decorate one for you. Let me see what flavors we have today. Can you hold a moment?"

"Yes, but I'm in a rush, so please make it quick." I glance at my watch. I'm going to be twenty minutes late for my massage.

"Hi, yes, we have vanilla with buttercream, chocolate with fudge frosting, and strawberry with buttercream."

"No vanilla with chocolate frosting?"

"No, ma'am, that's all we have today."

"You'd think you'd have vanilla with chocolate frosting. It's such a basic combination."

"I'm sorry, ma'am."

"That's disappointing, but I guess I'll make do. I'll take chocolate with fudge frosting. Whoever heard of not having a vanilla and chocolate combination?" Anger fills my chest, causing me to spit my words out like daggers.

"Ma'am, what do you want the cake to say?"

"*Happy forty-eighth birthday, Isabell.* Wait no. *We love you, Happy Birthday*, err no, maybe *Forty-eight and Fabulous*? I don't know. What do you think?"

"Ma'am, we can do any of those. Which would you like?"

I glance at my watch again. I need to walk out the door this instant.

"Just *Happy Birthday!*" I bark. "I'm going to have my housekeeper pick it up and bring it to the party location. I need to get going. This call has made me late." I give Katie my credit card information.

Hanging up, I see a notification from Facebook. I must have more comments on my post.

> **Hillary Roberts:** My sister-in-law owns Breaking Free Bakers, and I find anonymous mom's slander indefensible. If I am correct in my assumption of who this mom is, be aware that she is bat sh*t crazy. To rectify this unfortunate incident, Breaking Free Bakers will offer free gluten-free brownies or cupcakes all day today! One per customer. Come by and see for yourself how delicious Breaking Free treats are!

> **Barbara Rose:** I agree with @Hillary Roberts, anonymous mom may have had a bad experience with Breaking Free, but there is no need to disparage it on a public page that reaches thousands of moms in Hamilton Beach.

> **Jennifer Katz:** Amen, shame on anonymous mom.

I never shy away from a fight, so decide to jump right in.

> **Isabell Whitmore:** I'm not sure why people are upset with anonymous mom? This was her experience, and she has the right to warn others about poor service. Free speech. It's a thing.

"Ms. Isabell?"

I look up and find Mary staring at me. "I'm going to need to leave. My son's school just called. He's not feeling well."

Ugh, I think. I need someone to pick up my cake. "Can't you find anyone else to get your son?"

Mary's eyebrows scrunch together, and her eyes practically cross. "No, there's no one else who can pick him up. I apologize." She turns away from my scowling face.

"Fine," I say at a clip. "But I need you to do one thing for me. Go to Wheatless Wonder, pick up my birthday cake, and deliver it to Ocean Club One. I'll text you the address. Also, be sure to confirm the cake is chocolate with fudge frosting."

She looks at me. I can tell she's irritated by the way she's chewing on her lip. "Yes, ma'am, I will."

A LAYER OF expensive creamy lotion penetrates my legs as steam from my shower dissipates into the air. Brody will be here any minute to do my hair and makeup. I hear my phone buzz from the closet. Walking into the gorgeous space dedicated to my wardrobe, I find my phone sitting on the marble island surrounded by perfectly arranged rows of shoes, purses, scarves, and designer clothing.

It's a text from Laura. She's probably irritated I haven't called her back to let her wish me a Happy Birthday. I wonder if she's mad I never met up to talk about Nora?

> **Laura:** Nora's having a hard time and asked me to go to dinner. Sorry to cancel on your b-day. Need this time with Nora. Let's celebrate another day.

Oh well! It's better anyway. Laura's so intense. I hate the way she always holds eye contact a little too long, her gaze blazing with a fire that makes me squirm.

Two hours later, Brody trails me to my front door. "The total for your hair and makeup is four hundred dollars. Just Venmo me."

I hurry upstairs as soon as he leaves. It's past six o'clock. If I don't leave the house in a half hour, I'll be late. If only I didn't need to squeeze in calling about the cake.

My arms push through the sleeves of my new Hervé Léger dress. It's a lovely deep emerald. I can barely breathe while wearing it. The lady at the boutique said it brought out my eyes. I agree. My family will fawn over how gorgeous I look when they see me.

The girls have plans with their friends after school and will meet us at Ocean Club One. Warren has basketball practice. I thought he'd come home and shower before dinner. Harris, of course, is coming straight from work.

Buzz. My phone alerts me that my Uber Black is arriving in one minute. I'm going to be fifteen minutes late to dinner, but it's okay. I deserve a grand entrance on my birthday.

Tracing my lips with gloss, I shove the makeup into my hot pink Chanel Maxi Flap bag.

Where's the car? The Uber app tells me the driver is now ten minutes away. *What the hell is happening here?* I text the Uber driver, demanding he arrive immediately. I'm already late! The driver better not try to make small talk. My patience is running thin.

Finally, sitting in the Mercedes on my way to dinner, my phone buzzes again. It's a message from Lola.

> **Lola:** Running late but we'll be there

My body fills with heat. Late on my birthday. So disrespectful. I do everything for these girls—buying them Lululemon gear, paying for their manicures and facials. I even got Harris to drop their recent punishment, and they can't even make it to my celebration on time. A jolt of electricity flies to my fingers as I respond in a fury.

> **Me:** Late to your own mother's birthday dinner. Sounds right. You're spoiled brats.

The ellipses flash on the screen, and I wait for Lola's reply. They disappear just as the car pulls up to Ocean Club One. Just wait until Lola and Grace arrive. I'll be giving them the cold shoulder the entire meal.

As I step inside, I'm suddenly disappointed. When I reserved the table, I forgot to specify an outside unobstructed view of the water. I'll need to cause a stink and have us moved if my family isn't seated at one of the preferred tables. Where you sit at a fancy restaurant has become a status symbol.

"Hi, I have a reservation for six under Whitmore." The host shuffles menus around as I speak. "My husband and son should already be here."

"Yes, let me look at the reservation list."

"Also, we will need to move to an unobstructed water-view table, if we're not already seated at one."

The host's eyes bulge at my comment, but I'm used to people reacting this way to my requests. It doesn't rattle me.

"Looks like you're the first to arrive, Mrs. Whitmore."

It's *my* eyes that bulge as the host delivers this piece of news. I do my best to contain my surprise as he continues.

"The good news is I have a wonderful table for you and your family tonight. One of our best tables, right by the water. Follow me."

The host grabs several menus and leads me to a large deck that nestles next to the water. My heels click clack against the dark wood floor as I walk. The outdoor space is contained by a ceiling, arched high and finished in the same wood that covers the floors. Each table is set with heavily starched, bright white tablecloths with arrangements of deep blue hydrangeas in the center. I take a seat in one of the wide-backed wicker chairs.

"I see we're waiting for additional guests to arrive." A petite young waitress smiles at me, highlighting her perfect bone structure and youth.

"Yes, my family should be here shortly." I look at my phone as if to confirm this information is correct.

"Great, can I bring you anything while you wait?"

"I'll have sparkling water."

"Sounds good. I'll be right back."

A few more minutes go by, and I realize it's now seven-thirty. A full half-hour past the reservation time. *Where is everyone?* Before I even work out what to say to my family to evoke the most guilt, the waitress is back with water, except instead, she's carrying champagne.

"Mrs. Whitmore, right?"

I nod to confirm.

"Your husband Harris called. He sent over this bottle of our finest champagne. He apologizes, but he's not going to make it." The awkwardness of the conversation stretches her words thin.

"Oh," I say, my wobbly tone giving away my disappointment. "Did he say anything else?"

"It was his secretary that called."

My face flushes in embarrassment, and I rush to fill the silence. "That's what happens when your husband is rich and powerful," I blurt out.

The waitress looks at me sheepishly. "Well, I'm sure your other guests will be here shortly. Can I open the champagne and pour you a glass?"

I push a long-stemmed fluted glass forward, and she fills it generously before she steps away.

Warren, what happened to him? I send him a text.

> **Me:** Where are you? My birthday dinner????

Within a few seconds, I get a text back.

> **Warren:** Oh, Mom, sorry. Totally forgot. Max's dad took us sailing after basketball. Just got back. I'll see you tonight when I get home. So sorry.

Heat courses through my body, making my head throb.
I text Grace.

> **Me:** Are you coming????

> **Grace:** No, Mom, we're not. Why would you want to have dinner with spoiled brats??

"Ma'am?" The waitress approaches as I slam my phone on the gleaming white tablecloth. Why does she insist on hovering?

"Would you like to order an appetizer while you wait?"

I swallow hard, trying to figure out if I'm going to divulge to this twenty-nothing-year-old that everyone has stood me up for my birthday.

"I'll take an order of caviar, and please refill my champagne glass. Also, there should be a cake in my name. Could you bring it to the table?"

She looks at me, confused, but nods.

My body slumps against the chair as I gulp my second glass of champagne and start on my third. The liquid permeates my entire body, engulfing me in pleasant warmth. I guess I'll just sit here, drink champagne, and eat caviar and cake until my heart's content. I scroll through the new comments on my post, hoping it has erupted into a firestorm.

> **Hillary Roberts:** FYI, everyone, I'm sure @Isabell Whitmore is the mom who posted anonymously.

Seriously??? Hillary outed my anonymous status. A stab of rage consumes me. That's completely unacceptable!

The waitress returns and sets the cake box on the table, then leaves. My knees hyperextend as I stand up and lean against the table's edge. I gently lift the cardboard sides of the cake box and flip up the flap. I take in the beautiful rosebud-shaped frosting flourishes that surround the cake's edge.

I'm looking forward to eating a large slice while I finish my bottle of champagne and figure out how I can get revenge on Hillary Roberts and every self-righteous mom on Laura's stupid Facebook page. Harris, Laura, my kids…I don't need anyone. This is perfect.

My eyes settle on the scrolled words written in rose-colored pink on the center of the cake, and my face grows hot.

"Just Happy Birthday."

CHAPTER 36
Laura Perry

OOKING THROUGH JULIE'S file, I grab the document I need her to sign and place it by my purse. Suddenly, I remember I also need Isabell's birthday gift. She told me to drop by after I finish at Julie's. Missing her party was the right thing to do. My dinner with Nora was a definite step in the right direction. Since therapy, she's more willing to talk openly about her feelings, and I'm more willing to listen and embrace her exploration of deaf culture.

"And when we ordered, Heidi used the notepad app on her phone, so I did the same." Nora relayed the details about her recent outing with Heidi as we sat for our dinner at Southern Cal Sushi.

"I'm glad you're enjoying your time with Heidi," I said. And it was true. Nora was getting back to her cheerful self.

Nora grinned. "It's great. Heidi's introduced me to several of her friends. They are teaching me so much. I want to become fluent in ASL."

Although I felt momentarily unhinged, I pushed through the discomfort, just like our therapist advised. The scary feelings are just a knee-jerk reaction. I sat and waited to feel the next thing, the thing that may be truer than fear. "To be honest, Nora, I wish we had taught you some sign language. You needed to express yourself, but I was so focused on following the rules, I didn't even stop to consider this basic human need. I apologize."

"What?" she asked, obviously confused. The restaurant was noisy, and even with her implants she sometimes missed things.

"I want to apologize," I repeated my words, making sure she heard.

Nora put her fork down. Her eyes pricked with tears. "I appreciate that, Mom. I'm grateful I have implants, but I wish I grew up more in touch with the deaf community."

"That makes sense," I said. "I don't know why I was so afraid to let you understand that part of yourself."

Nora wiped the corners of her eyes dry. "I know everything you did was out of love. I'm just glad we've finally gotten to this place."

"Me too," I said. Years of regret I didn't realize I was carrying slid off my shoulders. "Daddy and I support you. In fact, maybe we should learn sign language too?" I shrugged my shoulders and grinned. The weight of the rules was lifting, and the thought of learning sign language excited me.

We sat for a moment in silence as we reviewed the dessert menu.

"I'm glad we're having dinner together tonight, Mom."

"Me, too."

"I love you," she said, making the sign for the words as she spoke.

"I love you too," I said. And although I was still completely intoxicated because she could hear me, I knew everything would be okay if she couldn't.

As I reminisce about our successful dinner last night, I hear Nora's car screeching into the driveway. The sound of her tires burning the concrete pulls me away from my thoughts. Nora chose not to wear her implants to school today. I hope it went well.

As she walks in the door, I can tell she's upset. Her eyes are red from crying. She steps inside and plops herself into the chair across from where I'm standing.

"I totally forgot about the debate competition. I couldn't participate." Her shoulders round toward the floor.

Grabbing a pen, I jot down a note, since Nora's unable to hear.

Why don't you save not wearing your implants for the weekends? You need your implants during school.

Nora's lips thin. "You're going to have to trust me. I'm not in kindergarten anymore. I'll figure it out."

An image of Nora's first day of kindergarten flashes in my mind. She was nervous and kept asking me how I would love her while she was at school. I placated her fears by putting her red plush heart from her surgery day inside her backpack.

"I bet you want to say I told you so!" Nora looks up and me with an angry glare, snapping me back to the present. "I bet you're happy I learned my lesson and couldn't do the debate competition."

I take a deep breath before responding. Nora is the captain of the junior debate team, and word-sparring is her absolute passion. "That sounds hard," I reply, careful to avoid saying anything that will cause her to take her disappointment out on me. But her words sting badly, and I take a physical step backward to dull the pain. "I thought we were moving forward and getting past this?"

Unable to hear, she stands abruptly and runs up the stairs.

I start to chase after her, but then decide to give her a few minutes to cool off. Instead, I grab a handful of lemons and sugar. Lemonade usually works as a peace offering in this house. As I slice the lemons and squeeze their juice into a large pitcher, my nostrils flare from the acrid smell. I mix everything, hoping Nora will appreciate my gesture.

Ten minutes later, I knock on her door, softly at first, in case she's put on her implants. But there's no response. I knock again loudly, hoping she'll feel the vibration of the pounding and let me inside. I wait a few seconds more, but nothing changes. Finally, after several more moments, I crack her door open. She's sitting on her bed with her back to me. I can see she's on her computer, FaceTiming with Heidi. Heidi's arms and hands are flying around in a whirl.

Placing the pitcher of lemonade on the dresser, I step closer to Nora. Her body stiffens, and Heidi freezes as soon as she sees me on screen. Nora signs something to Heidi and turns around to face me. Nora's picking up sign quickly. My chest fills with pride.

Both girls giggle. They're probably making a joke at my expense, but I'm okay with it. Nora turns back to face Heidi, and they continue for a few more moments. I sit on the bed next to Nora.

"Heidi wants to sign with you." Nora pushes the computer over and centers the screen on my face.

"I won't understand," I say, confused. But before I can protest further, Heidi's deep in conversation with me.

Immediately, I'm mesmerized by the elegant way Heidi moves her hands. But it's not just her hands that have me captivated. Her arms, body, and facial expressions move in a rhythm as complex as a Beethoven symphony. Her eyes pierce directly into mine, never wavering for even a moment. The intimacy of her steadfast gaze and unbroken attention makes me feel Heidi has a genuine and complete interest in knowing me. For a moment, I understand how much is lost when two hearing people communicate through voice alone.

Nora interrupts, signs something to Heidi, and then turns to look at me. "I'm sorry I blew up at you. Today was not a good day. I need to speak with my teachers ahead of time, so I know what's coming."

I nod my head in agreement, knowing she can't hear me without her implants. Pulling her in for a hug, she embraces me tightly, then pulls away and signs something to Heidi.

"If you want to stay and learn a few signs, Heidi said she's happy to teach you."

A soothing warmth floods my body.

I nod my head, yes.

"Great!" Nora says as she reaches across her bed and digs under a pile of sweatshirts strewn haphazardly on top of her duvet. Her hand searches for a moment until she finds what she's looking for. "Here," she says as she places the red heart plush from her surgery day in my lap.

Looking at the stuffed toy, I realize I've spent my life communicating with Nora through hearing and speaking. But, at this moment, my hands will say what's in my heart.

I shape my fingers and lift my palm with the sign for *I love you*.

"THE HOUSE LOOKS gorgeous."

Julie leads me into her kitchen. We both take a seat in the high-backed stools lining the peninsula.

"Thanks. It's coming together." Julie's eyes proudly sweep across her home.

I pull my file folder from my tote bag and find the paper I need Julie to sign. "Sorry, we missed this. It just transfers the flood insurance policy from the previous owners to you."

"No problem," Julie says as I hand her a pen.

"So, how are the kids adjusting? Do they like Hamilton High? I think Nora and Talia have a class together?" I lean back on my stool, focusing my attention on Julie.

"Honestly, it's been a whirlwind. It hasn't been the easiest time for me. Eric and I have been struggling."

She drops her eyes from mine, and I wonder if she regrets telling me.

"Oh no. I'm sorry. I've been going through a hard time as well."

Julie leans toward me, placing a hand on my shoulder. "Sorry to hear that. Care to chat? I can open a bottle of wine, and we can trade stories."

This is exactly the support I needed when I was at the gardens. It feels good to be here, in the flesh, with Julie. "Sure! I've got thirty minutes."

"Great, your friend Isabell dropped by a few weeks ago and gave me a bottle of wine. I never took it out of the gift bag. Let me grab it." Julie gets up and disappears into her pantry.

"Got it!" she says as she walks toward me, holding a bright pink bag with sparkly tissue paper. "Oh my, what's this?" She pulls out a thick glossy sheet of paper and lays it in front of me.

"Oh, my gosh!" I cup my hands over my mouth to squelch my laughter.

Julie hunches over, crying tears as she giggles.

I pick up the paper and describe what I'm looking at. "Let's see, it's an eight by ten photo titled *The Whitmore Family*. Isabell attached a sticky note that says, *So you can get to know us.* A short bio underneath reads as follows: *Harris is the lead partner and founder of Whitmore Software, and Isabell works tirelessly to maintain the estate at 23 CoCoplum Way.*"

Julie's almost hyperventilating as she peers over my shoulder and looks at the glossy photo. "Is this a promotional piece selling her family?" Julie wipes tears from her eyes.

"Open the wine!" I say through bursts of laughter as I continue. *"Grace and Lola are seniors who hope to create their own brand and market products as influencers. Warren is a junior who plays as point guard for the Hamilton Hornets."*

Julie pours us each a massive glass of wine as we continue to laugh. "I've never seen anything like this. Did you know Isabell had a family spec sheet?" She looks at me, equally amused and horrified.

"No! Absolutely not," I say. "I know they're often asked to share information about their family for different high-profile projects. She must have had these made to keep it easy." I wave my hand in the air as if maybe, just maybe, there's a logical reason for this over-the-top family sell sheet.

"Crazy! I know you're good friends. Sorry, I can't stop laughing." Julie pushes the photo aside and sits back down.

"It's okay," I say. "She's an old friend, but we've grown apart." I run my hand through my hair, feeling disloyal to Isabell, but it feels good to tell the truth.

"There's something to be said for old friends, though." Julie smiles.

"Yes. She's always been larger-than-life. But she was a good friend while growing up and in college. Something happened when we lived in New York, and she's never been the same."

"What happened?" Julie meets my eyes questioningly.

"To be honest, I don't know, and I don't want to guess. But she shut off emotionally. She's become this rude, self-absorbed person, but I stick by her, because the real Isabell is in there somewhere." I take a large sip of wine, swallowing my tender feelings for Isabell.

"I get that," Julie says. "You're a good friend, Laura."

"Oh, thanks. Anyway, did you want to chat about what's going on with you?"

Julie stays quiet. I don't push her to disclose anything else and just stare ahead at the fantastic view of the ocean in front of me. She shifts on her stool and turns toward me. "Have you ever had a difficult time accepting something about Troy?"

We sit in silence again as I take a moment to think. I consider her question, while also reveling in the intimacy of a back-and-forth conversation between two people.

"I hope I'm not oversharing?" Julie fills in the quiet between us. "You probably don't want your clients getting too personal." Her eyes dart to the floor in embarrassment.

"Oh, no, Julie. Not at all. First, I've not had that experience with Troy, but I'm having that issue with Nora. As you said, I'm trying to accept something about her I'm not entirely ready to accept. But we're working through it."

Julie nods, and her body relaxes.

"And second. Our relationship has moved beyond Realtor and client. I liked you right from the start and consider you a friend." Staring into Julie's eyes, our faces only a foot apart, I realize we've allowed ourselves to be vulnerable with each other. This is the rocket fuel for emotional closeness missing from social media.

I BANG ON Isabell's door. No one answers.

That's strange. Isabell told me to come over at this exact time. I planned my entire day around bringing Isabell her gift in person.

Pulling out my phone, I send a text.

Me: I'm at your front door. No one home?

Waiting for a minute, I decide to leave Isabell's gift by her front door. When I get back in my car, my phone pings.

> **Isabell:** Sorry! Got an appointment with my eyelash girl. See you tomorrow at the fundraising lunch.

Rage stomps through my core, as if it's trying to extinguish a fire. I get out of my car and race up the large staircase that leads to Isabell's front door. Grabbing the gift, I hurl it into the air as far as I can.

I watch as it crashes on the ground several feet away. The mug I bought to commemorate our obsession with watching *Friends* when we lived in New York is surely broken. I picture the words embossed on the cup scattered into shards—*You're the Rachel to my Monica* and walk away exhilarated. I'm finally ready to break free of this relationship.

CHAPTER 37

Gabriella Martinez

TURNING OFF OUR outdoor porch light, I see our neighbors outside in coordinated *Frozen* costumes. Shelly's dressed as Anna, her daughter and son are outfitted as Elsa and Olaf, and her husband looks ridiculous as the reindeer Sven. His glowing red nose twinkles in the fading sky.

Halloween has always been my favorite holiday, although it's stressful once you have kids. The traffic is atrocious. And the pressure of getting your kid into their costume, feeding them dinner, and taking pictures, before meeting up at the neighborhood pre-trick-or-treating party, is enough to make Carol Brady lose her cool.

Last year, Lucas laid in the middle of the road, screaming at the top of his lungs, when the M&M's he opened spilled onto the ground. I can still see the image of his Chewbacca body as he attempted to gather up the brightly colored candy morsels as they rolled down the street.

At precisely five o'clock, Carlita walks into the house carrying a large shopping bag.

"*Hola*, Gabby. Happy Halloween, Lucas," she says as she stoops down to meet him at eye level. "I'm sorry Daddy can't come, but we're going to have so much fun!"

"Yes, Abuela," he squeals in excitement.

"What's your favorite candy?" Carlita asks. She waits for his answer with rapt attention, as if his reply will be the answer to world peace.

"Reese's! No, maybe Twix? I don't know. Mom never lets me eat candy." He looks at me sheepishly, wondering if his comment angered me.

"But tonight, you can eat all the candy you want!" I say quickly. "Why don't you go upstairs? I'll be up in a moment, and we can put on our costumes."

"Okay," he yelps, and then dashes up to his room, excited by the promise of endless chocolate and sugar.

"Well, he's excited," Carlita says, watching Lucas run upstairs.

"Yes, I'm excited too," I say. "I love Halloween."

Carlita looks at me with a smirk on her face. "Yes, Gabby, we all know you like to dress up!"

I can't help but laugh. She's right about that.

"So, I've got news to share before I put on my costume," Carlita continues as she holds up her large shopping bag and walks toward the bathroom.

"Do I need to sit down first?" I say, only half-jokingly. I never know what Carlita's going to throw at me.

"Remember that piece Maggie O'Donnell did on me for the *Hamilton Herald*?"

"Yes, of course," I say, remembering how embarrassed I was to see my mom's dating life splashed across the newspaper's pages.

"Well, the *Herald* wants me to do a weekly dating advice column for seniors! They got a tremendous response to the article Maggie did, and they love my blog. They say the column will be a home run. It's a paid job. Can you believe it?!" She's beside herself with excitement.

Pausing, I consider the things I've done and will continue to do that will make Lucas disappointed or embarrassed. The relationship between a parent and child is complex. Each person has their own viewpoint and sensitivities. I think about Carlita's bright spotlight and the energy that always swirls around her.

"Yes," I say. "I can believe it. You are amazing, Mom. You're extra in all the best ways. *Amo a mi familia.*"

Ten minutes later, Lucas and I walk down the stairs in our costumes and meet up with Carlita by our front door. We are a strange combination, *Harry Potter*, Princess Leia, and Marilyn Monroe. We are individuals, but we are bound by love and family. The three of us grab hands and walk outside, ready to reap the rewards of trick-or-treating.

CHAPTER 38

Julie Wu

M Y ARMS THROB as I carry multiple grocery bags at once. Heaving everything onto the kitchen island, I look around to see if anyone can help. I find Talia and Van sitting on the couch, staring at their phones. "You two better have plans other than Instagram for the evening," I say as I put away Talia's organic crackers and several cans of black beans.

Talia looks at me. "I'm leaving in a second to meet Blair and a few other people at the Town Park shops. Is that okay?"

"Of course!" I say, thrilled Talia is making her way in this new sunny alternative universe.

"And Talia's going to drop me off at Jack's house on the way," Van adds. "I'm going to hang with my brahs."

"I don't know what a *brah* is, but I'll assume you mean friends."

"Yes, Mom, with my friends." He smiles his cute smile and turns back to whatever he was doing on his phone.

"Where's Dad?" I ask, realizing he's not home.

"Dad went to Home Warehouse to get shelving for the garage. Not sure when he'll be back." Talia stands, comes over, and hugs me. She's wearing her favorite lime green tank top. I can tell she's in good spirits. "We're heading out now," she says. Van gives me a wave.

"Don't forget, curfew is at eleven. Text or call if anything comes up."

"We will."

The front door scrapes as they leave. And just like that, my new, beautiful, California home is empty. My brain beats with the events of the past months. I can practically feel it pulsing inside my head.

Eager to quiet its methodical thumping, I head outside and drop into one of the lounge chairs on our deck. But before I can relax, I hear the gentle rumble of our sliding glass doors opening.

Eric appears and sits down at the bottom of my chair. "Hi."

"Hi."

"Where are the kids?" he asks.

"They went out for the night with friends."

"That's good. They're making friends."

I nod. He looks at me, searching deep in my eyes, probably for a way to gauge the state of our relationship.

"How was your individual session with Dr. Martinez the other day?" He brushes his hand through his hair and rests his head on his palm.

"It was okay. I'm trying my best. I feel so many things at the same time."

"Care to elaborate?" he asks.

I hesitate before I speak, uncertain if this conversation will lead us into another argument. I smooth out my voice, so my words have soft edges. "What if Talia finds herself in a situation like the one we were in our senior year? Don't you want her to have the same choices we did?" I look at the ocean. The sound of the waves crashing against the shore helps keep my emotions in check.

"Of course, Julie, the answer is yes, without question. I guess where we differ is that I don't believe the conservative leadership will achieve an abortion ban. Think about it. You don't agree with everything the Democratic Party stands for, yet, as a whole, you feel they represent you better."

"But Roe vs. Wade was overturned. They are achieving this part of their platform." My words sound monotone. I'm trying to stay calm.

"That's not how I see it. While I'm shocked it was overturned, the states will be stuck in legal battles for years. And you know I don't agree with it."

"But your support of these candidates makes you complicit, whether you agree with restricting abortion or not. Aren't you outraged?" I turn my body away from his.

"The extremist nature of politics is not my fault." He wraps his left arm around his right shoulder as he speaks, as if trying to hold himself together—as if my words are going to break him.

Dr. Martinez's question from our last session bursts through my mind. Do I need Eric to reject this part of himself to stay married to him? Do I need his conservatism to break away and shatter?

Suddenly, Eric stands up and reaches toward me. "Here, let's walk on the beach. The ocean is so beautiful. Seems a shame to sit up here while we talk."

I grab his hand, inhaling deeply. I forgot how good it feels to have our bodies connect. We walk hand in hand as Eric continues.

"I understand what you're saying, Julie. The world is polarized, and the pendulum has swung so far from the center for both parties. The pendulum will swing back toward the center, and those who've taken such extreme positions, Republican or Democrat, will suffer a backlash. Most people believe in choice. Most people agree individuals should be able to determine their destiny."

"I hope you're right," I say.

Eric stops walking and plants his feet in the sand. "So, I've been thinking about what I can do personally. I've been running my brain ragged, coming up with ideas to prove I'm on the same side as you."

"Really?" I turn toward Eric and look into his golden brown eyes. He smiles, and I'm instantly transported back to Mr. Rifkin's classroom all those years ago. Something softens inside me.

"Yes, and here's my proposal. We should earmark money each year to donate to organizations fighting this battle."

"I like that," I say, trying to stay open to his efforts. "I'd like to specifically support organizations focused on minority women," I continue as I kick sand around with my foot.

"Also, many Republicans are pro-choice. I get politics. I work with lobbyists every day. I'm going to explore how I can take an active role in organizing this segment of the Republican Party."

I squeeze Eric's hand. A space is opening inside me. Sometimes change is a small incremental step in a different direction.

Suddenly, my thoughts shift to our personal journey. "Do you ever wonder what our life would be like if we kept the baby?"

Eric's face sinks in for a moment, as if he's in terrible agony. "Sometimes. To be honest, though, not very often. I've made good choices in my life. I've made bad choices in my life. I define that choice as neither good nor bad. I define that choice as incomprehensible."

I move toward him, sensing his pain. The sun shines brightly behind him, begging me to speak my truth. A moment later, I push words out I've never dared to speak. "I sometimes dream I'm holding a baby. I see the face and know the gender. And even in my dreams, my conscience tells me this is the baby we would have had. Even in my sleep, I know this is the baby we abandoned."

Eric encircles me in his arms. "Why haven't you ever told me that before?" He grabs my hand and leads me back to the dry part of the sand. He sits, and I lower my body next to his. "I know one thing is certain, Julie. I could not imagine a life without you as my wife. And who knows how having a baby at sixteen would have affected our relationship? Maybe we wouldn't have brought the two amazing children we have into this world. Maybe it would have torn us apart. Maybe our relationship would have ended."

I nod slowly. "But maybe we would have endured. I guess we'll never know."

He looks at me pensively. "Yes, we may have had a similarly great life, and that's the cruelest of all truths."

Eric's words remind me of his emotional depth. A surge of deep and binding affection fills my heart. Still, I feel unsettled.

"It's difficult to accept there's a world out there where we had the baby, and it all worked out. I struggle because I flip back and forth between feeling grief for what we lost and feeling grateful for the choice we had. And I can't help but connect the abortion to my youth. The event is just another truth I need to hide about myself."

"Julie," Eric says as he moves his face to within inches of mine. "You don't remember everything clearly. You think you faded into the background in our small town, but that's not true. You were the smartest and most respected student. You were valedictorian. Our town celebrated your acceptance into Yale. You only remember the ones that didn't." Eric exhales as I consider his words.

Suddenly, it hits me. It's time to embrace myself. It's time to accept myself. I will no longer hide. I am proud to be Jewish. I am proud to be southern. I am proud to be raising culturally diverse children. I am many things simultaneously.

"Yes," I say as I lean back into his chest. "I guess, when I think about the abortion, I don't have to force myself to choose only grief or only gratefulness. I can choose both."

CHAPTER 39

Indira Acharya

GLANCING AT THE mourners, the white garments of my family and Hindu community contrast sharply with the traditional black clothing of my friends. Our Brahmin stands with Kabir and me over my mom's open casket. The pungent smell of perfumed flowers mixes with sandalwood, overwhelming me. My knees buckle slightly, and Kabir catches my elbow, steadying me.

It suddenly feels as if I am a helpless child who Kabir must steer at every turn. I've severed myself from my mind. Memories and what ifs are too painful. All that's left is a body trembling in anguish.

As the funeral concludes, Kabir and I stand aside as guests pay their respects. From here, our immediate family will attend the cremation, where my mom's soul can enter the next world. Glancing at my daughters seated in their simple white Punjabi suits on a bench before me, I can't help but see my mom's lips, her sharp eyes, and thick hair.

I'm lost in an image of my mother's face when I feel the warmth of Fatima's hand in mine. We haven't seen each other since we made love. She pushes her body against mine, and her lips settle next to my ear.

"I know you need time right now. I'm not going anywhere." Her voice makes me tingle, but the convergence of my mother's death with the beginning of our relationship has shattered the feeling I had of walking on air only days ago. I am now walking through the devil's fire.

Fatima pulls her face away from mine and presses an envelope into my other hand. I look up at her, but I know my eyes are void of emotion. She nods, understanding that my pain is too much at this moment. I cannot hold anything else. Not even her love.

I PEER THROUGH the rearview mirror as Kabir drives. It's been a long day, and each of my precious girls is drifting softly to sleep as the car hums along the highway.

I turn my head toward the girls. "As soon as we get home, let me help you get out of your clothes. I don't want to see Punjabi suits rolled up on the floor." My voice drags as we make our way from the funeral.

"Your uncle's sleeping at your dad's house tonight." Kabir glances at me quickly before turning his eyes back to the road. "We'll go there first thing in the morning to receive visitors. Is there anything you need me to do for you tonight?" he asks.

I'm overwhelmed with an urge to feel his body touching mine. I place my hand on his arm, and the warmth of his skin soothes me. Kabir and the traditions of my culture have propped me up today. This man and the rituals of my heritage have put their hands on my back and been the pillars supporting me on the most difficult day of my life.

As soon as we arrive home, I help the girls to bed, drying their tears as I collect their mourning clothes. Walking to the laundry room, I drop the garments in the bin by the washing machine.

Kabir appears, already changed into his pajamas. "Do you want me to take care of that? Why don't you get into bed?"

"I need to settle down. I'll be up soon." Turning on the laundry room sink, I'm relieved to have a task to complete.

Kabir looks at me hesitantly. "Okay, but I'm happy to stay down here with you."

"You need to get sleep," I say, knowing Kabir hasn't slept a wink since we got the phone call from my dad at dinner several nights ago.

"I want to soak these clothes overnight. I'm going to fill the sink, and I'll be up after that."

Kabir shuffles over to me and kisses the top of my head. "Goodnight, my love," he says before he turns his back and walks up the stairs.

His use of that phrase punctures a deep feeling of remorse, releasing it to spread around my body. Turning on the laundry room sink, I let the water run until it's the perfect temperature, just on the edge of warm.

After dropping my daughters' clothes into the water, I leave the room and walk through our kitchen. My mind rushes with thoughts of the day, and I suddenly remember the envelope Fatima gave me. I find my bag and pull it out. As I rip the paper open, I see the glimmer of a gold chain. Pulling it from the envelope, it hangs down, straightening out toward the ground. A delicate sun charm dangles before me. An engraving on the back reads, *you are the center of everything.*

Clasping the necklace and charm in my palm, I walk by the glass doors surrounding our kitchen table. As I take a step, a bright white glimmer catches my eye. I realize the base of our new pool, coated with white cement earlier in the day, appears lit up by the moon's soft rays.

I pull apart the doors and walk to the opening in the ground. The pool company will be back soon to fill our pool with water. This project has dragged on and I'm eager for it to be over.

As I stand at the unfinished pool's edge, I suddenly feel the need to step into the lustrous shine of the large hole. I walk down the pool's stairs and toward what will be the deep end. I lay on the hard surface. My mind rushes with thoughts of Fatima. She's a live wire that's turned on a switch, shining a blinding light on my truth.

But I am not cut from a lion's heart like the woman I deeply love. My heartbeat slows to a sluggish, repetitive thump. Tears pour out of my eyes as if commanded with the impossible task of filling this barren pool with water.

My relationship with Fatima cannot be. I love my life with Kabir. I love my culture and my heritage. The passion I feel for Fatima is not enough for me to abandon the essential components of my world handed down to me by my mom.

The pool's gleaming white walls shine all around me like diamonds. But I have little interest in their flashy sparkle. Instead, my eyes move straight overhead to the endless, deep, dark, starless black sky. I stare above me and let it swallow me whole, wishing it were my Fati.

CHAPTER 40
Maggie O'Donnell

"**MAGGIE, YOU'RE STILL** new to therapy. How are you feeling about things?"

I look at Dr. Martinez. She's quirky, but I like her. There's *Star Wars* paraphernalia all over her office. The poster with Luke Skywalker, with the label *Classic Daddy Issues* is my favorite.

"Are you asking if therapy's helping?"

Dr. Martinez nods.

"Well, I'll admit I used to check Doug's phone whenever I had the chance. I could tell he was hiding something. But I haven't had the urge since we've been coming here." I regret saying the words as soon as they come out of my mouth.

"You were looking through my phone?" Doug's shocked by my confession. His nostrils flare in anger.

"Yes, I'm sorry. I know that's wrong." Heat rises to my cheeks.

Dr. Martinez leans forward. "Doug, Maggie just confessed something that puts her in a vulnerable position. You have the right to be angry, but I want you to keep in mind she's taken a risk admitting she's violated your privacy."

The heat on my face races down my neck and courses through my body. If Doug knew about my post on the Hamilton Beach Moms'

Facebook page, he would never forgive me. I deleted it a few weeks ago. I will never, ever tell him about it.

Doug sighs, leaning back into the soft leather couch. "Maggie, please never look through my phone again. If you want to know something, ask me."

"Great response, Doug. Maggie, can you agree to that?" Dr. Martinez waits for me to respond.

"Yes, absolutely. Of course. I really do apologize, Doug."

"We've only got a few minutes left in our session," Dr. Martinez says, "but, Doug, I want to ask you the same question I asked Maggie. How do you feel things are going?"

Doug taps his finger on his knee and squirms around. "I'm glad Maggie knows the truth. I didn't realize how difficult it was to keep my secret. Lately, I feel lighter, and I have more energy. I'm not tired all the time." Doug turns his face upward and almost smiles.

"Wonderful," Dr. Martinez says as she brushes her wavy hair away from her face.

"But," Doug continues, "now that Maggie knows the truth, I wonder if she can really accept this." His shoulders scrunch together.

"Well, why don't you ask her?" Dr. Martinez looks at Doug.

He turns toward me, hesitating for a moment. "Does knowing this make you not love me? Does it make you want to leave me?"

"No," I say, the word escaping my lips as easily as breath. "I love you, and I don't feel like the answer to this challenge is to end our marriage."

I place my hand in his. I can feel the heat in his fingertips.

"Remember the song I played you on the morning I asked you to marry me?" he asks.

"Of course, 'You Are the Best Thing,' by Ray LaMontagne." I smile at the memory of us in our first apartment, playing house, and starting our careers.

"I mean it now and always. You're the best thing that has ever happened to me. I love you."

I think about our past, the relationship we have, and the life we've built together. I consider what Dr. Martinez said the first time I met her. She explained that Doug's compulsion to wear women's under-wear does not have to define something crucial about our marriage, and I wholeheartedly agree.

"I love you too, Doug," I say. "And acceptance is part of love. I think so, anyway?" I look at Dr. Martinez for confirmation.

"I love that sentiment, Maggie. Yes, you're right."

THE SHRILL OF my phone alarm wakes me early the next morning. My body fills with anticipation. Rolling over, I look at Doug and smile. Picking up my phone, I pull up the song he deserves to hear. It's the first time I've played a song for *him*, and it has been years since we've participated in this ritual. I hope the song, so perfect in its message, can express the words that capture how I feel. I'm unsure what lies ahead for us, but I know our relationship will weather this storm.

Hitting play, my ears perk up as the music wafts slowly through the air. As the meaningful Billy Joel lyrics for "Just The Way You Are", ring out in the silence, I am water, flowing around this obstacle rather than trying to change it.

Doug turns to me, the smile on his face a treasure I will hold in my heart always.

"A song for me," he says. "Finally, a song for me."

CHAPTER 41
Laura Perry

"WHAT'S YOUR NAME?" I glance at the woman standing in front of me. "I'm sorry, it's hard to hear with the chatter." Looking around the lobby of Edge of the Water Hotel, I see hundreds of women gathered and enjoying themselves. I can't help but smile.

"My name is Maggie O'Donnell."

"Nice to meet you, Maggie. Grab a card out of this jar. The number you pull will be your table for today's lunch."

Maggie looks at me hesitantly. "Oh, but I have a friend coming. We were planning to sit together."

"Right, lots of women have been making similar comments. We want everyone to meet new people. I hope you'll play along and sit at the table number you draw from the jar." I pick up the container and edge it toward Maggie.

She shrugs her shoulders and smiles. "Sure. Could be fun." Reaching her hand in, she retrieves a slip of paper and opens it. "Table eleven," she says, and then makes her way to the growing crowd in the lobby.

My eyes follow her, but then I see Isabell charging toward me. She's decked out in a bright blue, tight-fitting, cotton dress and dripping with expensive jewelry.

Not in the mood to deal with her, I shuffle around papers, so I look busy.

"Laura!" Isabell says in a high-pitched squeal. "Sorry I missed you when you dropped by. I thought you said you left my gift by my front door. I didn't see anything?" The glass of champagne she's holding teeters from side to side.

"Maybe someone brought it inside?" I say flatly. "Check with Harris or your kids."

"Can you believe I'm forty-eight? Look how fantastic I look!" She shimmies her body around in a circle as if she's an expensive piece of art I should inspect before I make a bid at auction.

I want to tell her to leave me alone. I've had enough, and she's not the center of the world. But, instead, I shrug and half-grin. Now is not the time.

"Grumpy much?" she says as she gulps the rest of her champagne. "Anyway," she continues, "this event is going to be amazing. It's going to be like fireworks exploding on the Fourth of July. All these women, with all their opinions and self-righteous attitudes. What could go wrong?" She wobbles on her feet for a moment as she lets her question hang in the air. Her expression is unnerving.

The cogs inside my head spin with anger. "What are you even talking about, Isabell?" I snap. "And it's clear you're drunk. Maybe you should go home?" I make my anger sound like a question.

"Can't a girl have fun?" she says as she steps back from the check-in table. She shakes her hands around excitedly, as if she's a five-year-old girl meeting Cinderella. "I wouldn't miss this event for the world."

"Listen, I'm swamped," I say, losing patience. "I need to find Gabby and finalize details." Standing, I move away from Isabell and walk toward Gabby.

"Fine!" Isabell calls out. "I'm sitting at table eleven when you're ready to apologize for being so rude."

I turn and watch as she walks to the bar in the lobby. Suddenly, my body burns, as if there's a fire smoldering in my gut. *Why is she acting so strange?* There's an air of a threat in her behavior. It's unsettling. I should tell Gabby.

My pace increases, fueled by a fear I can't explain. As I approach Gabby, I see she's talking to Maggie O'Donnell. I step toward them but hear Gabby say something about patient confidentiality. *Maybe Maggie's a patient of hers?* I'll just give them space.

Glancing around, I notice a few more women crowded around the check-in table. I push my concerns about Isabell's odd behavior aside and hurry back to my post.

"Hi, I'm Indira Acharya. I'm here for the event."

"Oh, wait," I say curiously. "Are you Dr. Acharya? You did my dad's hip replacement last year. He's doing wonderful."

"Yes." She blushes at my compliment. "Glad to hear the surgery was successful."

I instruct Dr. Acharya to pull a number from the jar and move on to the next person in line.

"Almost time for everyone to be seated." Gabby buzzes by me.

Suddenly the wait staff appears, leading everyone into the ballroom where we're having lunch.

"There's a few things to arrange at the auction tables before we join everyone," I say to Gabby. "Follow me."

She nods and steps next to me.

"Oh, and I need to talk to you about Isabell. She's acting bizarre."

CHAPTER 42
Gabriella Martinez

JOIN LAURA AND we walk to a row of tables displaying various items for auction.

"Let's call up the table who donates the most money and congratulate them in front of the group after dessert," Laura says as she places a glittery necklace with an emerald-colored stone on the silent auction table.

"Did you want to talk about Isabell?" I ask.

"You know what? Let's just forget about Isabell," she says. "I'm not getting caught up in her drama."

"Okay." I pause, wondering if I should press her for more information but decide to drop it. "Yes, let's call up the winning table. We can present each person with their prize and let the crowd clap and cheer. I still can't believe Edge of the Water Hotel is giving the winning table overnight spa weekend packages! This prize will certainly motivate people for the table competition!"

"Well, I was married at Edge of the Water, and I always have my out-of-town clients stay here during house hunting. I'm very friendly with the hotel's manager."

"Excuse me, sorry to interrupt, but the guests are seated. The hotel staff is serving lunch." The hotel's event planner points Laura and me to the ballroom where the event is taking place.

"I guess there's just one thing left to do," I say, as I pick up the jar with the table numbers. "There are only two place cards left. We each need to choose one."

Laura reaches her hand into the bucket. "Drum roll, please!" She pulls out a thick white card and opens the crease. "Table eleven," she says hesitantly. "Same table as Isabell. So much for mixing it up." She smiles, but the expression in her eyes doesn't match the upward curve of her lips.

"Here, why don't we switch tables," I say. "I understand why you don't want to sit with Isabell." I pull the last place card out. I gasp when I read it. "Oh no, I'm also at table eleven." Laura and I giggle in unison.

"What are the chances that the last two cards are for the same table?" Laura sighs. "Well, that's okay. You can temper Isabell with your therapy skills. Be aware, though, I saw her doing shots at the hotel bar a half hour ago." Laura's eyes narrow into slivers as she speaks.

"Shots at a lunchtime event?"

Laura hooks her arm through mine. "Oh, let's just forget about Isabell. It's time to eat!"

The ballroom buzzes with excited chatter as Laura and I walk to table eleven. My feet glide as I notice how the moms in the room are intermingling and enjoying each other's company.

When we get to table eleven, I see three empty chairs.

"Isabell's missing," Laura whispers in my ear as she crosses to the other side of the table and takes one of the empty seats.

"Hi, Julie," Laura says as she folds herself into a chair next to my patient, Julie Wu. They must know each other.

I sit in one of the other empty chairs, and the women quiet. As I survey the faces, I notice Maggie O'Donnell seated across from me. She's unsettled by my presence, but as I explained in the lobby, everything we talk about is confidential. I move my gaze around to the other women.

"Hi! I'm Gabby, and that's Laura. But you probably already know that," I say to the table happily.

The women at table eleven smile and nod.

"I promise we got seated together randomly!" Laura jokes. "Strange, right? So, what were you discussing before we interrupted?" Laura glances at the woman sitting across from her.

"We were formulating our plan to win the table fundraising competition. We have a two-pronged strategy. High bids in the silent auction and direct payments to the Venmo account you set up to collect cash donations."

"Perfect strategy," I say, pleased to see the competition is working as planned. "And what's your name?" I glance at the woman speaking, noticing how her thick dark hair frames her face.

"I'm Indira," she says as she plays with a small gold charm dangling from a necklace she's wearing.

"One chair is still empty. Who's missing?" Julie asks as crisp salads are brought to our table.

"Isabell," Laura says ominously.

"Oh," Julie says in surprise. "Isabell's my neighbor," she clarifies for the table.

"This isn't the infamous Isabell that's always stirring up controversy? I'm sure she wouldn't come to this event," Maggie jokes.

"Oh my. So, I'm not the only one who notices her comments?" Indira agrees with Maggie.

My fingers tap the table, letting out nervous energy. This is exactly the negative side of the coin we want to move away from. "Actually, it is that Isabell," I say, trying to diffuse this line of conversation. "She's just a straightforward communicator."

"Exactly," Laura says. "Isabell's blunt."

I glance at Laura, satisfied we have steered the conversation away from a gossipy bashing session.

LAURA AND I sit on a plush wintergreen couch outside the ballroom as the attendees finish dessert and coffee. "Why don't you tally up the silent auction bids, and I'll tally the Venmo donations," I say. "I can't wait to see how much money we've raised for the food bank."

As my eyes scroll the list of donations, I'm surprised to see an entry with several zeros. "*Dios mío*, look at this," I say. "Someone made a ten-thousand-dollar donation on behalf of table eleven under the name "anonymous mom."" I move my phone toward Laura and show her the entry. We both stare for a moment, confused. Seconds tick by, and then, we blurt "Isabell."

"What happened to her, anyway?" I ask. "She never showed up for lunch." I peer around the lobby, but Isabell is nowhere to be seen.

"I have no idea," Laura says, shaking her head. "I saw her at the bar hours ago. But we can't worry about that now. Let's go back inside and announce that table eleven's the winner." Laura grabs the stack of papers she tallied from the silent auction and puts them in a file folder.

I stay seated, wondering why Isabell would make such a large donation under the name "anonymous mom." My body prickles with a strange feeling.

Laura looks at me questioningly. "What's wrong?"

"What's Isabell up to?" I can feel the way my shoes are rubbing against my toes uncomfortably. My senses are heightened.

"Oh, don't worry about it," Laura says. "Ten thousand dollars is nothing to her. Maybe she's trying to make amends for all the controversy she's caused on the page? Let's go back in and announce the winners!"

CHAPTER 43

Laura Perry

"**GOOD AFTERNOON, LADIES** of Hamilton Beach!" My legs shake as I stand and address the group. "My co-moderator, Dr. Gabriella Martinez, and I thank you for coming. I'm going to keep this brief so everyone can continue to chat. I love our community, I love our Facebook page, and I love the fact that we are giving back!"

The women clap enthusiastically, and I beam at the crowd.

"I'm glad everyone finds the Hamilton Beach Moms' Facebook page helpful. The collective advice and wisdom you share truly amazes me."

My ears buzz with another round of enthusiastic clapping.

"As you know, we came together today to support our community food bank. I am thrilled to announce we've raised close to $45,000!" My heart skips happily in my chest. "We beat our fundraising goal by $15,000!"

The room erupts in cheers.

"Now I'm going to announce the table that won our fundraising competition. Boy, you ladies love a good contest!" I giggle, and the room rings with laughter.

"Congratulations, table eleven! You won!" I glance at table eleven, as all of the women in the room hoot and holler in excitement.

"I'd like to call up everyone from our winning table and present each of you with a gift basket with treats and gift cards from our wonderful sponsors. Plus, your voucher for your spa weekend! When you hear your name, please join me. Julie Wu, Maggie O'Donnell, Indira Acharya, Isabell Whitmore, and our very own page moderator, Gabriella Martinez!"

The women at table eleven stand and make their way toward me. They crowd together as every single mom in the room stands and cheers wildly.

"Thank you, table eleven," I say. "Gabby and I will put our spa packages up for bid on the Facebook page, since it hardly seems fair that we planned this event and won the competition."

The women in the room nod, satisfied.

"Thank you to all the moms of Hamilton Beach!"

CHAPTER 44

Gabriella Martinez

S URVEYING THE CROWD, I'm overcome with a sense of ac-
complishment. The event is going amazingly well. The attendees
are in the perfect space to embrace the plans Laura and I have
to integrate the Facebook page into real life.

Laura motions for me to stand next to her. "Now, I'd like to hand
the microphone over to my co-moderator, Dr. Gabriella Martinez.
She has some exciting ideas to share with you."

Taking the microphone from Laura, I look at the hundreds of happy
faces staring at me. The randomized seating and table competition
did what Laura and I had hoped. Now, it's time to tell everyone about
our plans to make this page more than an online forum.

I bring the microphone to my lips. "Let's hear it again for Laura,"
I say. "She started this page five years ago and has worked tirelessly
to make it the best place for moms to get advice and support." A roar
of clapping erupts around me. Some moms stand and shout adoring
comments at Laura.

When the room settles, I continue. "As you know, I joined the
page a short time ago. I'm excited to announce that Laura and I have
a bold idea to launch this page off our screens and into the real world."

Suddenly I see blank stares all around me. My stomach knots,
but I continue.

"We're going to start interest group clubs that meet in person regularly. Some ideas are a book club, a running club, a coffee and chat club, a stroller-walking club. But we're open to anything. Each group needs a chair to organize meetups, but it won't require much more than that."

Several women squirm in their chairs. *Do they hate the idea of in-person clubs?* The room is silent. My stomach twists.

A short, stout woman in the back stands. I'm terrified of what she's going to say. "Can we have a club for moms addicted to Target?"

Everyone laughs.

A moment later, another woman stands and addresses the group. "I would love a meetup for swapping clothes my kids have outgrown."

Cheers ensue.

"How about a group for divorced and single moms?"

"Yes! I really need that," another woman shouts back.

As the crowd hums around me with ideas, my heart surges with joy. It's working. These women want to connect and support each other beyond the virtual space. I look at Laura and see she is dabbing happy tears from her eyes.

Pop. Screeeeeeeeech.

My ears vibrate from the loud sound blasting from the speakers. The microphone pulses in my hand. Everyone is startled by the interruption. Looking around confused, I see Isabell stumbling toward me in three-inch heels and a dress meant for a sixteen-year-old.

Is she drunk or unsteady in her shoes? She's holding another microphone, and as she steps close, my microphone reverberates again with high-pitched squeals. Deafening sounds bounce off the room's walls and windows.

I look at Laura, who rushes toward Isabell.

"Hello, Moms of Hamilton Beach." Isabell presses her body against mine as she screams into her microphone. My nose tingles with the scent of whiskey.

The room freezes.

"Isabell, what are you doing?" Laura pleads. "Go sit down." She reaches toward Isabell's arm, but Isabell pulls it back aggressively.

"No, Laura, I have something to say to these women." Isabell sneers at the faces in the room and then swallows hard. "One of you outed my anonymous post the other day. That's unacceptable. I will not allow anyone to treat me with disrespect." Her words are long and sloppy. It's clear she's drunk.

Laura looks at me with fear. "I'll fix this!" she says with a shaky voice. "I'm going to get security." She runs out of the ballroom.

I turn my microphone off and meet Isabell's eyes. "Let's go outside for a minute. Let's talk this out in private." My heart pounds in my chest.

Isabell looks at me and slowly lowers her microphone to the side. Relief washes over me. Stepping toward the exit door, I motion for Isabell to follow.

She takes one step but then thinks better of it. I can see the left side of her mouth rise as her lips purse together, as if she's taking me up on a dare.

She quickly brings the microphone back up to her face. "No one is going to get away with outing my anonymous mom post!" Her words reverberate over and over through the air. "As retribution, I've had a tech friend work out a way to get you back." She pulls the microphone away from her face and waves it around accusingly. "I'm sick of how you all hate me for the comments I make. I'm sure most of you agree with me behind closed doors, but you're just too chicken shit to show your true colors. So, let's spill secrets. Let's see what we're really made of."

I run to the speaker system to find a way to shut it off, just as Laura arrives with security.

Isabell continues. "In exactly thirty seconds, my tech friend will put a link on the Hamilton Beach Moms' Facebook page that reposts every anonymous mom post ever made with the name of the person who posted it."

A collective gasp overtakes the room. I see looks of shock and fear all around me. Maggie's face pales. Indira runs out the door.

"And that's what you call a mic drop!" Isabell cackles as two security guards forcefully escort her out of the room.

My ears explode with a loud ringing, but is it the noise coming from the microphone on the ground, or the deep, relentless pounding in my head?

CHAPTER 45

Isabell Whitmore

"**G**ET YOUR HANDS off me!" I struggle against the grasp of two security guards as they lead me out of the hotel. "Leave the premises, or we'll call the police." They pull me outside into the salty air and release their beefy hands from my arms.

I quickly step inside the Uber I have waiting. "Good times!" I scream as I slam the door to the army green Hummer idling in the hotel's driveway.

As the larger-than-life vehicle pulls away, I see Gabriella and Laura dash outside toward the security guards. Gabriella's arms are flailing with anger, and Laura's making that face she makes when she's completely dumbfounded.

"Ha!" I can't help but chortle in laughter.

The Uber driver narrows his eyes in the rearview mirror. "Looks like you had a wild afternoon. Did security kick you out of the hotel?"

"They sure did!" I say, feeling satisfied with how my plan unfolded. I bet all those women are scurrying away from the hotel awash in shame over their exposed anonymous posts.

I text my IT boy toy.

> **Me:** It was amazing. Those women got what they deserved!

I see the ellipses pop up, but then they disappear.

> **Me:** Meet you at our spot. I'd like to repay you—wink wink.

I give the Uber driver the address for my rendezvous point with IT Boy. Looking at my phone, I see the ellipses pop up again and then disappear. *What the hell?* Doesn't he want to have victory sex? We won this!

The text goes silent.

I lean toward the Uber driver. "Actually, just take me to 23 CoCoplum Way. I'm going home."

I'm confused when the Hummer pulls up to my house. There's a limo waiting in the roundabout by the front entrance. As I step out, I see Lola and Grace dragging suitcases toward the limo driver. He grabs their bags and loads them into the trunk as they crouch and enter the car.

"Where are you going?" I screech. Taking a giant stride toward the limo, the spike of my left heel sinks into the grass, and my body goes flying onto the ground. *"God dammit!"*

As I pull myself up, I notice the blue silky cap sleeve of my dress has torn and is hanging at an odd angle. Brushing off dirt from my waist, I charge toward the limo.

"You're probably wondering what's going on?" I hear Harris's calm voice.

I spin around and see him outside our front door with a travel bag slung over his shoulder.

"Where's everyone going?" I say, baffled.

Harris slowly walks down the grand staircase. He's cool and composed. "The kids are in the limo. We're leaving to go to our beach house in Mexico. You're not welcome to join us." He presses his lips together tightly. Descending the staircase, he moves to within a few feet of me.

I stare at him, my mouth agape.

"This marriage is over, Isabell. I've put up with enough over the years, but this stunt you tried to pull with my new IT hire is the last straw."

My eyes widen in surprise as he shakes his head in disgust.

"Yes, Isabell, I know about your affair. And thank God I've been monitoring your emails and texts. If not, I wouldn't have known about your plan to blow up that Facebook page." His voice simmers in anger.

I'm stunned into silence.

"That link you had your boyfriend send out, I had it deactivated. It led to nothing more than an error message. All the secrets in this town are safe." Harris spits his words out at me one by one.

A rush of disappointment explodes in my chest. Suddenly, I'm exhausted. I lower myself to the ground and sit with my legs crossed, as if I'm in kindergarten.

"And don't think that I did this to protect you. The only reason I intervened was to protect my software company. Who knows what those anonymous posts would have revealed about my business partners and clients?" He stares at me blankly, waiting for my response, but my throat squeezes tightly, making it impossible to speak.

"The kids and I will be home next week when this blows over," he says, as he strides toward the limo. "I'm leaving now." He opens the door to the car but hesitates before he gets in. "Is there anything you want to say for yourself?" His face shines with the glow of victory.

Turning away from his prideful gaze, I stroke the ripped silky sleeve of my dress but remain silent.

Looking up at the sky as if perplexed, he gets into the limo, slamming the door behind him. I watch with a blank stare as the car drives away.

"ISABELL! ISABELL!" THE shrill voice of someone calling my name blares in between the sound of choppy waves crashing on the beach. The bottom of my blue dress is soaking wet as the moving water around me rises over my hips.

"Isabell!" I hear the voice again and realize someone's in the water behind me. It's hard to see in the inky dark sky.

"Isabell, oh my god. Come back to shore."

Feeling a hand on my shoulder, I turn and see Laura standing in the water next to me. She takes the bottle of wine from my hand and holds my arm.

"Let's get you inside. You need a shower and to put on dry clothes."

As we walk onto the sand, Laura runs her hand through my clumpy hair, pushing it away from my face. "Thank goodness, Julie and Eric saw you out here. They said they tried to get you to come to shore. I came as soon as they called." She smooths her finger under my right eye, wiping away drips of water and runny mascara.

Lunging toward Laura, I pull her body tightly against mine and sob. She squeezes me, rubbing my back in a circular motion.

Breathing heavily, I push out a few words. "Can we just sit right here?" My body crumbles to the ground from the alcohol I've been drinking since the fundraising lunch this afternoon.

Laura sits beside me, hugging her knees to her chest. The sound of the waves continues, but silence stretches between us.

"I know I don't deserve your friendship, Laura," I say as I run sand through my fingers.

Laura stays quiet, squeezing her arms around her legs, and continues to look at the water.

"I'm a terrible, awful person," I continue consumed by guilt. "I'm so sorry about what I did today. You should never forgive me." The humid air swallows my words.

"You *can* be difficult," Laura finally interjects in a flat tone.

"Difficult is an understatement," I huff. "Just ask my latest housekeeper, Mary. She quit." My voice sounds grainy and slow.

"You're a pro at finding new housekeepers." Laura laughs a bit, trying to lighten the mood. "You do it almost every month."

"But don't you see?" I say, facing her. "That's exactly it. I can't keep a housekeeper, because I'm a bitch."

"You have a strong personality. And I'm sorry to say, but you're often unkind," Laura agrees regretfully.

"I deserve that," I say. "I'm rude, I make snide comments on Facebook whenever I can, I'm self-involved." My voice trails off, but I know this list could be much longer.

Laura releases her legs and stretches them out toward the ocean. "Well, I guess the first step is realizing what needs to change."

"Did you know my entire family stood me up for my birthday dinner the other night? I went to the restaurant, but no one was there." Tears collect in the corners of my eyes.

"That sounds awful," Laura agrees.

"And now they left and went to our beach house in Mexico. Harris wants a divorce. He's the one who made the link inactive. If it weren't for him, this town would be like a ship going down in a storm." I hang my head in shame.

Laura sighs loudly. "I'm very thankful Harris intervened. I probably wouldn't be here if the link had worked. It's hard to understand how you're capable of coming up with such an appalling plan."

Her tone is distant, and I'm terrified I've lost her too. "You're right. There's no excuse for what I did. I deserve what I get." A slight wind blows, making my wet clothes uncomfortably cold.

"I can't help but think back to New York," Laura says. "What happened? You bottled it up and refused to tell me." Her voice competes with the sounds of the ocean.

Suddenly, my body shakes, and I let out a distorted-sounding wail. "Yes, New York. It's where it all went wrong, and now I have no one."

"Do you want to tell me what happened?" Laura reaches for my hand, folding it within hers.

I sit silently for a moment. When words finally leave my mouth, they are soft, barely a whisper. "I've never said it out loud. I'm not sure I've even admitted it to myself." My heart thumps against my chest.

"If you can't tell me, that's fine," Laura replies in a soothing tone. "But you need to talk to *someone*. You've already lost so much because of what happened."

I push my palm deep into Laura's grasp, feeling heat from her hand. My body beats with fear, but I know I have to stop running from my past. The words wind their way up my throat and shoot out of my mouth. "It was my boss and his business associate," I say.

Laura turns and looks at me, and I know, at this moment, I am not alone. That I didn't have to be alone all this time.

"I was drugged. I was raped. I was a victim." My voice trails off without further explanation as silent tears fall from my eyes. Words that were questions in my mind have transformed into true and unalterable statements.

Laura wraps her arms around me and pulls me into a tight hug. "You are brave for telling me," she says. "We'll get you the support you need."

I cry softly into her shoulder.

"Listen, let's get up and go inside. I want you to take a shower and put on clean clothes. What do you think? Can you manage that?" Laura stands and reaches her hand out.

I lift my head and look at her through red-rimmed eyes. "But why would you even bother to help me? I've been a terrible friend. It's like you're Cinderella, and I'm an evil stepsister."

Laura gently grasps my arm, helping me stand. Facing me, she places her hands on my shoulders. "You're right. You haven't been a great friend, but we have a long and complicated history. And I love you despite all of it. There has to be a way back to who you were before New York. We'll figure this out together."

"But you didn't answer my question. Why would you help the evil stepsister?"

Laura pulls me closer as we walk to my house. "Because, Isabell, it's a myth right out of a Disney fairy tale that the evil stepsister can't transform herself into a loving friend."

CHAPTER 46

Laura Perry

SIX MONTHS LATER

"**H**AVE FUN TODAY."

Taking her car keys from the hook by the door, Nora smiles widely.

"Be extra careful driving if you're not wearing your implants," Troy cautions as he steps to the door.

"I've decided I should wear them when I drive." Nora pushes her hair aside, showing her implants are in place. "Got to run, so I'm not late for school."

Good choice for driving, I sign as I watch her gather her backpack.

Thanks, Mom. Love you, Nora signs back.

Picking up my purse, I throw my phone into my bag, and leave shortly after. My car glides along the coastal highway as I drive to Seaside Coffee for the Hamilton Beach Moms' monthly meeting. My heart feels light and happy when I consider how the page has evolved.

Stepping inside the coffee shop, I walk straight to the meeting room in the back. Seaside Coffee's manager bustles around my group of close friends, taking coffee orders and setting out a mix of pastries.

"Morning, Laura!" Gabby waves me toward a table where most of the women from table eleven sit.

"Hi." I fill my plate with an enormous blueberry muffin and join them. "There should be about twenty new people attending today," I say excitedly. "One person also contacted me about announcing a new club."

"Sounds great! What's the new club?" Julie asks as she takes a gulp of coffee.

"It's an art club," Gabby pipes in. "The goal is to visit interesting art exhibits around Southern California."

"Oh, that sounds fun," Indira replies.

"The clothing drive for immigrants was super successful," I say as Indira takes a bite out of a huge banana walnut muffin. "What's the *Give-Back Club* organizing next?" Pride about the things the moms in this town are doing buzzes through my core.

"A school supply event," Indira says. "We're collecting wish lists from the schools. We want our teachers to have everything they need."

"Ladies, is everyone ready for our big interview?" Suddenly, Maggie is standing before us, along with a friend of hers who's a writer for the *Los Angeles Times*.

"Ready!" Gabby grins.

Maggie sits, and her friend does the same. "Everyone, this is Valerie."

A wide smile spreads out on Valerie's face, as both she and Maggie inch their chairs closer to the table.

"I'm really excited about this piece," Valerie says as she pulls out a notepad. "Maggie told me we have thirty minutes before your meeting begins."

I nod my head, confirming she's correct. "This place will be packed with moms looking to join clubs soon. We should jump right in."

"Sounds good to me." Valerie uncaps her pen. "So, table eleven! I'm so pleased to meet you. I'm going to ask a bunch of questions." She leans forward and begins. "Let's start with connections. Before you sat at table eleven, did any of you know each other? I heard the seating was random." Valerie turns her gaze toward me. "Laura, I'll let you start us off, since you planned the event."

"Oh! Okay," I say nervously. "Yes, I planned the event, along with my wonderful page co-moderator, Dr. Gabriella Martinez." I look at Gabby and smile. "Let's see. I sold Dr. Martinez, or Gabby, as I call her, and Julie their homes. So that's how I knew them."

Valerie writes in her notepad and then looks at Gabby. "Gabby, or should I call you Dr. Martinez?"

"Gabby is fine," she replies.

"I heard you're a marriage and family therapist. Did you see any of your patients at the event? I suppose that would be awkward?"

I shift in my chair uncomfortably. Maggie warned us that Valerie might push the envelope with her questions but assured us this was standard reporter behavior.

"I see my patients out and about all the time," Gabby says, unruffled by Valerie's question. "I always keep matters private."

Valerie quickly moves on. "Okay, who wants to go next? How about you, Maggie?"

Maggie adjusts the scarf draped over her shoulders. "As you know, I'm a local reporter. I interviewed Indira shortly before the event about her volunteer work at the refugee center."

Glancing at Indira, I notice she looks lost in thought.

"And," Maggie continues, "I had interviewed Gabby's mother, Carlita, who does the *Hamilton Herald*'s senior dating column."

"Oh, Gabby, you're Carlita's daughter?" Valerie bounces in her chair excitedly. "She's a real spitfire. How do you feel about her popular column?"

I'm curious about Gabby's response.

"To be honest," Gabby says, "I wasn't supportive when Maggie first interviewed my mom. But seeing how proud my mom felt after they offered her the column shifted my focus. My mom's a unique individual. The column is perfect for her."

"Wonderful," Valerie continues. "Indira, did you know anyone else besides Maggie?"

"No, only Maggie."

"This is all great," Valerie says glancing at us. "Give me a few examples of how you use the Hamilton Beach Moms' Facebook page. Anyone at all. Don't be shy."

Indira begins to speak. "Here's a silly example. My husband and I are taking surfing lessons to reconnect. I posted on the page, looking for a local instructor. I had a few names within an hour of posting."

"How fun!" Valerie grins widely.

"And I used the page to get tickets to an REO Speedwagon show," Maggie comments. "The show was sold out, and I was desperate to take my husband. REO's music holds a special place in our relationship."

"Classic eighties rock. That's my jam," Valerie replies. "Anyone else?"

Julie clears her throat. "I've found the page's shift to an umbrella for clubs to be a great source of support. I lead one of our clubs."

"I'd love to hear about it." Valerie taps her pen back and forth.

"It's called *Political Divide*." Julie tosses her head back and laughs. "It encourages people with different political views to come together in conversation. It gets heated sometimes, but our group is respectful of differing opinions."

"That's interesting. Where did you get the idea for a mom's club about political differences?" Valerie asks.

Julie shifts in her chair. "I made an anonymous post about the political divide in my marriage. It started a firestorm. The page practically imploded, and my post had to be taken down." Shrugging, Julie looks at me for support.

I jump right in to help my good friend. "Yes, the post was taken down, but ultimately, it's what led Julie to create the club, and I must say it's one of the more popular ones."

"That sounds intense," Valerie replies.

"Yes, it was," Julie admits. "But I've seen the way people can come together, even when they disagree. It's been great."

"I'd love to come to one of the *Political Divide Club* meetings. It sounds like a great story."

"Anytime," Julie says cheerfully.

"Anyone else?" Valerie scans everyone's faces again.

"Yes, the clubs have taken off," Gabby says enthusiastically. "Word has gotten out to surrounding communities, and now clubs are popping up all around Southern California. It's exciting!"

Valerie scratches something down on her notepad and continues.

"Speaking more on the topic of anonymous posts." The volume of Valerie's voice drops. "I'd like to talk about what happened at the event. I don't think I can write this article without including Isabell Whitmore."

Although Maggie gave us a heads-up, everyone at the table sighs. And even though my relationship with Isabell is on good terms, I squirm in my chair.

"Go right ahead and ask us whatever you want," Gabby says with confidence. "We have nothing to hide. The page has changed so much since the fundraising lunch. And, luckily, the link Isabell posted led to nothing more than an error message."

My heart picks up speed as I recall almost shutting down the Facebook page after Isabell's stunt. But, luckily, Gabby convinced me to use the incident as a way to make the page into something better.

"Well, what happened to Isabell?" Valerie asks.

Everyone at the table looks at me. I've stood by Isabell's side as she works through her trauma and charts a new course. I'm incredibly proud of what she's accomplished so far. "I'll take this one." My limbs tingle with nervous energy. "Isabell's a childhood friend."

"So," Valerie peers at me. "What does Isabell say about what happened?"

Pausing, I think about how much Isabell's life has changed. She's renting a townhouse in the Parkside neighborhood and spending as much time as she can connecting with her children. She stays out of the fray, knowing she's not welcome most places.

"Isabell sincerely regrets her actions and is working hard to get to a better place. That's all I can say."

"Public records show she's recently divorced. Did her husband leave her because she tried to expose the anonymous posts?"

Maggie grasps Valerie's arm, signaling that her questions have gone far enough.

"The page no longer allows moms to post anonymously," Gabby says in an assured tone. She will not let Valerie push us on the topic of Isabell. "And I believe it's better this way. Occasionally, a mom will reach out to Laura or me and ask us to post something anonymously, but we've gotten good at pointing these moms toward better resources."

Valerie sits up straight in her chair. "But where do you think moms are finding support now that they can't post anonymously?"

Gabby flashes an expansive smile. "I like to think the clubs have helped the moms of Hamilton Beach find friends they can lean on in real life. They no longer need a virtual forum."

"It's a nice sentiment," Valerie says. "But I guess we'll never know if anonymous posts have died down because of closer relationships or Isabell Whitmore."

"We can each believe what we want to believe," Maggie says with a bit of irritation in her voice.

"Did someone say my name?"

Turning around, I see Isabell standing in the doorway. Everyone ruffles around uncomfortably. *Why is she here?* My stomach clenches.

"Hi, everyone. I know you're surprised to see me. I'm here to announce a new club idea." Isabell shifts from side to side as she speaks.

Valerie scribbles furiously in her notepad.

Even though Isabell's made progress, her presence is unnerving. Last time she was with this group, things went very wrong. *I need to fix this.*

I jump out of my chair. "Isabell, can we talk for a minute?"

As I pull her aside, I inhale deeply and remind myself *I don't have to fix everything.* Events will unfold as they will. Most times, just like with Isabell's anonymous post link, things work out.

I steady my voice as Isabell and I step to a corner. "Why didn't you tell me you were coming?" I ask.

Isabell pulls at the loose-fitting top she's wearing. "I wasn't sure I had the courage to show up. But, after a session with my therapist, I think starting this new club is exactly what I need."

"What's your club idea?" I ask, as a slight buzz runs through my chest.

"Well, before I tell you, let me say it's going to be run by my therapist. Not me."

"Okay," I reply.

"I want to start a *Me-Too Hamilton Beach* group."

"Really?" I ask. My mind spins with all the things that could go wrong. Then, miraculously, it starts to spin with the things that could go right.

Isabell continues. "I hid my turmoil for so long, and it ruined me. I hope this club will keep other women from doing the same." She pushes her long blond hair behind her ear and looks at me curiously. "So, what do you think?"

I put my arm around her and pull her into a hug. "I think it's a great idea, Isabell. I'm proud of you."

Suddenly, my phone rings. Looking down at the number, I see it's a potential new client who left me a voicemail yesterday. "I'm sorry, I need to take this."

Isabell nods and steps away. She stands awkwardly in the corner of the meeting room, knowing her poor reputation among the women filling up Seaside Coffee.

"Perry Properties. This is Laura."

Looking up, my heart floods with warmth as I see Gabby stand and invite Isabell to sit with the ladies of table eleven.

A voice pipes through my phone as I watch Isabell take her place at the table. "Hi, Laura. My name is Sabina. My husband and I are expecting our first child in a few months. We're looking to move out of LA."

"Congratulations," I say. "That's exciting. How can I help you?"

"It's funny. We weren't considering Hamilton Beach. It's a bit far out. But I've been hearing a lot about this town. It sounds like a tight-knit community, and that's exactly the type of place we want to be."

"It certainly is," I say as I watch Isabell and the women of table eleven laughing and enjoying each other's company. "It certainly is."

THE END

Keep reading for a sneak peek of Jenifer's next novel
Moms Who Read Romance Novels

Thank you for reading Anonymous Mom Posts. If you loved my book please leave a review here. Ratings drive book sales. Thanks!

www.amazon.com/Mom-Posts

Moms Who Read Romance Novels, coming soon! Visit my website at authorjenifergoldin.com to stay up to date on all my book news.

Follow me at

jenifergoldinwrites

Author Jenifer Goldin

jenifergoldinauthor

Moms Who Read
Romance Novels

CHAPTER 1
Ellory Brayson

M Y VOICE WAVERS. I stand and lean slightly forward against the back of my chair. This is the power pose I use whenever I need to activate my celebrity persona. Parting my lips, I read from my latest best seller. This time my voice is dense like a stone sinking to the bottom of a lake.

> *My appetite for him was insatiable. We were worn out but couldn't resist another moment of pure bliss. Clasping my hands tightly around him, he throbbed in my grip. I pushed him inside. My body contracted in pain, outlined with a perverse pleasure. I looked directly into his eyes. My body pulsed and released in an unending wave. Then my body shuddered again. But it was not from pleasure. It was from the way his eyes glowed, like truth-seeking orbs. He could never know the truth. The truth would destroy us.*

Lifting my head, I glance at the women who have come to Blast Off Books to get signed copies of the last book in my *Prince of Silicon Valley* series. My eyes wander over the crowd. The audience stares back at me with their mouths slightly agape. Their eyes are glassy, and their bodies are angled forward as if the scene I just read was a magnet pulling them toward me.

To be honest, I hate live readings. It's one thing to write a sex scene in the privacy of my office. And even that takes intense focus and preparation. I drink two glasses of wine to loosen up before I peck at my computer's keyboard. Sometimes I watch a steamy love scene for inspiration. The show *Outlander* has been a recent favorite. Or my classic go-to, *About Last Night* with Rob Lowe. My readers would be surprised to learn I'm not a sexual extrovert. In fact, my sex life is nonexistent. If my fans knew the truth, they'd shun me as the world's biggest fraud.

"Does anyone have questions for Ellory?" My childhood best friend, Tabby, owner of Blast Off Books, steps beside the chair where I'm standing. As the audience collectively exhales, expelling the last bit of sexual tension coursing through their bodies, I run my hand over the charm bracelet in my pocket. Its meaning feels heavy in this setting.

A woman in the back stands, shaking her hand in the air. Tabby encourages her toward us. I notice she's younger than my average reader. Late-twenties maybe? She's got a full, curvaceous body that fills the surrounding space. She moves gracefully and smiles so widely, I can't help but spread my lips out wide and smile in return. Tabby hands the microphone to the woman.

"Hi, Ellory," she says as her warm features draw me in. "My name is Harper. I'm such a huge fan. I've read all your books. Even the *Psychic Passions* series."

My muscles immediately tighten. I ventured into paranormal romance for that series, and it was awful.

"Anyway," she continues, "my question is, do you believe everyone will experience a great love in their lifetime?" She cocks her head, thinking for a moment. "I mean, look at you. You married an actual prince and have the most incredible love story."

My mouth turns downward as Harper mentions my husband, Prince Maximilian, a royal from a small monarchy in eastern Europe. *Yes*, I think to myself with dismay. *It really is the most unreal love story.* Pushing the thought away, I look at Harper. I've seen her kind over and over. Lonely and starving for the kind of love that only exists in romance novels.

Uncrossing my legs, I inhale deeply and tap back into my power pose. "I love this question, Harper. And it's one I get a lot. Everyone can have a great love story, but if you have rules about who it should be, or a specific timeline it must happen by, or any constraints that narrow the possibilities, your great love may slip through your fingers." I pause for maximum effect as Harper nods. "So, yes, everyone can have a great love story, but most people are going to miss it." It's my pat answer. I've given this little speech at least five hundred times over the years.

"Well, you certainly didn't miss yours." Harper bounces in place, too excited to contain her enthusiasm.

An image of Prince Maxy's face flits through my mind. He's the reason I lost my friendship with Tabby. He's the reason I'm back in Jupiter Cove, trying to make it up to her. I gently shake my head to loosen my clenching jaw. "Are you single?" I ask, knowing, of course, the answer is yes.

"Yes." Harper shifts her weight from side to side but somehow remains perfectly poised.

"Well, all I can say, Harper, is stay open and see what cues the universe gives you. Don't ignore them."

My mind wanders again to my broken relationship with Tabby. I hope being here gives me the opportunity to say all the things I need to say.

I'm lost in thought when I hear another voice through the microphone.

"Hi, Ellory. I love your books. So happy to see you tonight." A short woman with tan skin and overly highlighted hair smiles at me. "I love your characters. I love your plotlines. But I have to say, I also really love steamy love scenes. You seem to write less and less spice with each new book."

The crowd laughs nervously.

Before I can respond, the woman jumps up from her chair. Rushing toward the microphone, she almost knocks over a display of Colleen

Hoover's books. As she approaches, she passes the microphone and faces the audience. "Ladies, I love smut. Who's with me!"

Everyone's eyes lock on my face, wondering how I'll respond. *She's not wrong.* The love scenes in my latest books are tame compared to my earlier work. It's hard to write about passionate sex when you're not having any.

Heat creeps up my neck. I'm suddenly thankful I'm wearing a stylish scarf over my silky Chanel top. I can't let thoughts of my sham marriage overtake me now.

"I hear what you're saying and thanks for the input." Blank faces gape at me. I need to say something else to diffuse the moment. "I personally prefer the term *erotica*, but, yes, smut sells." I force a breathy giggle, hoping no one catches on to my discomfort.

The entire room explodes with laughter.

A tall, slender black woman, well past middle age, raises her hand. "I love smut too," she shouts proudly.

"And I love erotica," another woman squeals with a snorty chuckle.

More laughter from the crowd. Relief washes over me. Crisis averted.

The evening continues as more women ask me questions about love and relationships. It's as if they think I'm Cupid and can pull back my bow and solve all their love problems. I'm relieved when Tabby gives me the signal that it's time to wrap up the question-and-answer session.

Feeling like a fraud, I end the book-reading the same way I always end these events. "May you all find your happily ever after."

I almost choke as the words leave my mouth. *I know better than anyone there's no such thing as happily ever after.*

CHAPTER 2

Tabitha Wilson

"WELL, LADIES, THANKS for coming to Blast Off Books," I say. "I'm happy you could be here to welcome back Jupiter Cove's Ellory Brayson. We've been friends since second grade, so it's a real treat to have her back."

My eyes sweep over Ellory's glamorous image. It's hard to remember she was the one who loved climbing trees, throwing rocks, and daring boys to race her to the creek. She's traded Band-Aids for fancy scarves. I'll never get used to it.

"Ellory flew in from New York this afternoon. I'm sure she's exhausted. We're going to end here."

The group groans in disappointment.

"But I have one more announcement I know you'll find exciting." The faces before me brighten. I make my voice sound enthusiastic, even though I'm feeling hesitant about Ellory's reappearance in my life. "Ellory's almost done with a new book. A stand-alone. It's different from her usual novels, but she's been working tirelessly on creating another cast of characters for you to fall in love with."

This is exactly what Ellory's publicist told me to say when we planned tonight's event. And although I find it patronizing, I will play along. Ellory has agreed to sell all hard copies of the last book in her *Prince of Silicon Valley* series through my bookstore for now. The money it will provide could not come at a better time.

The women in the crowd clap and cheer.

"And," I continue, "Ellory is renting a house in Jupiter Cove for the summer while she puts the finishing touches on this new book."

"Oh my god," a woman in the back blurts. "This is the most exciting news ever!"

"Wow, the most exciting news ever?" Ellory laughs along with the crowd. "I'm very flattered."

"Yes, I agree. It's exciting to have a world-famous romance author living here and finishing her book." I smile at Ellory, but my chest tightens. A wave of uneasiness courses through my body. I ignore my feelings, knowing all that matters is the money. It's my last chance to fulfill my dream.

I continue with my prepared script. "But there's even more exciting news. Ellory will pick a few readers from this group to review her manuscript, give notes, and help with editing. It's a contest of sorts, called Ellory's Editors. Those chosen will be the first to read Ellory's new book, and they will help shape how it unfolds."

The women eagerly bob around in their seats. A couple of people in the audience clap. And one woman gasps with excitement.

I glance at Ellory and hand her the microphone.

"I'm so pleased to see your reaction," she says to no one in particular. "A few logistical things to know before you drop your name into the hat. You'll need to read the book in the next three weeks. If your life is busy and you can't meet this timeline, it's probably better not to apply."

The crowd nods in understanding.

"The editors and I will meet two or three times over the summer. We'll discuss plot holes, dead end storylines, and what ideas you may have for making my book better. And my publicist will run a social media campaign, highlighting Ellory's Editors. I'm excited and can't wait to collaborate with some of my biggest fans." Ellory reaches out an arm stacked with three Hermes bracelets and hands me back the microphone.

I wonder if she still has her charm bracelet. I think. "Can everyone who's interested raise their hand?" I ask.

Almost every hand shoots up, and I have to take a step back from the force of air molecules shifting so abruptly.

"Alright then!" I laugh with forced enthusiasm. "My daughter, Ila, has been awaiting her cue. She'll hand out the applications."

"Stepdaughter," Ila replies gruffly. She peers at me through squinty eyes.

"Oh, teenagers," I say, brushing off Ila's rude response. "Return the forms to me before leaving tonight. Now, everyone, please go enjoy the delicious coffee and treats." I glance at the refreshments, inhaling the scent of chocolate.

As the women sip coffee and chat, Ellory rushes toward me. She purses her lips together, then exhales. "I'm finally writing the book I've always wanted to write." She threads her fingers through her impossibly gorgeous hair. "My fan base is one hundred percent romance readers. If the book doesn't have forced proximity, a love triangle, or enemies to lovers, all wrapped up with a happy ending, it's going to flop." Her shoulders slump, but she immediately straightens as a gushing fan approaches.

Is Ellory feeling insecure? I must be misreading things. She's got a spine made of steel.

"I'm over the moon about this competition!" A slender woman, who looks to be in her thirties moves toward Ellory with her copy of *The Prince of Silicon Valley: Book Four.* "Would you mind signing this for me?" She bends her tall body toward us as she hands Ellory a black fine-tipped Sharpie. "I missed the signing before the talk. My husband was supposed to be home by five but was late as usual. I couldn't leave my kids alone."

"I remember those days," Ellory says with a conspiratorial wink. "How old are your children?"

"I have a six-year-old, twin three-year-olds, and a baby!" The woman leans back, smiling as if she's just told a hilarious joke. I suppose you get lots of big reactions after you tell people you have four young children.

As if on cue, Ellory holds her hands to her face, stunned. "Wow! How do you do it? I bet your house is nonstop."

The woman leans close to Ellory. "I'm fairly certain I'm going crazy." She screws her eyes together and shrugs as she pushes a long blond curl away from her face.

"Well, we're glad your husband eventually came home. Hand me your book so I can sign it. What's your name?"

"Faye."

Opening the Sharpie, Ellory presses its black point to a blank page in the front. *To my favorite mom, Faye. Thanks for being a fan, Ellory.*

"Thanks so much," Faye says as she places the book in a beat-up diaper bag. "I really need something other than being a mom right now. Here's my application."

"Thanks," I say as I take the form from Faye.

"Great, well, I have to get home. My husband has texted ten times about getting the kids to bed. He's helpless." She shrugs her shoulders and walks toward the store's door.

I turn toward Ellory, suddenly realizing applicants will be disappointed if they aren't chosen. "How are you going to decide who to choose for Ellory's Editors?"

"It doesn't matter," Ellory says at a short clip. She lowers her voice to a whisper. "This is all for social media. It's not like any of these women could provide input that will improve my book. They have zero understanding of what the publishing industry demands."

And just like that, I'm reminded of how much Ellory has changed since becoming a world-famous romance novelist. I never know when she'll shift into *Ellory Brayson, self-obsessed celebrity.* She acts like she's the main character and we're all just playing bit parts in the story of her life.

An image of the peach maid of honor dress I was supposed to wear to her wedding flies through my mind. It hangs in the back of my closet, with the tags still attached all these years later.

I need to stay one step ahead of Ellory.

Want to read more of
MOMS WHO READ ROMANCE NOVELS?

Visit:
https://bookhip.com/MRMCQTB
for more free chapters

Acknowledgements

Anonymous Mom Posts exists because of the unending support I have received from both family and friends.

First and foremost, I must thank my husband for allowing me the time and space to write, and for providing the financial support necessary to publish this book. Thank you to my mom, who has been an enthusiastic reader and worked every connection she had to make this book a reality. (Thank you SS). And thank you to my dad, for believing in me.

Thank you to my children, who have supported me as I have gone through many emotional ups and downs while bringing this book to publication. They have learned a ton about rejection and perseverance. To my brother Andrew and sister-in-law Carrie. You've generously given your time to read and provide feedback, and I am thankful. To my brother-in-law Joel and my sister-in-law Allison. Joel, you are my legal eagle, and Allison, I appreciate your feedback and willingness to pass my stories on to others for input.

To my friends, beta readers, and people I have met along the way. I am indebted to you for your suggestions, willingness to lend an ear during the tough times, and your general support. Amy Beyer, Sara Bier, Michele Blondheim, Lori Cahill, Heather Carlin, Stephanie Feinberg, Marcia Fleishman, Giselle Gryngarten, Teresa Huff, Kathy Kalmon, Samantha Katz, Scott Kirpatrick, Robyn Klugman, Gennye and Matthew Krasner, Meredith Lee, Jodi Loar, Heather Lourie, Debra

Pristach, Amy and Evan Rosen, Laurie Rubin, Lorna Sherwinter, Stephanie and Michael Tavani, Elisabeth Warrick, Dana Webber, Jen Woodrum, and my therapist.

To my sensitivity readers. It's scary to write a character outside your own lived experience but it was important to me to have this book encompass women from diverse backgrounds. Thank you Kshiti Buch, Leona Neelam Maple, Jen Nelson, Julith Perry, Susan and Lily Stibal, Taye Timko, and Camille Ward. And thank you to Salt and Sage books for providing the medium to bring writers and sensitivity readers together.

Thanks to my public relations guru Lora Sommer.

Thank you to my copy editor Shannon Cave.

Thank you to all my advanced readers. You caught a few things I would have missed!

To the literary agent out there that provided multiple rounds of edits. You gave generously of your time and taught me so much about writing. You pushed me but made this book so much better. Thank you.

Thank you to Mark Dawson for creating amazing courses to help self-published authors embark on this crazy adventure.

Thank you Stuart Bache from Books Covered for the amazing cover design.

Thank you Stephanie Anderson from Alt 19 Creative for the beautiful interior pages.

And finally, a special thank you to my website designer and self-publishing mentor Jessica Lepe. You answered millions of questions and helped me navigate the world of self-publishing. Thank you.

Made in the USA
Columbia, SC
22 March 2023